MARGARET

The Forgotten Smile

VINTAGE BOOKS
London

Published by Vintage 2014

2 4 6 8 10 9 7 5 3 1

First published in Great Britain by Macmillan in 1961

Vintage
Random House, 20 Vauxhall Bridge Road,
London SW1V 2SA

www.vintage-classics.info

Addresses for companies within The Random House Group Limited
can be found at: www.randomhouse.co.uk/offices.htm

The Random House Group Limited Reg. No. 954009

A CIP catalogue record for this book
is available from the British Library

ISBN 9780099595496

The Random House Group Limited supports the Forest
Stewardship Council® (FSC®), the leading international forest-
certification organisation. Our books carrying the FSC label are
printed on FSC®-certified paper. FSC is the only forest-certification
scheme supported by the leading environmental organisations,
including Greenpeace. Our paper procurement policy can be found at:
www.randomhouse.co.uk/environment

Printed and bound in Great Britain by
Clays Ltd, St Ives plc

TO DAVID DAVIES

The dialect of Keritha is spelt, as nearly
as possible, as it was pronounced.

PART ONE

'THERE'S NOTHING THERE'

Little we see in nature that is ours.

WORDSWORTH

1

A large uncouth artefact stands in a little garden outside the Museum of Antiquities on the island of Thasos. It has the head of a seal, a body like a horizontal sausage roll, rudimentary wings, and human legs plunged into heavy boots. Few visitors think it beautiful.

It had, however, an enduring fascination for Selwyn Potter, who never failed to inspect it whenever he came to Thasos. Seen from the front, so that the bird-like rump was concealed, it reminded him of someone whom he must know quite well. The morose expression on the seal face was tantalizingly familiar.

This long-standing riddle was solved one spring morning, when he saw Dr Percival Challoner come stumping out of the museum to peer at the thing. The association became abundantly clear; they were as alike as Tweedledum and Tweedledee. In another era, in another life, Selwyn had sat for hours, attentive to information trickling out of that glum mouth.

Now these fantastic twins stood confronted as though each waited for the other to begin a cross mumble, some obscure quotation from the Palatine Anthology. Selwyn strolled up to them and got one in first.

Tweedledee took no notice but Tweedledum begged his pardon, in modern Greek, without looking round.

This had always been Dr Challoner's technique, in any country, with foreigners who insisted upon addressing him. He begged their pardons and went on doing so until they shut up. He also knew the word for thank you, in French, German, and Italian, but had not troubled to learn it in Greek.

Selwyn obligingly translated:

'The holy bird can give his swift wing a rest here.'

Foreigners who talked English were the worst nuisance of all since nothing could shut them up. Nor did Dr Challoner relish this singularly tasteless translation of Mnasalcas. He gave a disapproving grunt and turned to go out of the garden, pursued by Selwyn who was anxious to find out what Tweedledum thought of Tweedledee.

'Was he once very holy, this bird, do you think?'

Now, after many years, he heard the thin titter with which his one-time mentor reproved ignorance. It was like putting a penny in a slot.

'Te-he-he! A bird?'

'Isn't he a bird?'

'A griffin, possibly.'

'I thought a griffin had four legs.'

'The hind legs have obviously been destroyed.'

'What do you think of it?'

'It's not in the least remarkable. I was merely wondering . . . I had an impression I've seen it before somewhere.'

You see it every morning when you shave, thought Selwyn.

'Perhaps,' he suggested, 'you've seen something like it in some exhibition of contemporary art?'

This was another penny for the slot and it drew from Dr Challoner a smug assertion that he knew nothing whatever about contemporary art. He had always taken a kind of pride in confessing total ignorance of any subject save one; upon late Greek poetry he claimed to be an absolute authority, and this claim was, it seemed, partially based upon a determination to know nothing whatever about anything else.

The dear old responses had something of the charm exerted by a treasured musical box, lost, forgotten, and rediscovered. To elicit yet another was an irresistible temptation.

'A Greek griffin,' suggested Selwyn, 'saying what it thinks of the Turks?'

Prompt as ever the rocket went up.

'*Greek?* What exactly do you mean by *Greek?*'

Selwyn smiled and went glibly into the old routine:

'Oh, I wouldn't say Achaian, or Dorian, or Ionian, or Aeolian. I don't suggest he's strictly a Hellenic griffin but ...'

'*You!* Why ... you're English! I know you!'

This really disconcerted Selwyn who had assumed the recognition to be mutual. If he remembered people it was natural to suppose that they must remember him. Nor could he understand why anybody should mistake his nationality. He had but a hazy notion of his own effect upon others. That his waistline was abnormal he knew because he found it difficult, in England, to buy trousers off the peg. He also knew that his hair was stiff and curly since hats had a way of bouncing off it as though recoiling from a nest of springs. Of the general effect he was unaware. To take him for a florid young Levantine was very natural in a place like Thasos.

'I'm Potter,' he explained, a little crestfallen. 'You know me. You coached me once. Selwyn Potter.'

Dr Challoner riffled through his mental card index. Potter? Potter? Ten years ago? More? A fat young man with a scholarship from a grammar school. Promising, as so many of them were. Fizzled out, as so many of them did. Why should anybody remember Potter?

'Let me see,' he said, doing his best. 'You got the Beaulieu?'

'The Glanville.'

'Ah yes . . .'

And how many times, since then, had brilliant young men carried off the Glanville Award before fizzling out?

'Ah yes. And what are you doing now?'

'Oh . . . loafing round the islands.'

'On vacation? I mean, what do you *do*?'

This meant, apparently, how did Selwyn earn his dinner. He said glumly:

'I teach.'

He did not say where. Had he taught in a reputable institution he would have named it. Some miserable Dotheboys Hall, reflected Dr Challoner, unrecognized by the Board of Education, catering for boys who had failed to qualify for any secondary or grammar school, for parents too snobbish to accept the inevitable – that was a beach frequently combed by holders of the Glanville who had fizzled out.

'I see. Well . . . pleasant to have met you.'

With a last suspicious glance at Tweedledee Dr Challoner stumped off, unaware that his former pupil had been looking forward to a much longer conversation, although they had very little in common.

Selwyn had once read Greek with eager pleasure until all pleasure vanished abruptly from his world, leaving him footloose and solitary. He had always valued the older man's grasp of verbal subtleties and had listened to him with respect, although obliged to laugh at him occasionally.

Dr Challoner's felicity lay elsewhere. He got most pleasure out of scoring off an opponent, was uneasy in the company of people who knew as much, in his own field, as he did, and dreaded the bare possibility that anybody could ever know more. Promising young men occasionally gave him qualms of apprehension; they might become potential rivals if they should emulate his own austere determination to know nothing whatever in any field save one. But they could generally be trusted to waste time and energy upon history, archaeology or philosophy. They deserted the printed word for the plastic arts. They even made excursions outside the classics. They came and they went. He dealt out the required information, tittering sometimes at their inaccuracy, and tolerably certain that they would fizzle out.

Selwyn's disappointment was short-lived, for he had not expected very much. The brief warmth engendered by the meeting soon evaporated, and he subsided once more into a sadness so complete that he scarcely knew himself to be sad. No part of him remained detached from it to observe or to comment on the rest. In a frozen melancholy, the prevailing climate of his existence at this time, he wandered down to the harbour and exchanged island gossip with some men who had come in with a haul of squid. In some ways he was a good mixer; he had the easy tap-room geniality often to be observed in melancholics. These peasants were going over to the mainland and offered to take him with them. He would have accepted, since he had had enough of Thasos, if Dr Challoner had not reappeared, trotting down the quay and bleating for him in querulous anxiety.

'Potter! Oh . . . I say! Potter!'

A little boy in the boat thought this summons very funny and repeated it in ecstasy.

'Potta! O-ai-se Potta!'

His father cuffed him into sobriety. People like this were common enough upon Thasos. They came in boatloads, took a look at Tweedledee, climbed up to the Acropolis, walked round the island, and sailed away again.

'I say, Potter, can you speak the language? I saw you talking to these people. I wonder if you could help me. I'm in rather a fix . . . most annoying . . .'

'I speak it well enough. What's the trouble?'

'I want to get to an island called Keritha. I thought I could get a boat from here, but they tell me no boats ever go there.'

'They wouldn't, in a regular way. There's a post boat goes to Zagros, twice a week. That's the nearest island to Keritha.'

'So I gather. I must hire a boat, and I don't know how to set about it. I have the address of an agent here; I've just seen him. A most incompetent person. Can't speak English. Only French, of a sort. I thought he'd fix me up with a boat and an interpreter, but he just shrugs his shoulders and tells me to go to Zagros. Nobody, according to him, ever goes to Keritha.'

'I dare say not. There's nothing there.'

'But I must go. It's a business matter.'

Selwyn turned to the squid boat and explained that he could not go to the mainland, since he must stay and look after this old character. The men nodded and continued to throw their cargo on to the quay, more or less in the direction of the old character's ankles. The boy, risking another cuff, yelled:

8

'Zany!'

'What horrible creatures,' exclaimed Dr Challoner, recoiling from the squid tentacles.

'They're good eating,' said Selwyn.

'Zany! Zany!'

'Why does he keep shouting *Zany*?'

'He means foreigners. Xenoi, originally.'

'Good heavens!'

This unorthodox encounter with a perfectly respectable word, hitherto only to be met with in print, quite flabbergasted Dr Challoner. He crept away up the quay followed by Selwyn, who demanded:

'Did you say you had business on Keritha?'

'I did. Is that a newspaper kiosk over there? Could I get a *Times*, do you think?'

'You could try. But . . . Keritha! There's nothing there. Never has been. No ruins, no sites. Never once mentioned in history or literature . . .'

'Have you been there?'

'No nearer than Zagros. There's a church and a shop on Zagros. I got to know the schoolmaster there; he goes over to Keritha to teach school two days a week and he told me what a God-forgotten place it is.'

'Can you help me to get a boat?'

'I'll ask around and see what I can do. You wait for me at that *taverna* behind the kiosk.'

There was no *Times* to be had, nor anything nearer to it than an elderly copy of the *New York Herald Tribune*. Dr Challoner was not surprised. The difficulty of obtaining *The Times* every day had, long ago, given him a distaste for all foreign travel. It had exasperated him in places far less barbarous than Thasos. He rejected the *Tribune* and went to

9

the *taverna* where, for the price of an abominable cup of sweet black poison, he could sit down.

This, he reflected, was foreign travel at its very worst. He might hope to know more about late Greek poetry than anybody else, but he had never felt the faintest inclination to visit the land of its birth. He could, by reading, ascertain all that was necessary; any visual gaps could be filled by good photographs. It might, originally, have belonged to a lot of dead foreigners, but he considered that it had now become the personal property of people like himself, who settled *hoti's* business decorously in a thousand libraries from Upsala to Princeton.

As he tried to swallow his nasty foreign coffee he wished that he had had the foresight to bring a tin of Quickcafe in his suitcase. Potter might know, perhaps, whether such a civilized amenity could be purchased on Thasos; Potter might, if that was so, write down on a piece of paper some sentence which he could show to these people: *Bring me a cup and a spoon and a jug of hot water.*

Sighing, he thought of his quarters at home − of the breakfast table with Quickcafe, toast and marmalade, bird-song and daffodils in the Fellows' Garden outside, and an uncompromising photograph of the Parthenon over the fireplace.

Presently Potter came into sight again, exuberantly seedy, lounging along the quay. A belt or braces! thought Dr Challoner, watching his progress. One or the other! A paunch, inexcusable in so young a man, cannot be trusted to keep the trousers from slipping below the navel.

'We're in luck,' said Selwyn, subsiding heavily upon a chair. 'There's a boat in from Keritha, going back today. I've fixed it all up. There'll be some cargo, but they'll have room for us, if you haven't too much luggage.'

'I've a couple of suitcases. But . . . are you coming too?'

'I'd better, if you're going on business and can't talk Greek. I'm sure nobody on Keritha even speaks French. In fact I dare say their Greek is pretty queer; that schoolmaster says they've a lingo all of their own; a lot of words you don't meet anywhere else.'

'Very good of you. But I don't want to upset your plans.'

'I have no plans,' said Selwyn, who was determined to find out what Challoner might be up to. 'I've always wanted to go to Keritha, and this is a very good chance.'

'And will this boat bring us back?'

'Oh no. We'll have to come back via Zagros. We can easily get somebody from Keritha to run us over. And then from Zagros catch the next post boat here. There's one on Thursday.'

'You mean sleep on Zagros? Is there an hotel?'

'Good heavens no. But somebody will put you up. The schoolmaster might.'

'Where did you sleep when you were there?'

'Me? Oh, I don't remember. I just . . . sleep around.'

'I never thought I should have to spend a night . . . I thought I could stay here . . . though this is bad enough, and run over to Keritha for the day.'

'I suppose you've never been so far off the map in these parts before?'

'I've never been in these parts before.'

'You *haven't*? Really? How very odd!'

'I've never felt the least desire to come. What is there to come for? All this . . .' Challoner waved towards the quay and the squid, '. . . what has this to do with literature?'

'It had a lot to do with it once.'

'Not now.'

Never at any time, in Dr Challoner's private opinion. Poetry has never been written by yokels who throw fish about on quays.

Selwyn mused for a while and then said:

'All over long ago? Dead and gone?

> '. . . On thy voiceless shore
> The heroic lay is tuneless now,
> The heroic bosom beats no more?'

'Quite! Quite! I know the lines.'

When minded to quote poetry Selwyn was not to be deterred by an obviously unwilling audience. He flung himself back in his chair and rolled out the final couplet while his trousers crept further down his hips.

> 'And must thy lyre, so long divine,
> Degenerate into hands like mine?

'Is that how you feel?'

Dr Challoner felt nothing of the sort. No lyre, falling into his domain, was likely to degenerate. He repeated impatiently:

'Quite! Quite! I know the lines, of course. Pity Byron was such a cad.'

2

The boat was small. The cargo included several crates of Coca-Cola and a tempestuous billy goat. At the sight and smell of this creature Dr Challoner would have cancelled the trip had he been able to retrieve his suitcases which were stowed away under the crates. Nobody listened to his protests. He was pushed aboard amidst a terrific altercation carrying on between the crew and some people on the quay. In the course of it they put out to sea but the volleys of invective between ship and shore went on as long as any shout would carry across the water.

'What was all that about?' he asked as silence fell.

'Just the time of day,' said Selwyn. 'Who's dead, and who's getting married. Also some important citizen has bought a refrigerator. You needn't keep your feet tucked up like that. The goat won't bite.'

'Isn't it unusually large?'

'He's a famous goat. They're very proud of him on Keritha. He's been lent to somebody here for stud purposes.'

As soon as they were well out to sea the goat settled down. The sun shone fiercely. Selwyn had clamped an enormous straw hat upon his unruly curls. Dr Challoner draped a handkerchief from the back of his hat to protect his neck. The sky was dazzling and the sea was a very dark blue shot through with streaks of green and bronze like a peacock's tail. The distant islands, scattered about the horizon, were pale lilac and pink in the triumphant light.

'This is very . . .'

Dr Challoner paused, abashed by the word which he had been about to use. He sought for an alternative.

'Very striking. Remarkable.'

Selwyn nodded. He would have made no bones about calling it beautiful and had thought it so for years. He still came to look at it as often as he could, just as he still did many things merely from habit.

'If I'm to be your interpreter,' he said, 'you may as well tell me why we are going to Keritha.'

Since the goat had gone to sleep Challoner ventured to stretch out his legs before answering.

'I have some property there. A house. At all events a house. And possibly some valuable . . . until I get there I hardly know what to expect. I had an uncle who used to live there. He died this spring and left me the house and its contents.'

'You had an uncle on Keritha? How very odd!'

'I suppose so. My grandfather . . . he was a very eccentric man, my grandfather . . . he went there.'

Selwyn suppressed a grin, supposing the eccentric grandfather to have been quite a gay blade.

'Insane, really,' lamented Dr Challoner. 'Very well off. Had a huge house in Kensington. No profession. Nothing to steady him. My grandmother, his first wife, must have had a time of it. She was a perfectly sensible woman, as far as I know. A Miss Greighton. But she could do nothing with him. Always off on some fad or other. *He took Schliemann seriously!*'

'A lot of people did,' suggested Selwyn.

'Should have been laughed out of court . . . never went to any university . . . never learnt Greek till he was past thirty . . . the untold harm that man has done! No qualifications whatever.'

'Too bad he hit on Troy when all the qualified people were insisting that there was no such place.'

'It was *not* Homeric Troy,' bellowed Dr Challoner. 'He missed that, for all his digging.'

'Still, it was there, where he said it was. Would you rather Priam's gold was still buried because the qualified people had dug up the wrong place?'

'It was not *Priam's* gold, and I'd much rather it was still buried. Dug up by an ex-grocer! Advertised to every Tom, Dick, and Harry under a totally false description. Looted by the Russians in '45? Scattered now, nobody knows where, in Omsk or Tomsk. If qualified people had handled it nobody would have taken the slightest interest in it.'

'Too right,' agreed Selwyn, reflecting that gold handled by Challoner's buddies would immediately become so tarnished with dullness that nobody, not even Russians, would trouble to loot it. 'But go on! Did your grandfather dig up Keritha?'

'He did. After consulting the Odyssey. Just as Schliemann consulted the Iliad before digging up Hissarlik.'

'Thought it was a sort of Baedeker?'

'Upon my word I believe so. I don't know what he expected to find, but he bought the island and dug for months. Found nothing, of course. Only coins. A lot of obols, of various periods, scattered about.'

'Kensal Green.'

'What?'

'Local cemetery. Coins last longer than bones. Local yokels buried with an obol apiece under the tongue.'

'Ach!'

Dr Challoner recoiled from this suggestion. People in classical literature might have been buried with an obol as Charon's fee, but he blenched at the idea that anybody, at any time, had ever actually been so silly.

'Anyway, that's all he got for his pains. Except a second wife. My grandmother was dead by the time he went to Keritha. When he gave up his digging he brought home with him an island girl he'd married out there.'

'Married?'

This was a surprise. Selwyn had pictured a bastard left behind on Keritha.

'He brought her back? To Kensington?'

'To the Addison Road. A mere peasant. I doubt if she could read or write. *And* they had two children. Alfred and Edith. My uncle and aunt. Younger than I was. My father, the son by the first wife, was grown up and married by that time.'

'Look! There's Keritha! Behind Zagros.'

A long low island had appeared to the south with a mountain rising in its midst. Selwyn explained that this mountain was Keritha which lay behind its neighbour.

'The two islands must be quite near to each other,' said Dr Challoner, squinting into the strong sunlight.

'Further than you'd think. You'll see when we get round Zagros. It's quite a high mountain really. Not as high as Samothrace, of course; but Keritha is like a smaller model of Samothrace – very much the same shape.'

The boat changed course, turning westwards to round the long cape of Zagros.

'And did you all play together in the Addison Road?' asked Selwyn. 'You and your little uncle and aunt?'

'Not much,' admitted Dr Challoner glumly.

That pair had been a life-long grievance to him. He hated any kind of irregularity. No other boys of his acquaintance had uncles and aunts younger than themselves and conspicuous freaks into the bargain.

Alfred wore sailor suits for years after the date at which he should have been put into Norfolk jackets, Edith went about in a long black pinafore affair. Neither of their parents seemed to know what to do with them. Their mother sat upstairs in a room full of ikons. Their father rode his hobby horses. Attempts were eventually made to civilize the two bewildered children. They were dispatched to a Public School and a Convent. Edith was even presented at Court. They continued, however, to be a couple of fish out of water, inevitably doing and saying the wrong things, although apparently themselves aware that silence and inactivity had best be preserved whenever possible.

'No harm in them really,' conceded their nephew handsomely, recollecting that Alfred had left him a good deal of money as well as the property on Keritha. 'They were merely ninepence in the shilling, both of them. We never went there much. My father was on cool terms with my grandfather, who had given that foreign woman all my grandmother's jewellery, on top of a great deal of money. After he died the three of them cleared out. Went back to Keritha and built this house there. Thirty-eight years ago. That was the last we saw of them. Now they're all dead. I don't know when the foreign woman died, but my aunt died just before Christmas and my uncle soon after. The actual island they gave back to the people there, some time ago. But the house and everything in it . . . if it was only the house I shouldn't have bothered to come. No earthly use to me. But there's that jewellery. Must be worth a pretty penny if it's still there.'

As they rounded Zagros the islanders fell into an animated discussion. Presently one of them called out to Selwyn that the price of the trip had been doubled.

'You pulled a fast one on us,' he complained. 'If we'd seen the old bird we'd have stuck it on. You just said an old man.'

'So he is, isn't he?'

'Lousy with money. You never said he was a tax collector.'

'He's not. And you never mentioned the goat.'

'What's he want on Keritha, anyway?'

'Wait and see.'

'What are they saying?' demanded Dr Challoner.

'They want to know why you're going to Keritha.'

'Tell them it's none of their business.'

'He wants,' Selwyn told them, 'to visit the grave of his uncle, Alfred Challoner. Know him?'

'Potter! What are you telling them? Why . . . what on earth . . .'

Their companions were scrambling towards them over the crates and the goat.

'They want to shake hands with you. They seem to have thought a lot of your uncle. They call him the Lord Freddie.'

Dr Challoner was compelled to shake several brown and smelly hands and to receive obvious compliments.

'What *are* they saying?'

'They say he saw his angel when he was in the middle of ordering repairs to his vineyard wall. I think they mean

18

he suddenly dropped down dead . . . They say he made a grand corpse. They put him away in style. Classiest funeral ever seen on Keritha. They got candles from Thasos, great big ones . . .'

Selwyn fell silent, fearing that some of the details shouted down the boat might sound callous when translated. Nor was he quite certain that he understood them; Milorthos Frethi had, it seemed, been buried with fifty lepta *peiratikion*. Unfortunately this was the only word caught by his companion.

'But what's that about pirates?'

'Safe conduct money really. Passage money . . . It might be passage money to − over there. I don't know.'

'They took him over to Zagros?'

'No. He's buried here. But they seem to have spent a lot bringing . . . *pragmata* . . . goods, for the funeral.'

Obols, thought Selwyn, remembering the stories told by the schoolmaster on Zagros who complained that the neighbouring island was at least three thousand years behind the times. This could not be true, since even obols must, at some point during that interval, have been adopted as a newfangled notion.

The islanders returned to their end of the boat, which had by now rounded the cape of Zagros. A wide space of water between the two islands was now visible. Selwyn, feeling hungry, produced some bread and cheese which his companion refused to share. The proximity of the goat had turned Dr Challoner's stomach.

'When did Charon turn ferryman?' asked Selwyn, munching. 'Pretty late, wasn't it? A good bit after Homer. Who was he originally?'

'Death probably, or the messenger of death,' said Challoner.

'He's often identified with Thanatos. Even as late as Bianor
. . . *Panta Charon apleste . . .*'

'Oh yes. I remember. Why did you grab young Attaus in
such a hurry? He'd have been yours in the end, you know,
even if he'd made old bones.'

This barbarous translation, the smell of the goat, and
Selwyn's manner of eating bread and cheese were too much
for any civilized man. Dr Challoner fished a bottle of tablets
out of his pocket and sucked one hastily.

Keritha drew nearer. It towered superbly over them as
they ran in under its lower slopes. These were thickly wooded
with chestnut, pine, and ilex.

'No houses on this side,' commented Selwyn with his
mouth full. 'Yes, there are though! Look! Smoke curling up
above the trees. Circe's Palace!'

One of the men, following their glances, shouted:

'*To Palati tou Frethi.*'

'Oh! It's yours. It's Freddie's Palace.'

They passed a small headland and the house came into
view. Its stately aspect, its graceful proportions, took them
both by surprise. There were glimpses of bright spring
flowers in sheets falling down the slopes to the sea. A deep
cleft or ravine cut the mountain to the right of it; here
they caught sight of water falling in a thin intermittent
thread.

'Must be a spring up there,' commented Selwyn. 'It's all
so green. Doesn't look as if it ever dried up in the summer.'

'I'm surprised,' said Dr Challoner. 'I hadn't expected . . .
I thought it was just built by the local people.'

'It's in the local style. White walls, red tiles . . . but he
must have had taste, your uncle.'

'Taste! He never heard of such a thing. A pure fluke, I

20

suppose. Palace though!' Dr Challoner tittered a little. 'That's coming it a bit strong.'

'More like Plâs in Welsh, perhaps. Plâs Freddi.'

'But that smoke! Potter! Somebody must be there. I thought nobody lived there now.'

Their companions, when questioned, said that Madam Eugenia lived there, and all the servants and the tax collector.

'A tax collector!' cried Dr Challoner in dismay, when this was translated. 'What's he doing there?'

'I believe they only mean a foreigner,' said Selwyn. 'Come to think of it, the schoolmaster on Zagros told me they don't call foreigners zanies on Keritha. They call them tax collectors. I dare say tax collectors are the only people who have ever bothered to go there, and they've generally been foreign.'

He put some further questions and reported:

'She's a female tax collector and she's lived in Plâs Freddi for some years. A friend of The Lady. Your aunt, I suppose. Let's hope she hasn't pinched all the jewellery.'

Some such thought had already occurred to Dr Challoner but he considered the comment typical of Potter's taste.

The house vanished behind the next headland. A flat little peninsula came into view. There were fields, olives, fruit blossom, scattered houses, a jetty and one or two boats. The whole population of Keritha seemed to be awaiting their arrival.

As they approached the jetty one of the men in the boat got up, pushed the goat aside, took a bottle of Coca-Cola out of a crate and flung it overboard, as though this were a piece of routine.

'What did he do that for?' asked Dr Challoner.

Selwyn would have liked to know, but inquiries were

impossible. The exchange of shouts from ship to shore had struck up. It had reached a deafening volume by the time that they bumped against the jetty. The sexual prowess of the goat seemed to be the main theme of the moment but a good deal was said about the pious pilgrimage made by these two tax collectors to Milorthos Frethi's grave.

The goat had to be landed first, an operation which took some time. Selwyn soothed his fretful companion and surveyed the population of Keritha. He had previously imagined the party in the boat to be all of one family, since they were curiously alike. Now he saw the same features everywhere and perceived the effect of inbreeding over many centuries. They had squarish faces and their eyes were abnormally wide apart, which stamped them with an expression at once innocent and sly. The candid brows, the wide-spaced eyes, seen full face, had a child-like effect. Seen in profile these eyes looked round the corner in a disturbing way. They might not, he supposed, make very much of what was happening under their noses, but they were unusually perceptive of anything behind their backs.

At length the goat was restored to his home ground and led off in triumph. Selwyn jumped out of the boat. Dr Challoner was hauled out. There were more greetings – endless hand-shakings, after which they were conducted to a couple of donkeys.

'Are we supposed to ride on these?' asked Challoner reluctantly. 'Where? Up to the house?'

'No. To the grave, I think.'

'You'll have to, or your name will be mud on Keritha. Not one of them will ever lift a finger for you again.'

'I don't ask them to lift a finger for me.'

'Yes, you do. You'll want them to take you away from here. If they don't, nobody will.'

'Oh, very well. Which reminds me. We must pay those people who brought us over.'

'I think not. Just now I believe we're the guest of the island. Later on you might distribute some tactful largesse.'

With a shrug Dr Challoner mounted a donkey. It was so small that he had to curl his feet up, lest they trail on the ground. Then, catching sight of his suitcases on the jetty, he tried to dismount again.

'They'll be all right,' Selwyn assured him.

'These people . . . are they honest . . . Oo-ugh!'

The donkey, in response to a thwack from an old woman, started forward in a disconcerting trot.

All Keritha accompanied them as they took a rough track across a shoulder of the mountain. They jogged along amidst a torrent of square, wide-eyed faces, grey-beards, youths, withered crones, plump girls, skipping children, and babes in arms. Selwyn steadied himself on his donkey and shouted:

'They're terribly proud of this grave. When we get there we can't gape like a couple of fishes. We shall be a ghastly flop if we don't say something or do something.'

'What will they expect?'

'I haven't a clue.'

'Do you know anything about their religion? Greek Orthodox?'

'Not much. And I've a notion they aren't orthodox so you'd notice it. I don't suppose it matters much what we do, only we must make a ceremony of it. After all, we're tax collectors. Nobody will be surprised if we act a bit funny. What about poetry? I'll say a line or so, and you take it up. You can spout plenty. I've heard you.'

23

'Greek? They won't understand a word of it.'

'No. Might as well spout Beowulf in the local on Saturday night. But it will sound like something. That's all that matters. Question is: What? I doubt if the heroic lay would suit your Uncle Freddie. What about one of the Bucolic . . .'

'I shall do nothing of the sort.'

They jogged on, past a couple of homesteads whence more people ran out, with boisterous cries, to join them. The torrent formed itself, imperceptibly, into a ritual procession of the whole community. It took on a simple, innate dignity. The old men went first. The young men followed with the donkeys in their midst. Then came the girls. Women and children brought up the rear.

They had a knack for it, reflected Selwyn. Processions were in their blood. Whereas, amongst many tax collectors, the most solemn occasions are often celebrated by nothing more impressive than a self-conscious straggle of people, walking slowly one after another.

The pilgrimage ended at a little plateau carpeted with anemones, and commanding a fine view of Zagros sprawling on the peacock sea. They were assisted from their donkeys and conducted to a tall stone set up to face that view. Upon it was carved, with considerable grace, an inscription in English:

HERE LIES
EDITH CHALLONER OF KERITHA
Born 1898. Died 1959
also
HER BOTHER
ALFRED CHALLONER
Born 1897. Died 1960
The bright day is done and we are for the dark.

Their nephew was surprised and bewildered by his own dismay. This stupid blunder, the mis-spelling of a single word, was cruelly typical of that unhappy pair. Despite their patient efforts to conform, to behave like rational people, they had always contrived to be figures of fun. Their lifelong failure was now perpetuated in their monument. The site was exquisite, the stone a good shape, the lettering graceful, and the whole effect ridiculous.

He had always resented their uncanny faculty for making fools of themselves and of everybody connected with them. Now, standing by their grave, he could have desired to think of them without resentment. In this place, at this moment, the dignity of death should be acknowledged. He wished vaguely that he had brought a wreath. Potter had been right in suggesting that ceremony of some kind should be observed. He looked round sharply, afraid that the fellow might be laughing.

Selwyn was not laughing. Having studied the monument gravely, he crossed himself. Keritha followed suit, and so a few seconds later, did Dr Challoner in a couple of brusque jerks. The assembly became quite silent, waiting for something to be said. After a short pause Selwyn lifted his voice and launched upon the Greek of a former day:

'Ah me! When the mallows wither in the garden,
And the green parsley,
And the curved tendrils of the anise. . . .'

He paused and waited. If Challoner would not play ball he would finish it himself, but the old boy ought to have it pat enough since he was always yakking about the Ausonian Song.

The old boy took it up in a gentler voice than usual:

'On a later day they live again,
And spring in another year.'

A sigh went over the listeners as though they understood.
Selwyn turned and flung the lament away over the seas to
Zagros.

'But we men,
We the great, or mighty, or wise,
When once we have died
In hollow earth we sleep.'

Again he waited and again Challoner took it up:

'Gone down into silence.
A long and endless and unawakened sleep.'

A moment of stillness followed, so profound that the sea
and the sky, the earth and the stones and the trees might
have been listening too. They were both not a little astonished at the resonance and authority of their own voices;
it was as though the assembly on the plateau had become
a single creature which had found utterance through them.

That creature was satisfied. So much was apparent in the
atmosphere. They had declaimed some obviously pious words
in a strange tongue which still had power to awaken echoes
in the nerves, if not the minds, of their companions. Keritha
took its leave, not with more handshakes but with grave
bows, and trooped downhill. The mourners were left with
the donkeys and one little boy, who explained that he would

now show them the way to the house. They mounted again and set off on a track through the pine trees.

Challoner felt as though he were emerging from a dream. Selwyn was excited at perceiving a cow tethered a little way below the path. It seemed to him that the island must be unusually well watered if it afforded grazing for cows as well as goats. He questioned the boy, who told him proudly that Keritha had three cows, all the property of Milorthos Frethi who was so very rich that he ate butter every day.

'Her Bother Alfred!' exploded Dr Challoner. 'That must be put right.'

'How?' asked Selwyn. 'Unless you put up another stone.'

'I shall. It can't be left like that. I won't have my uncle made a laughing stock.'

'Nobody here thinks that.'

'Any civilized person coming here will.'

'Cost you a packet to have another one put up,' said Selwyn unkindly.

This was probable. Dr Challoner's thoughts turned uneasily to the mysterious foreigner in his house, the possible disappearance of the jewellery, and doubt as to whether this wild-goose chase might not leave him out of pocket.

The trees were intermittent, giving frequent glimpses of the sea below. The track ran straight eastward round the mountain. Selwyn remembered the deep ravine and the waterfall which they had seen from the boat, and wondered how they were going to cross it. This problem was solved when they came to a plank bridge with no railings, just wide enough to admit the passage of a loaded donkey. Since neither of them had a good head for heights they alighted, preferring to walk across while the boy led the donkeys over after them. But before they could set foot on the planks he barred their way, demanding sugar, nor would he budge when they told him that they had no sugar. The offer of money moved him not at all. If they had no sugar, he declared, they must take a path which plunged down beside the ravine almost to sea level and came up again on the other side.

'I don't suppose he's particular,' said Selwyn. 'Give him one of those tablets you sucked on the boat.'

'Those? They're bicarbonate of soda.'

'Try him with one, anyway. We don't want to go down that path if we can help it.'

A tablet was offered to the boy, who took it rather dubiously but moved aside to let them cross the bridge. The chatter of the falling water grew much louder for a moment and sank again. When they had got safely across Selwyn peered over to watch the thin thread drifting down. Nobody there? he thought dreamily.

The boy joined them with the donkeys. They mounted again. In a few minutes the track, rounding a huge boulder, brought them to the house amidst its blazing flowers.

They were expected.

Upon the terrace, waiting for them stood a tall, grey-haired woman. She looked like the mistress of an English country house welcoming week-end visitors. Her voice was a voice from home – well bred, a little abrupt, but pleasant.

'Dr Challoner? I'm so glad you've come. They've brought up your suitcases.'

She then turned to Selwyn, who was gaping at her in astonished recognition. A flicker of uncertainty crossed her handsome rosy features.

'Mrs Benson!' he exclaimed. 'Don't you remember me? Selwyn Potter. I'm Judith's friend. Your daughter Judith. We were up together. I came to a party at your house once. In Edwardes Square.'

'Oh yes. Of course,' she said hastily. 'I remember. But it was a long time ago, wasn't it? Just after Judith came down.'

'Ten years ago. I broke something or other. I forget what.'

'I don't,' she said with the forthright candour of her type. 'It was a Louis-Quinze table. Come in, both of you, and have some tea.'

3

Half an hour with Mrs Benson put Dr Challoner into a much easier frame of mind. She gave him tea and excellent buttered scones. She told him all that he wanted to know and much which he lacked the wit to ask, including a short account of his uncle's death. She suggested solutions for all his problems. He could not believe that she had purloined his jewellery or that she had given anyone else a chance to do so.

Keritha had been her home, she told him, for more than two years. She had been installed there as friend and companion to Edith, who had needed some such solace, had died slowly, half blind and in great pain. Alfred had followed her, six weeks later, dying of a coronary thrombosis. The three of them were old friends. Kate Benson, in the days when she was Kate Mortimer, had lived next door to the Challoners in the Addison Road. She and Edith had been very fond of one another as children although they lost touch later, for many years, before this final reunion on Keritha.

'My own children,' explained Mrs Benson, 'are all grown up now and out in the world. They don't need me, and Edith did.'

So Mr Benson must be dead, concluded Selwyn, wolfing

buttered scones. Ten years ago there had assuredly been a Mr Benson in the background, although he had not, perhaps, shown up on the inauspicious occasion when Selwyn, vehemently discussing some point, had crashed his fist down upon a valuable little table. Mr Benson evoked no memories. All the rest of them did. This lady had presided over an excellent buffet supper for young people. She was not so grey then; had once obviously been a red-head bleached to a nondescript sandy hue. The younger daughter, a schoolgirl, had beautiful dark red hair. A son, busy opening beer bottles, had been sallow and dark. Judith had been dark too – a pale incisive brunette. He had made her acquaintance during their undergraduate days and believed her to be his friend, although he never received any token of regard from her save this one invitation to her home in Edwardes Square, soon after they both came down. The invitation was not repeated nor was she available when he tried to ring her up. That the damaged table might have something to do with this never occurred to him at the time.

That one visit had made a considerable impression on him. It was an unusual experience. His friends, having perhaps a regard for their furniture, did not invite him to their homes. He had little idea of family life or of what went on in it. In Edwardes Square he got a glimpse of something which he found astonishing and attractive. In retrospect he came to idealize it. They all appeared to be nourished and sustained by some dish which they had in common, which they took for granted, and which was supplied by Mrs Benson in a cheerful, matter-of-fact way.

She had reshaped his notion of a mother, whom he had always supposed to be a tender, slightly sentimental, creature ordained to preside over the lives of infants. He could remember nothing of his own. By the time that he was four years old he knew that most children in Isleworth, where he lived, had got one but that he had Aunty Madge instead. She was not really his aunt. Her husband was a man called Blackett to whom Selwyn's father had foolishly lent a thousand pounds without security. When Selwyn was flung upon the world, a penniless orphan, Sydney Blackett squared his conscience by making himself responsible for the child's upbringing. This decision was a permanent grievance with Mrs Blackett. According to her calculations it would have been cheaper to give Selwyn a thousand pounds, which was probably true but beside the point, since a thousand shillings would have been more than Sydney Blackett could ever have got together. Selwyn was a bad bargain and he ate enormously. Having a conscience of sorts she put up with him as best she might; if he fell down and cut his knee she did not 'kiss the place to make it well', but she produced lint and plaster. The Blacketts were neither kind nor unkind to the child. He was neither grateful nor ungrateful to them. He grew up unacquainted with warmth or affection and never missed them.

A mother's function remained vague to him until he got a glimpse of Mrs Benson surrounded by her lively family, adult and semi-adult. She bound them together, preserving them as a group whilst speeding them off on their separate paths. He thought her wonderful. She seemed to foresee what everybody would want.

She did so still. As soon as she could, without tasteless precipitation, she put Dr Challoner out of his pain. The jewellery, she told them, was all in a wall safe. She had a key and a list. Another key and a duplicate list were lodged

in a bank at Athens, a precaution which she had herself
suggested to Edith some time ago. Things of that sort, she
said, should not be left to chance. There were also duplicate
lists of other valuable objects – books, coins, ceramics, and
curios, which had come originally from the Addison Road.
Some of the furniture, moreover, was worth a good deal.
An expert should be got in to value it. As for packing and
crating, she could recommend a good firm in Athens.

Dr Challoner looked doubtful. He had no use or space
for these objects in his bachelor's burrow in college. The
idea of so much bulky and valuable property daunted him.
It could be sold, but that might involve a lot of trouble,
unless this useful creature could be persuaded to do all the
work for him. It seemed that she had stayed on at the house,
after Alfred's death, in order to keep an eye on things until
somebody should turn up to claim the inheritance. Hoping
to enlist her further aid, he thanked her with unwonted
civility for all the trouble that she had taken.

'Oh, but I'm afraid I've let you down over one thing,'
she protested. 'The grave! That stone! Yorgos, who brought
up the baggage, said you'd gone at once to see it. I'm afraid
it must have given you rather a shock. I printed it all out
for Lakis – he's our stone-mason – just what was to be put
under the inscription for Edith. Of course he knows no
English. But I ought to have gone and stood over him while
he did it. I would have, if I'd known he'd do it so quickly.
They aren't generally so prompt. I was horrified when I
saw it. I fear you must have been.'

'It can't be left as it is.'

'I suppose not. And they're so proud of it. Did they all
escort you to look at it?'

'Quite a crowd came.'

'It would be a great occasion for them, and they do love occasions. I expect they hoped you'd be delighted.'

She paused and looked at him uneasily, adding:

'I shall hear from them how they thought it went off.'

He perceived that his antics at the grave, of which he now felt rather ashamed, could not be concealed for long. In that case he had better make a clean breast of it.

'I . . . we . . . we thought they obviously expected some kind of ceremony. All that we could think of was to recite some . . .' he blushed and his voice sank almost to a whisper, '. . . some poetry. They seemed to like it.'

'Oh? What a good idea! Greek poetry?'

'Er . . . yes. Just a short pastoral passage.'

'Freddie would have liked that. Theocritus?'

This got her a suspicious glance. Dr Challoner did not approve of women who talked glibly about Theocritus, but was mollified when she said:

'Freddie was so fond of him.'

'You're very near the mark, Mrs Benson. Moschus. The lament for Bion.'

'What? Not that bit about how the plants die and come up again next year, but we don't?'

'Yes. *Ai! Ai! Tai malachai men hotan kata kepon olontai.* It seemed suitable.'

Selwyn jumped up, nearly upsetting the tea table, and strode out through the open window into the garden.

'You couldn't have chosen better. Such a favourite poem of Freddie's. Every autumn he used to come in and quote: "Oh dear! The parsley is all dead in the garden."'

'Quite! Quite! Mallows, not parsley. And Oh dear! is hardly a suitable rendering of *Ai! Ai!* Alas! perhaps.'

'That's how Freddie translated it,' she retorted, looking a

little put out. 'But was it you or Mr Potter who thought of . . . oh yes, and why is *he* here? I was never so surprised in my life.'

Dr Challoner explained Selwyn's presence and added:

'I doubt if I'll need him any more. He'd better get himself a boat over to Zagros.'

'He won't get one tonight. He must stay here till tomorrow.'

'That's quite unnecessary. I never invited him.'

'But his bag has been taken to a guest room. I expect the maids have unpacked it by now. Yorgos said there were two of you.'

'In that case I suppose he'd better . . . I'm sorry to inflict him on you.'

'Tell me – what has happened to him? I've not seen him for a good many years and, today, I was quite shocked. He looks so different. So gone to pieces somehow. He was always odd looking. Uncouth. But such a brilliant, lively creature.'

'He was my pupil at one time, but I've not seen him since he went down. I've no idea what he's been doing with himself. He looks as if he'd come a cropper of some kind.'

'I've always had him a little on my mind. I rather liked him, although he broke my table. I felt he'd never had anyone to take an interest in him or tell him how not to be a lout. But my children didn't want to ask him again. They thought him a bore.'

'Have you indoor plumbing here?' asked Dr Challoner, who also thought Potter a bore.

She explained the sanitary arrangements, which were less primitive than he had feared, and took him up to his room.

In College he slept on an iron bed in a bleak little box looking out on a row of dustbins. A scout brought him tepid shaving water in the mornings and he had to take a very long walk if he wanted a bath. Here he was provided with a stately bed of cedar wood. There were many chests and cupboards for his few possessions, comfortable chairs, a large writing desk, and an incomparable view from the window. In the adjoining bathroom water was heated by a log stove. The smoke from this he had already seen, curling up amongst the trees. It was all a deal too foreign for his taste.

Having explained that these were formerly his uncle's quarters, Mrs Benson went down to find her other charge. Selwyn was lounging on a bench a little way down the garden slope. He learnt that he was to stay the night but it was tactfully indicated that tomorrow he must get a boat over to Zagros. This hint he ignored. He meant to stay as long as he could in a house where butter was eaten every day.

'How's Judith?' he asked.

'Oh, she's married. A barrister called Brian Loder. They have two children. Andrew is married too. And Bridie . . . you remember Bridie? My younger daughter? She trained at the R A D A. Now she's doing quite a lot in Radio and Television. She's in that radio programme: *The People Next Door*. I don't suppose you ever listen to it.'

'I've heard bits of it, once or twice. Can she manage the accent?'

'They don't have an accent on that programme.'

'I know. It must be very difficult to sound like somebody who is neither U, nor non-U, nor urban, nor suburban, nor provincial, nor rural. Completely sterilized diction.'

'A lot of people do sound like that nowadays. Actually

I've never heard Bridie. She joined the programme after I came here and we don't get it on our radio. She's the girl the younger son is engaged to. The intellectual son. She lives in terror that the authors will decide to make them break it off, for then she'd lose her job.'

'Have you been here all this time, without ever once going back?'

'I went back for three months, during the first winter. Our house, in Edwardes Square, is sold.'

'I know.'

'How did you know?'

'I called there, the summer before last, and found you'd all gone away.'

'Yes. It had got too big for us. My husband has a flat in Chelsea.'

'I thought he was dead,' exclaimed Potter the lout, adding hastily: 'I mean . . . I'm very glad he isn't.'

For a few seconds their mutual confusion was so great that they could say nothing.

'So why am I here?' she asked, getting her breath back. 'Various complicated . . . my health, for one thing. I was ill when I went back. But *you*? What have you been doing all these years?'

He made no reply. She would not, probably, have asked, if she had not been so flustered. During the ensuing pause each knew that some unspeakable disaster must have befallen the other. They exchanged glances of apology.

'How do you like Keritha?' she began brightly. 'It's pretty, isn't it? But of course there's nothing here.'

'So everybody keeps saying. I don't know why. I've heard a rumour that the people here are three thousand years behind the times.'

'Oh well, it's such a little place. Nobody ever came here. So it's always stayed pretty much the same.'

'History must have washed up a thing or two from time to time. Obols . . . Christianity . . . and Coca-Cola . . .'

'Yes. But only like things washed up on a high-tide line. A few more each century. It never washed all over Keritha, quite blotting out the past. The people took anything that came along and added it to what they'd got. They never scrapped anything. I should think they've got a very low I Q. There's nothing particularly important or interesting about them.'

'Methinks the lady doth protest too much. What did Milorthos Frethi think?'

'He disliked people who come asking impertinent questions.'

'Dr Challoner wants to know why we gave the sea a bottle of Coca-Cola at the end of the trip. I think I must tell him it was an offering to Poseidon. It would annoy him so very much.'

She flushed angrily.

'I'm sure they've never heard of Poseidon. I thought you were a good-natured person, even if you did go about breaking furniture. Why tell people what you know will annoy them? If you'll come in I'll show you your room.'

Turning away, she went up to the house again. He followed, apologizing:

'I'm sorry. I won't say anything. But I don't think I was good-natured, you know. Only dumb.'

His room was almost as princely as that assigned to Dr Challoner and his appreciation was eloquent.

'What a lovely archaic bathroom! Will the maids come and give me a bath?'

'I'm sure they'd like to. But if anyone does, it ought to be the staid housekeeper, surely?'

'Who's she? Eugenia?'

At this he got a startled look.

'The people on the boat said she lives here,' he explained.

'Oh? Well . . . yes . . . I suppose you might say she's a very staid housekeeper. But she won't give you a bath.'

'Shall we see her?'

'I don't know. She has her own rooms, across the court at the back. I think she'll stay in them unless Dr Challoner sends for her.'

Left to himself, Selwyn sprawled on a chair by the window, languidly wondering about several things. Why had Mr Benson been thus jettisoned? Who and what was Eugenia? Was there, after all, 'something' on Keritha to justify Freddie's distrust of busybodies?

These old customs, superstitions, folk-lore, survivals of paganism, were not particularly remarkable. They could be observed everywhere, from Woking to Paraguay. The busiest body could do no more than prate about some former Numen on Keritha, long extinct, commemorated now in a few meaningless words or gestures. Milorthos Frethi? What could remain for him to guard?

The scene at the grave flashed out vividly and was dismissed. For a moment Selwyn Potter had escaped from the prison house of a single existence, had melted into some other, larger, person, had spoken in a voice not his own. If Keritha should offer more moments of that sort his stay there would be short. They were dangerous.

In a panic he began to count. One, two, three, four, five, six, seven, eight, nine . . . That was a great safeguard, counting, when he was alone. It was not so fatiguing as his defence when in company: his performance in the role of a man to whom nothing much can ever happen – noisy, insensitive, and flippant. He kept on counting until the gong rang for dinner.

PART TWO

'HAPPY BIRTHDAY, MRS BENSON!'

Ladybird, Ladybird, why do you roam?
I'm off on a ramble to visit the moon.
Ladybird, Ladybird, fly away home;
Your house is burnt down and your
    children all gone.

1

Kate Benson first came to Keritha on a cruise organized by a firm called *Wanderers Ltd*, which undertook to cater for those who yearn for the unbeaten track but shrink from physical hardship. She had seen one of their advertisements and sent for particulars, since the idea had occurred to her that she ought, for a time, to 'get away from everything'.

Everything was Edwardes Square and the Benson family, which had ceased to be the agreeable entity which Selwyn had so much admired several years earlier. It had become less well integrated and less good-humoured. All the birds had flown from the nest. Judith and Andrew were married. Bridie lived in a students' hostel. There were no more buffet suppers for young people. Kate, for the first time since her marriage, had nothing much to do. A sensible woman, she thought, would make use of the bleak leisure thus bestowed and broaden her mind by travel.

They could all manage very well without her for a while. If obliged to do so, they might make up their minds, settle amongst themselves, how much they still expected of her. This was an open question. Although all three were resentful of any interference with their personal lives, each one of the three was constantly invoking her interference in the lives of the other two. It was still her function, apparently, to set all right if anything went amiss.

An attractive brochure arrived from *Wanderers Ltd*. For three weeks in June a boat called the *Latona* would dawdle about the Eastern Mediterranean and the Aegean, calling at small and little-known ports or islands. There would be no guides, no sites, no ruins, no antiquities. Picnic lunches, bathing, and a leisurely enjoyment of the scenery were the main pleasures offered to patrons unconventional enough to appreciate 'something different'.

Kate liked the idea and promptly booked the cruise without saying a word about it to the children, since they would certainly tell her that she ought to have done something else and she was tired of standing up for herself. Judith and Andrew were scolding her for letting Bridie train at the R A D A, predicting a waste of time and money; Bridie was not cut out for the Stage. Bridie and Andrew held her responsible for the bad manners of Brian Loder, Judith's husband. He had called Holy Communion 'Holy Theophagy' in the presence of a touchy churchgoer who happened to be Andrew's best client; none of Kate's own children would have been permitted to do this and her plea that a son-in-law cannot be dragooned was dismissed with scorn. Judith and Bridie prophesied Andrew's probable death from food poisoning; his wife never scrubbed her draining board and her kitchen stank to high heaven. A mother who really loved her son would have dropped a hint about it a long time ago. Poor Kate felt that she could do nothing right, and had no wish to hear their comments on the cruise, although she was not sure whether it would be condemned as too cheap, too expensive, too short, or too long.

She did, however, mention the project to her husband

before finally committing herself. He merely asked for the date, made a note of it in his pocket diary, and agreed that it was an excellent idea. For years he had been agreeing with everything that she said before she had quite finished saying it. This had formerly been convenient, when the children were small and when she was always busy. There had been no time to waste upon arguments or discussions with Douglas, nor had she ever been disposed to pay him much attention. She came of a matriarchal tribe. She was one of the five daughters of Old Mrs Mortimer, who had dominated West Kensington from 1885, when she came there as a bride, till 1947, when she dropped down dead in the middle of a successful altercation with the dustman. And Old Mrs Mortimer had been one of seven daughters born to Old Mrs Nayler, who had dominated East Anglia from 1854 to 1910.

In this century-old clan of sisters, mothers, aunts, and cousins, little attention was paid to husbands, who earned money, begot children, and did as they were told. Kate alone had been something of a deviationist. She had never, complained the Naylers and the Mortimers, managed to behave quite like everybody else. As a child, in the Addison Road, she had insisted upon making friends with the weird Challoners next door, at whom all sensible people laughed. By turns tempestuous and humble, she was seldom satisfied with herself. That Mortimer standards in ethics, taste, art, music, literature, and social deportment were high enough to content any reasonable creature, so much she would allow, but she would not dismiss, as tiresome eccentrics, those who demanded something better. She had been known to rebel against the Mortimer-Nayler axiom that a mother, should her children's interest be at stake, is morally justified, in any action, however shady, in any lie, however black. As she grew older she continued to form friendships beyond the family circle; her unaccountable affection for people 'who did not belong to her' remained a standing grievance with her sisters. Nor, when she married, would she allow her husband's shortcomings to become a topic of tribal merriment and discussion.

These oddities, however, were only apparent to the clan. She ruled the roost in Edwardes Square, and Douglas did as he was told, largely because she had incomparably the stronger character of the two. In the eyes of the world she was one of the Mortimers – efficient, self-satisfied and domineering. People who liked that family sometimes maintained that Kate was the nicest of them. Those who did not, generally allowed that Kate was the least intolerable.

Now that she was more at leisure she would have welcomed a little rational conversation with Douglas, from time to time, but he no longer wanted to talk to her and shut her up by a technique of monotonous agreement. Of course she must take the June cruise, since the *Wanderers* had nothing to offer in July. Certainly she must be free in August, so that she might take Judith's children to Cromer while their parents got off on a little holiday by themselves. Naturally he would himself prefer August for his annual trip to Skye with an old school friend. Undoubtedly Andrew and his wife would need Kate's services in September, when they would be moving from their flat to a house which they had bought. Yes, to be sure, June was the only possible month. She must know, better than anybody else, whether the change would be beneficial and whether the expense would be justified. Yes . . . certainly . . . of course yes.

There was only one person in the world who ever got

any unofficial counsel or advice from Douglas Benson. This was a Mrs Shelmerdine, a client and an old friend, with whom he often drank a glass of sherry on his way home from Lincoln's Inn. She was very rich and he managed her money for her. She never knew what she could afford or how much she had in the bank. She could not have told the difference between a passport and a visa unless some man had explained it to her.

Ten days before sailing Kate drove up to Swiss Cottage with a sewing machine which she had promised to lend to her daughter-in-law. Andrew and Hazel, since their marriage, had perched on the top floor of a converted house there. They seemed to be settling down very well. Kate could have wished for her son a wife with more sense, but Hazel was a dear little creature and responsibility for her welfare had steadied Andrew. He no longer spurned all manner of work which was not 'essentially creative' and was resigned to security with a firm which built houses in dormitory towns, an opening secured to him at some sacrifice of Benson capital.

The sewing machine was heavy and the stairs to Andrew's flat were steep. Parking her car by the privet hedge in front of the house, Kate honked her horn twice, hoping that Hazel would recognize the signal and come down to lend a hand. No Hazel appeared, although a couple of young men, who were working in the garden, poked their heads over the hedge.

At last she got out and toiled up the stairs. These ended abruptly at a blue door with a comic brass knocker which annoyed her whenever she came to Swiss Cottage. She rapped, waited, listened, and rapped again. Footsteps pattered along the passage. The door opened. Hazel stood there, dripping wet and wrapped in a large bath towel.

'Oh . . .' she panted. 'Oh! It *is* you! I'm so frightfully sorry. I was having a bath.'

'I said I'd come at six.'

'I know. But I didn't realize it was six. Goodness, I'm sorry. Do come in. . . .'

Warm, wet, glowing, her tousled curls in her eyes, Hazel might have been five years old. Kate's heart melted, as it always did towards anything very young.

'You run and get something on,' she said. 'It doesn't matter. I'm in no hurry.'

She turned into the living-room, was, as usual, appalled by its sluttish disorder and repressed, as usual, an impulse to tidy it a little.

There seemed to be a smell hanging about which she did not like. It was not the accustomed stench of a dirty kitchen. It might be, in itself, an agreeable smell, but it had disagreeable associations. She stood sniffing until she identified it as something called Opal 5, much prized by Pamela Shelmerdine. Douglas was always buying expensive little bottles of it and sending them to the woman.

Kate despised jealousy. She did not, however, think about Pamela unless obliged to do so. The whole business was, to her mind, intolerably silly. Downright infidelity in Douglas she could have forgiven and understood. Had Pamela been his mistress there might have been some sense in it. With mere sentimental philandering she had no patience. Sherry, sighs, lingering looks, expressive silences, and flattering attention were all that any man had ever got from Pamela.

She captured the fools by asking helplessly for their advice and by encouraging them to talk about themselves for hours together. She had nothing to do save listen. She had no children. Servants did her housework. She had not even a husband since Mr Shelmerdine had died in Brazil after running away with his secretary. Ever since then Pamela's little house, close to South Kensington Station, had been a port of call for husbands whose wives had no time for them.

These husbands believed her to be a woman of wide reading and considerable culture on the strength of some trite quotations from the minor poets with which she made considerable play. She could always impress them by invoking Cynara, killing the thing she loved, thanking whatever Gods there be, wishing herself in Grantchester or hearing the bells on Bredon. Her theme song for Douglas was, so Kate understood, some flummery about a golden journey to Samarkand. They were going to take it some day, or had taken it, or sadly longed to take it. Some reference to it always accompanied those expensive little bottles of Opal 5.

To meet that smell in Andrew's flat was disconcerting, although it was a perfectly respectable smell, patronized by many women of impeccable taste. Hazel's preference had hitherto been for something called *Love Affair*, but there was no reason why she should not have decided to smell otherwise. Opal 5 did not invariably indicate humbug and mischief. Yet it repelled Kate so much that she stuck her head out of the window in order to avoid it. The young men in the garden below were planting dahlias.

Fifty-nine in June, she thought. I shall have my birthday on that cruise. I mean to enjoy that cruise very much. It will do me good. Soon I shall be dead. Everything has gone by too quickly. They are grown up. It's over. But we are all very fond of each other really.

To tell herself this was her defence against a haunting sense of failure. The children scolded and criticized. They bickered amongst themselves. Douglas had a grudge against her for being more of a mother than a wife. Her groping, untutored efforts to give them something better than she herself had known in the Addison Road might have been, after all, a mistake. They presented a less united front than other Mortimer households, although she clung to the belief that they had, amongst them, more genuine sympathy and affection, a firmer regard for one another's rights and feelings. They were, at least, quite honest. Nothing underhand had ever gone on in Edwardes Square. Her own mother had not scrupled to listen at doors, eavesdrop on the telephone, or read any letters which her daughters might have left lying about. Stephanie, Moira, Georgina, and Fanny had adopted the same tactics with their own children. Love, in their eyes, imposed no obligations in the way of candour and plain dealing.

So why did I have to be different? wondered Kate, hanging out of the window. They're planting those dahlias too close together. If it hadn't been for those two next door, my life might have been ... Freddie and Edith. Poor things! What's become of them? It's years since I ... Edith's eyes when she heard me tell a lie! ... Of course one had to lie to Mama or life wouldn't have been worth ... I felt so base. So vulgar ... not morals exactly ... aristocratic. There was something aristocratic about Edith. Some things she couldn't do. Not wouldn't *Couldn't*. So, ever since, I've felt uncomfortable about lying to people I love, yes, and I threw that croquet mallet at Fanny for laughing. My own sister! My awful temper! Thank goodness I never seem to lose it with children. I might have killed her and been hanged. I should hate to be hanged. But otherwise . . . I loathe Fanny. Yes I do. My daughters don't loathe each other. I've brought them up not to. We are all very fond . . . Ha! Ha! *Ha!* Fanny's laugh. Like a donkey braying. She still laughs like that. 'Ha! Ha! *Ha!* Edith Challoner's been presented. It's in the paper. Mustn't she have looked killing in a train and feathers?' So I threw . . .

Hazel reappeared in tapered slacks and a cotton jacket.

'We'd better go down and get that machine,' said Kate, reluctantly returning to the smell of Opal 5.

'Oh, you mustn't. I'll get Bob to bring it up. He's down there gardening.'

'Bob who?'

'I don't know. He and Simon share the ground-floor flat. Do have some . . .' Hazel dived into the kitchen, '. . . I got some tomato juice, for you specially, because you don't like gin.'

Tepid tomato juice in a smeary glass was produced. Kate, sipping it, decided to divulge her plans. Hazel at least would not scold or criticize.

'I,' she said, 'am off on a cruise in ten days' time. What do you think of that?'

'Oh? How simply fabulous!'

'I thought I might treat myself to a little holiday.'

'Oh, I am glad. Mummie went on a cruise once. To Bermuda. It was fabulous. They had everything. An orchestra and everything. And the food was absolutely fabulous. And then, in Greece, there's all the history and the ruins. You'll love that. Excuse me, I'll get Bob to bring up the machine while he's still out there. Can I have your car key?'

Kate finished the tomato juice and wondered why nobody had surnames any more. Bermuda was just the sort of place to which Hazel's Mummie would take a cruise. A boring woman.

All the history and the ruins . . . but had she mentioned Greece? She did not think so. How did Hazel know? Had she known of it already? Who could have told her? Douglas? She believed that he had not seen Andrew and Hazel lately.

'How did you know I was going to Greece?' she demanded, when Hazel returned with the sewing machine. 'I never said so. I merely said I was taking a cruise.'

The girl stared at her in manifest consternation.

'Has anybody . . .' began Kate.

Then she remembered one of her anti-Mortimer maxims: *Never catechize.* She put the question less aggressively.

'Perhaps somebody mentioned it already?'

'Ye-es,' said Hazel miserably. 'It must be that. I must have heard something . . .'

Go on, you fool! Find out who it was.

Opal 5?

No, no, no! Impossible. She mustn't come here. She sits inside that house of hers, in a flattering light, with a chiffon scarf to hide the wrinkles round her neck and a black lace mantilla to hide the bald spot on top. She and Douglas sit there talking rubbish. They don't talk about me. They can't. And she doesn't come here. She mustn't. Douglas is one thing. Andrew is quite another. If she came here I should . . . I should throw something. I won't ask any more, in case she does. Better talk about the sewing machine. Better explain it to her.

A demonstration followed which Hazel did not appear to follow very well, although she frequently declared the sewing machine to be fabulous.

'You can get all your curtain material for the new house

in the July sales,' suggested Kate, 'and have them run up by September.'

'Yes. I could do.'

'Though we've got some curtains put away at Edwardes Square which might do for some of your windows. That would save you a certain amount of trouble. You must come and look at them and see if you like them.'

'That's . . . that's sweet of you.'

'We'd better go up to the new house and measure the windows first. I could drive you up any time.'

'Absolutely sweet . . .'

'I'm off in ten days. We'd better do it as soon as possible. Would Thursday or Friday . . .'

'Sweet simply. Only . . . only . . . we're not buying that house after all.'

'What? I thought it was all settled.'

'No. Andrew hadn't signed anything . . . and he's changed his mind.'

'I never knew that.'

'It was only last night. He decided last night.'

She might have told me before, thought Kate. If she wasn't so hen-witted she'd have told me at once.

'I'm not sorry, in a way,' she said. 'To tell you the truth, I never much liked that house. Such an awkward kitchen. But you've got to turn out of here haven't you?'

'Oh yes. At the end of August.'

'Then you've got to find another house. I believe that one I wanted you to look at, the one in Chiswick, is still . . . I'll ring up and find out.'

'Oh . . . . oh . . . sweet of you! But I think . . . Andrew has found another flat, actually.'

'Another flat? Where?'

'I . . . I'm not quite sure. It isn't settled yet.'

'Hazel dear! You must know where it is!'

'In . . . in . . . in Bruton Street. I think it's in Bruton Street.'

'Off Berkeley Square? *That* Bruton Street? Oh no! You must be mistaken. He'd never look for a flat there.'

'A . . . a friend is arranging it . . . on special terms.'

'But nobody lives in Bruton Street. I mean not the sort of . . . What friend? Who suggested it?'

Hazel did not answer. She gazed at her mother-in-law in terrified supplication.

Any true Mortimer would have turned the silly little creature inside out forthwith. She had clearly been instructed to say nothing about this change of plan, which was evidence that Andrew expected his mother to oppose it. Nor was Douglas likely to approve. Bruton Street! The cousin of the head of Andrew's firm had been, at one time, a little inclined to suggest that the boy gave himself airs which must be dropped if he wanted to join Mortimer and Tyndale. Douglas had been disposed to agree and had been impatient over Andrew's reluctance to seize this solid opportunity. Of course the work would be small beer, demanding little inspiration and involving a great deal of drudgery. The same might be said of any profession. Douglas himself had never found a solicitor's life particularly inspiring. No firm on earth was likely to offer Andrew a cathedral or so to design, whatever opinion Kate might hold of her precious son's capacities.

It was common sense to interfere promptly before so silly a scheme could go any farther. Hazel might have promised Andrew to say nothing, but she must be bullied into breaking that promise. A mother, when her children's interest is at stake, is justified in any action, however shady.

Kate sighed and said:

'Well, I won't ask any more. I quite see . . . when one's plans are unsettled it doesn't do to tell everybody. People get worked up and implore one not to do things one isn't going to do anyway. So I'll bottle up my curiosity. I'm sure Andrew will decide sensibly. No, I won't have any more tomato juice, thanks. I really ought to be getting back.'

Hazel, trembling with relief, made no effort to detain her. As they went towards the stairs the telephone rang. On perceiving that the caller was Hazel's Mummie, Kate blew the child a kiss and went downstairs by herself. Telephone conversations with Hazel's Mummie were liable to outlast a night in Russia.

When she had got into her car she sat for a while, motionless, too much perturbed to drive away. She was far from sure that she had acted wisely and half ashamed of herself for not having extracted more details from Hazel. Douglas might think that she ought to have interfered.

Voices came to her from beyond the privet hedge. The gardeners must have thought that she had driven off long ago.

'Mums' day upstairs. Her Mum to tea in a Bentley. And his Mum in a Vauxhall with a sewing machine.'

'Oh, the Bentley wasn't her Mum. That was a Mrs Shelmerdine. She's fixing them up with a super flat in the West End. I heard them talking about it on the stairs.'

She should have had it out with Douglas forthwith, if only to protect herself from the virus of unresolved suspicion. Yet she dared not take the risk of discovering that he had been a party to such an underhand transaction. She preferred to believe that he could not possibly have known anything about it and that he would be very angry when it came to light. Even so she was furious with him. Her nose had not deceived her in the matter of Opal 5. Pamela had been to Swiss Cottage and had told Hazel about the cruise to Greece. Douglas must have told Pamela. They were all going round and discussing it behind her back.

Her fury was such that she relished the thought of the storm breaking after she had departed on her cruise. Douglas would have to deal with it unsupported. Since he had never attempted to deal with any domestic crisis he would be obliged to send a telegram begging for her return. That would give her an excellent excuse for cutting short a trip which no longer greatly attracted her, but which was now being forced upon her by family criticism and opposition. As the news spread their protests poured in.

Bridie considered that she should have taken a regular Hellenic Cruise; anything else was sheer waste of money. Nor might she bathe; at her age such diversions, even in the Aegean, were likely to bring on rheumatism.

The *Wanderers*, according to Judith, were notoriously inefficient. Brian's parents knew somebody who had sailed on the *Latona* and contracted diphtheria. Brian's parents wondered why Kate did not visit the Norwegian Fiords.

Fanny rang up from Sussex. She was the only one of Kate's sisters now living in England. Stephanie and Moira were dead, and Georgina was in New Zealand. What, demanded Fanny, lay behind this caper? Why should Kate want to spend three weeks on a ship, shut up with people who did not belong to her?

'Why does anybody take a holiday?' parried Kate.

'If you want a change, why not come to us? We're always asking you and you never will. The garden just now . . .'

'I want to get farther afield. Right away.'

'Right away? What from?'

Kate made no reply. She could picture Fanny down in Sussex, with her eyes popping out of her head.

'Has there been,' demanded Fanny, 'an upset?'

'No,' said Kate, picking up the telephone directory. '*No!*'

If Fanny had not been fifty miles away the directory might have gone at her head, as the croquet mallet had gone, on that memorable occasion.

An upset was the Mortimer term for husband trouble. It could mean anything: a husband who took to drink, wrote poetry in secret, lent too much money to a friend, sang in his bath, suffered from impotence, failed to cut his toe nails, was frightened of thunder, or threatened to become a Roman Catholic. No detail, however squalid and humiliating, was withheld from the clan symposium by anybody save Kate.

'Is it,' hissed Fanny, 'anything to do with that Mrs . . .?'

'NOTHING WHATEVER!'

'Don't shout. You're breaking my ear drums.'

Kate hung up. A few seconds later Fanny rang again complaining that they had been cut off.

'Have you been to see a doctor?' she demanded.

'No. Why should I?'

'It's so utterly unlike you, this cruise. Either you're ill or else you're unhappy. I want to know which so I can write and tell Georgina.'

'Oh, I see. Oh, very well. Tell Georgina that Douglas has been embezzling clients' money. I'm going because I don't want to be in the house when the police come for him.'

'Are you trying to be funny?'

'I'm not trying to be funny. I *am* funny. Ever so funny. You and Georgina have said so often enough. I'm going on this cruise because I want to see the Cyclades and the Sporades.'

'The what?'

'The Cyclades and the Sporades.'

'They sound like skin diseases. I don't believe it for a minute. You're terribly upset about something. I can tell that from your voice. You're going to do something silly.'

Kate hung up again and rushed out of the house to buy a needlessly expensive bathing suit.

The fatal day arrived. Since Bridie had borrowed the car for the week-end Douglas had to escort Kate to the station in a taxi. He failed, as usual, to secure it at the very early hour which she deemed prudent. Telephone calls to neighbouring ranks proved fruitless. Eventually he was forced to go out on a search in Kensington High Street. When he returned with a taxi Kate was fuming on the doorstep.

They set off, a little on the late side, but not as late as she felt they were. The *Wanderers*, when they reached the station, were not yet entrained. A glum group, standing in front of a barrier, seemed to consist entirely of wives scolding husbands for a late start and husbands maintaining that an earlier start would merely have meant a longer wait in this mob.

Kate giggled a little as she listened to these familiar exchanges. Douglas did not. He stood patiently beside her, carrying her over-night bag. Two large suitcases had been registered and would, so she believed, reappear in her cabin on the *Latona*. She herself carried a bucket bag which she would entrust to nobody since it contained her spectacles, her money, her tickets, her travellers' cheques, and her passport.

At last the barrier was removed. The crowd surged forward, stringing along the train in search of reserved seats. A moth-eaten-looking person, with *Wanderers Ltd* on his cap, stood at a distance, cynically watching them. He offered neither help nor advice. Kate, after running up and down a little with her bucket bag, found her seat in a compartment full of bickering couples. They all smiled at one another briefly, in acknowledgement of the fact that they were to be cooped up together on the *Latona* for three weeks. They then ignored one another, aware that it is never wise to become intimate with fellow travellers too soon. There might be people on the *Latona* whose looks they liked better. Wives told husbands where to put train cases. Kate stood at the window smiling down at Douglas on the platform.

How old he looks! she thought. He didn't always look as old as this.

Which was a ridiculous reflection although it was impossible to decide how he had always looked. The tall, dark, romantic young man who had, for a short time, swept her off her feet and had once eagerly awaited her at the altar was now a stooping, grizzled person who waited composedly for her to go away. The transformation had taken place by imperceptible degrees.

She poked her head out of the window to say:

'The chemist has the prescription for your pills.'

'Oh? Good!'

'All the addresses, for my letters, are on the hall table.'

'I know. You told me.'

With a visible effort he, too, smiled.

'Mind you don't get left behind by mistake on Naxos,' he told her. 'Stick to tomato juice.'

For a moment she did not perceive the allusion. His smile took her aback. It was an upshot beam on the clouds after sunset. It belonged to the days when he did not always agree with her.

'Oh yes . . .' she said, pulling herself together. 'Strong drink . . . Bacchus . . . Ariadne. Yes. I'll be careful.'

Keeping her head out of the window gave her a crick in the neck. She drew it in, wishing that the train would start. So soon as she was gone he would probably ring up Pamela.

'No, no. *Not* on top of my hat!' said one of the wives behind her, to a husband who was still fussing about with luggage.

The train slid forward so suddenly that Kate had no time to wave.

Brian's parents had been quite right. The *Wanderers* were remarkably inefficient and the cruise was an exasperating failure from the start. The *Latona*, reached after a chaotic journey to Trieste, turned out to be scarcely sea-worthy. Ten per cent of the registered luggage never reappeared. The remainder was flung at random into dirty cabins. The food was uneatable. Very seldom did any water, hot or cold, come out of the taps. After a week of it Kate was not the only passenger who thought wistfully of those Hellenic Cruises, once dismissed as too conventional.

Primitive places, little known and off the map, seldom offer landing opportunities for craft of any size, nor can transport from ship to shore be taken as a matter of course. On more than one occasion the *Latona* lay for hours, dismally hooting for men and boats miles away, fishing mullet.

'They seem to have left everything to chance,' complained Kate to Miss Shepheard, with whom she shared a cabin. 'They should have sent someone round in advance to make arrangements.'

'I think they did,' said Miss Shepheard. 'But the Greeks are terribly unreliable. They let everybody down.'

'They don't let *Eagle Tours* down. We saw that at Delos.'

An *Eagle Tour* had arrived at Delos, in a spick-and-span-looking ship, one morning when the *Latona* was forlornly hooting. The poor *Wanderers* never set foot upon that glittering island. They had been obliged to watch, in helpless fury, while boats, assembled in readiness, took the *Eagles* off.

'I shouldn't have cared to land on Delos,' said Miss Shepheard. 'Those *Eagles* made it look like an ant heap, all milling round and listening to guides.'

'We make any place look like an ant heap, whenever we do manage to land. And we mill round more than the *Eagles* did, because we don't know where to go. And we're behind on our itinerary. We ought to be at Skiathos by now. It's one of the places where we're supposed to pick up mail.'

'Not me,' said Miss Shepheard. 'I shan't get any mail.'

As a cabin companion she was congenial, since she was the least discontented passenger on board. At the age of seventy she had recently buried a father of ninety-eight to whom she had been a bond slave all her life. This was the first holiday that she had ever known and her cheerfulness was refreshing. Nobody else on the *Latona* was particularly congenial: Kate had scarcely troubled to discover their names.

'I want *my* letters,' she said.

It was her birthday, but she did not mention this in case Miss Shepheard might think herself obliged to buy some chocolates at the cruise shop. Never before in her life had she spent a birthday apart from her family; she felt unexpectedly forlorn.

They reached Skiathos in the afternoon. Mail bags were brought to the *Latona* and letters were distributed at the cruise office. Kate got three, from Douglas, Judith, and Bridie, and a large, ornate birthday card from Hazel. Meaning to savour them at leisure she put them, with her bathing dress, into the bucket bag and went on shore. Seclusion there might be easier to secure than it ever was on the boat, although the *Wanderers* were fast turning the little town into an ant heap.

After climbing steeply, through narrow streets, she came out upon a view of a woody bay, and sat down beneath the nearest olive tree. A few cruisers were already bathing on the rocky beach below. She decided to join them as soon as she had read her dear birthday letters; so far she had never gone swimming in her new expensive bathing dress. Bathing beaches were less plentiful than she had been led to expect, and jelly fish far more so.

Fishing her spectacles out of her bag she first examined Hazel's card, in the hope that a note from Andrew might lurk inside it. None did. The stupid, tasteless thing was inscribed, in Hazel's childish hand, with a greeting from both of them.

Men are lazy, she reminded herself, falling into a Mortimer generalization. Men are all alike. They don't think.

She expected most pleasure from Bridie's letter, so she saved it to the last and began with Douglas, who never had much to say.

My dear Kate,

I hope that this will duly reach you on your birthday, and that your cruise is coming up to expectations. Your postcard from Syracuse did not sound very enthusiastic, but rough weather may have accounted for that. You must let me know, when you get home, what you'd like for a present. Even if I could guess there would be no point in posting a parcel to the Sporades.

I go on very well. Mrs Piper cooks me excellent meals. All the lights on the top floor fused. I told her to get it seen to.

Otherwise there is no news. I had supper with Judith and Brian on Sunday. I did not see the children, who were in bed, but they are reported to be well. Brian and I had a slight brush. I rather think he has made a mess of a libel case we gave him. He has an unfortunate manner. If he thinks the judge an ignorant old fool he makes no attempt to conceal the fact. His conceit is likely to be a handicap to him. I can't give him cases if he's going to make a mess of them. He may be my son-in-law but I have the client to consider.

I gather that Cromer is off this year. They are joining Brian's parents on the Isle of Wight. I told Judith that you were keeping August free for Cromer. I expect she'll write to you.

I have a picture accepted at the Exhibition of Amateur Water Colourists. A sketch of the Coolins I did in Skye last year, I don't expect you remember it? As you say, I've sketched the Coolins rather often.

Your loving husband: D.

The news that Cromer was off annoyed Kate so much that she hurried on to Judith's letter. A fortnight alone with the babies had been a treat to which she had eagerly looked forward. But Judith, after an affectionate paragraph of birthday greetings, airily disposed of it. Nor was the pill much sweetened by a flattering tribute to Kate's efficiency as a grandmother.

This means that Brian and I won't be able to get off by

ourselves and it won't be much holiday for me, as I can't leave the children for half an hour with Mrs Loder. She's so nervous. She can't manage them for toffee. There's nobody like you, Mother, with little children. But Brian would rather go to Freshwater. He doesn't see his parents very often.

And now I have something very upsetting to tell you. I hate to do it on your birthday, but really it's urgent. If anything can be done at all, there's no time to be lost.

Andrew, if you please, is throwing up his job with Mortimer and Tyndale! He says he has always hated it. He's gone back to that daft old pipe dream of being an 'Interior Decorator'.

He's got a job with a firm just starting in Bruton Street. Mrs Shelmerdine is putting up the money and says that all her friends have promised to get Andrew to do their houses for them. She does have that sort of friend, I suppose. People who think it's smart not to know what colour paint they want. And he's not buying that house. He and Hazel are to have some kind of flat over the shop in Bruton Street.

It's cold, thought Kate, searching in her bag for a light wrap. Although the sun blazed down upon Skiathos the shock of this letter had sent a chill through all her nerves. Impossible! she told herself, two or three times. He can't. He mustn't. Douglas will . . . Douglas doesn't know yet. 'There is no news,' he said.

She read on:

Brian says it's a crazy scheme. It's got no security. Those smart people aren't reliable. They won't pay their bills, and another year they'll all go to somebody else. Brian thinks the mistake was to put all that money up for Andrew to begin with. It gave him the wrong idea of his own importance. If he'd learnt his job the hard way, as Brian has had to do, it would have been better for him.

Father came to supper on Sunday and we said what we could, but it was no use. He's been talked round, and he's in one of his sentimental: 'Ah! Youth! Youth!' moods. He says how differently most people would shape their lives if they had Andrew's chance to think again. A year ago, when Andrew got all that money, he was having a 'I'm a business man and no nonsense!' mood. He says now that too much pressure was put on Andrew. He's had a picture accepted lately for some exhibition and I dare say he sees himself as a frustrated artist forced by his mother to be a solicitor. He says that he and Andrew are both 'creative' types. And he won't write to you about it. He *says* he doesn't want to spoil your holiday. But I think he's frightened of what you'll say when you find out. He wasn't in a very sunny temper anyway. Brian took on a libel case for him and would have won it if the Judge hadn't been a senile idiot, but Father doesn't seem to realize that.

Anyway, *I* don't think you should be kept in the dark, in case you can think of any way to stop Andrew making such a fool of himself.

Kate flung off her little jacket again. Rage had countered that unnatural cold. A very large dose of adrenalin was coursing through her system. The scene before her had subtly changed its hue. A faint roseate haze lay over the white houses, the blue sea and the woody hills. She was, in actual fact, *seeing red*. This happened to her, occasionally. Bridie's letter, when she opened it, looked as though it was written on pink paper.

Judith says she's writing to you about Mrs Shelmerdine getting Andrew to throw up his job. I hope you can stop it. But I want to write about something else. It's been on the tip of my tongue for months, only I never quite dared. Now, this business of Andrew has brought me up to scratch.

Why do you let yourself be put into such a humiliating position? Why don't you and Father behave sensibly and get a divorce?

It's obvious that you don't need each other. I can understand that you stuck together, for *our* sakes, as long as we were children, so we shouldn't have a broken home. But there's no need for that now.

Then he could marry Mrs S. It seems she told Andrew that Father feels he can't ask you for his freedom, because you've been a good wife to him, according to your lights, though he has never been happy with you. Any move must come first from you.

I think it's a pity that you always try to pretend nothing goes on. Does this unrealistic attitude make anybody happy? People laugh at you about it, or else they pity you. I'm absolutely on your side, of course, but I can see that you two aren't suited. You're too good for him, and that's the truth.

There! I've said it! I believe all we Bensons would be much happier if we could call a spade a spade.

The red tinge of fury had faded from the landscape. Bridie's letter, though galling enough, need not be taken seriously. It was pure fantasy. Only Bridie, wallowing in Drama, could have achieved so complete a misunderstanding of the situation. Douglas and Pamela could not possibly desire a closer, more serious tie. Any conjugal strain would immediately shatter their sentimental duet. Gentle regrets there might have been – wistful sighs over 'this sorry scheme of things', but Kate herself was an essential third in their ridiculous game. Sometimes, when much exasperated with them, she had wryly amused herself by picturing their dismay should she die suddenly, leaving them with no excuse for delay in booking for Samarkand.

It's funny, she decided. Really it's very funny. Or it would be if there were anyone to share the . . .

Then the first blow came back at her. Andrew! His whole career! 'There is no news.' Oh, what a lie! He knew all the time. He knew before I went away. They arranged for it to happen like this while I was away. Oh, I'll never forgive them! Never! So it's all my fault because I put pressure on . . . why the hell must I be told what Brian thinks we should do with our money? It would do Douglas good, it would serve him right if he did have to marry her. He'd sup sorrow with the spoon of grief . . . old Nanny . . . who did she say that about? She was always saying it, whenever anyone . . . I believe she said I would, if I married Douglas! She never liked him, but poor Michael was dead and I wanted to get . . . and I *did* think I was in love . . . he'd sup sorrow with the spoon of grief after a week of married life with Pamela, and serve him right. It's funny. But Andrew! Oh, what shall I do? What can I do?

Nothing.

The *Latona* gave a warning hoot. Kate collected her belongings and crept back to the harbour. There was something which she meant to buy before going on board again, but she could not remember what it was.

A kiosk displaying postcards reminded her. She had meant to buy cards at Skiathos on which to write her thanks for those dear birthday letters which she had expected to get.

4

Keritha became an ant heap as soon as the *Wanderers* had disembarked. Boats, on this occasion, had been available. Picnic lunches were distributed. There was a rush for an attractive-looking bathing beach. A straggle of adventurers set off up a mountain slope.

Nobody except Kate took the track which turned north and led round the island. She longed for solitude, but did not mean to go far, since she was very tired. At the ravine and the plank bridge she paused and sat down. She would rest here, eat a few of the dry sandwiches in her picnic bag, and do nothing until it was time to return to the ship. The place was cool and solitary. It would have been beautiful, had she been attuned to beauty.

She had not intended to think about those letters still lying unanswered in her cabin. It would be so much more sensible to think of something else. She sought for other topics, found none, and took refuge in the well-worn reflection that 'it was all very natural'. It was the common lot. Children grew up and turned into strangers. That was Nature – an enemy bound to win in the end. One must not quarrel with other people for behaving very naturally, although one might never with a clear conscience behave very naturally oneself.

For half an hour she sat there, ascribing to her own

discordant mood a vague sense of uneasiness which haunted the ravine as though she were not, after all, quite alone. Some invisible companion did not welcome her presence. Even the waterfall, with its persistent little commotion, seemed to be hostile. That sharp, tiny chatter sounded like a succession of unfriendly remarks which ultimately got on her nerves so much that she sought another refuge.

Round the next corner she came unexpectedly upon a long, low pleasant house set amidst garden slopes. A woman in a black dress was feeding doves upon a terrace. The scene was familiar. Edith Challoner, in a long black pinny, used to feed doves fifty years ago in the Addison Road. Kate stood watching until a square, pale face was turned her way. Gaunt and aged though it was, she knew it at once for the face of her earliest friend.

'Edith!'

'Why . . . Kate!'

'It's you. It *is* you. Not changed a bit.'

Edith came tranquilly down from the terrace, took her hand, kissed her, and said:

'How nice! Would you like a bath?'

'No, thank you,' said Kate, remembering that Edith never said the expected thing.

'But there will be plenty of time before lunch. Freddie is out catching mullet.'

'Is he here too? This house?'

'It's our house. You'd much better have a bath. You'd enjoy it.'

Edith's remarks might be unpredictable but they were never silly. Kate had not had a bath since leaving London. On the *Latona* there were merely showers which nobody could manipulate.

'Well . . . perhaps . . .'

As they turned towards the house a fisherman came up from the cove with a basket of mullet. It was Freddie, and he too was very little changed. As children the Challoners had looked elderly. Now, upon the threshold of old age, some after-glow of childhood hung about them. He flinched a little when he saw Kate, but his sister said something quickly to him in Greek, whereat he smiled and said, in his turn:

'How nice! Where is your donkey?'

She explained that she had no donkey. They were both shocked to learn that she had walked all the way.

'If you'd told them on the quay that you were coming here, to see us, they'd have given you a donkey,' lamented Edith.

'I didn't know I was going to see you.'

'She's just going to have her bath,' said Edith to Freddie. 'Tell Eugenia we have a guest to lunch.'

'Oh yes,' said Freddie, as though a bath was the natural prelude to any hospitality. 'What wine do you like, Kate?'

'I leave that to you,' said Kate.

In the bathroom Edith produced two enormous towels and sat down in a chair by the window. A bath was apparently a social occasion and she was offering Kate her company. That had always been their custom; there had been a bathroom like this in the Challoners' London house. Kate and Edith had often, in childhood, amused themselves by sitting at either end of a vast tiled tub, sailing fleets of boats made from half walnut shells, with matchstick masts and curved paper sails. Kate had made argosies like these for her children and her grandchildren. Slightly disconcerted she shuffled out of her clothes and climbed into the water.

'Do you remember our walnut boats?' she asked. 'They were rather clever. Where did we get the idea?'

'Mama used to make them. All the children here make them.'

The bath was extremely pleasant. Kate rested her head on a ledge, which seemed to be put there for the purpose, and relaxed. A spell which she had always felt when with the Challoners began to steal over her.

'How long have you been here?' she asked.

'Oh. A long time. Ever since we came here.'

As if aware that this was inadequate Edith added:

'We came here with Mama when Papa died, and never went away any more. This is our home. We built this house.'

'When was that?' asked Kate sleepily.

'In the Spring. We came back in the Spring.'

'It must be lovely here then.'

'You can smell the flowers out at sea. We smelt them over the sea the day we came back.'

Kate closed her eyes and saw these wayworn travellers gliding over a laughing sea to the hyacinth slopes of Keritha.

'To your own native shore,' she murmured. 'But I meant what year was it.'

'Nineteen twenty-two. We couldn't have come much before because one of the wars was going on.'

'All that time. I never knew. The last I heard of you was a paragraph in the newspaper; you'd been presented. I hadn't the least idea you were here. I came to Keritha quite by chance. Isn't it strange?'

'No. Most things happen by chance. It's strange when they don't.'

The longer Kate considered this statement the less she found in it to refute.

'But we do always call it strange when something happens by chance,' she argued. 'I suppose we don't like to feel that so much really does. We'd sooner there was always some sort of pattern.'

'There's Freddie going for the wine,' said Edith, looking out of the window. 'We keep it down the well.'

'Yet chance sometimes makes patterns. Think of a Kaleidoscope! Edith! Think of a Kaleidoscope!'

'Why?'

To conduct Edith along any train of thought had always been impossible. Kate gave it up and announced that she had arrived on a cruise. This effectively shattered Edith's tranquillity.

'A cruise?' she whispered. 'Not . . . not a *Hellenic Cruise*?'

Her face was quite stiff with alarm and her tone suggested some kind of Black Mass.

'Oh no. Anything but. It's a cruise that goes to all the places Hellenic Cruises never go to.'

'You mean a lot of people have come? Are they here now?'

'They're swarming all over the island. Don't look so horrified. We shall all sail away again at six o'clock.'

'They . . . they never came here before . . . those things, those cruises,' murmured Edith in a shaken voice. 'Forgive me if I leave you. I must go and tell Freddie.'

She hurried away. Kate, dozing in the bath, reflected that this dismay was not surprising. The Challoners might well dislike an ant heap on Keritha. They could not be expected to like people, when people had been so very unkind to them, poor things.

It was as poor things that she had ultimately come to remember them. The walnut argosies belonged to very early days. Freddie, later, had vanished to school, coming back every holiday more silent, withered, and elderly. She and Edith had, for a time, attended a neighbouring day school, where her own life had been perpetually poisoned by humiliation on her friend's behalf.

If the ridicule showered upon Edith by pupils and teachers alike had been inhumane, their victim's inability to avoid it, her indifferent acceptance of the role of school freak, had been exasperating. Anybody else, considered Kate, would have made more concession to appearances, would have discarded the black pinny, would have puffed her hair out at the side with combs, as fashion then dictated, instead of pulling it straight back over her square skull. Edith might have tried to walk, stand, and sit as the herd did. Every gesture was alien. She accepted her mid-morning glass of milk, dispensed by Matron through a hatch, with a deep bow. On the very first day this bow caused titters in the milk queue. Yet she repeated it until forbidden to do so any more by Kate. She walked into Prayers as though taking part in some genuine religious procession. Her posture in class was so abnormally still that it earned her the nickname of 'The Statue'. Her answers were not merely wrong, but fantastic. Kate recalled a history mistress, a Miss Bynion, who had been fool enough to demand from Edith some comment on the battle of Hastings. After her long, customary pause, Edith exclaimed, her black eyes flashing:

'The Conqueror was a savage man from the north. After the battle he made a feast and a harper called Taillefer sang to him about "*Karlomain, et Roland, et ses vassals qui moururent à Roncesvalles*". Those people were French and the Norman liked to hear how the French had lost a battle. He didn't want a song about victory. Only defeat. Savage people can't really win victories because they don't know how to enjoy themselves.'

Miss Bynion, to whom all this was possibly news, said:

'Thank you, Edith. That may be very interesting but it won't get you through Matric.'

Edith, in the end, never took Matric. She departed to a convent. Her parents abandoned the Addison Road for South America where her father pursued, for some years, some wild-goose chase up the Amazon. She became, in retrospect, 'poor Edith', but her pathos grew less poignant as Kate learnt to be more mundane. Poor Edith, so it appeared, was very rich – an heiress.

Freddie, too, was remembered with less compassion as his wealth came to be understood. His persecution had been more severe than Edith's since non-conformity is always more heavily visited upon a boy. He was debagged, flung into rivers; his precious collection of gramophone records was systematically broken and methylated spirit was put into his tea. Not a word did he say about this purgatory but at one point, when about fourteen, he had rebelled. It was a drama which never reached the ears of the Mortimers although the servants in both households knew of it and of the sufferings which had driven him to revolt. Kate learnt of it long afterwards, from old Nanny Mortimer, grown garrulous in old age.

'Tried to hang himself. They cut him down and brought him round and his father gave him the choice of going back to school or a lunatic asylum for life. He chose school. Of course nobody had heard of Dr Frood then. If it was now they'd have sent him to Harley Street to get adjusted. But even Dr Frood would have had a job to adjust those Challoners.'

By that time poor Edith and poor Freddie had become rich freaks, who could afford to buy themselves some safe retreat in the company of people who would not, at least, mock them to their faces. So Kate had supposed for the last forty years and she had been quite right. Keritha must have been an excellent solution.

Climbing reluctantly out of the bath she wrapped herself in a towel and wandered to the window. Edith and Freddie were just finishing an earnest conversation in the garden below. Edith went back into the house and Freddie shouted:

'Yorgos!'

A young boy appeared to whom Freddie gave a brief order. Yorgos scampered off towards the village, grinning broadly, as though delighted with his errand. Kate had an impression that it was connected with Edith's tidings and the presence of the *Latona*.

She dressed again and went downstairs. Her hosts were waiting for her in the hall. Freddie had put on a crisp linen suit. Seeing them thus a second time, no longer dazzled by surprise, she noted a change in them both. They had become immensely dignified. In former days, they had never, for all their sufferings, lacked dignity of a sort. It was implicit in their imperviousness to mockery, their silent stoicism, their freedom from resentment or anxiety. They wore it like some tattered cloak of stately antecedents. Now it clothed them royally and silenced some slightly patronizing praise of their house which she had been about to offer.

In the dining-room a shrivelled old woman with something of the same dignity was giving directions to two young maids. Freddie said something to her, upon which she bowed very low to Kate.

'Eugenia,' he explained.

Kate bowed back, wondering if she ought not to have shaken hands. Eugenia seemed to be something more than an upper servant. As soon as they were seated she left the room.

The meal was delicious. It began with soup so good that Kate felt impelled to eat it in silence, since failure to offer it her whole attention almost amounted to a slight. She had enjoyed no meal since leaving Edwardes Square, and began to wonder if even the doves at Keritha would accept those nasty sandwiches in her picnic bag.

With the arrival of the mullet she was about to give an account of her cruise when Freddie began to talk of wine. He regretted that his own vineyard produced nothing save red wine, which would not do with fish. She should have some of it later, with cheese. The islanders, he said, had never exported their wine; it was merely produced for their own consumption and the younger people now preferred to drink Coca-Cola, whenever they could afford it.

'That American drink?' said Kate disapprovingly. 'What a pity!'

'Don't you like it?' asked Edith.

'I've never tasted it.'

'Then why is it a pity?'

'It seems so . . . so mass produced. Their own wine surely . . .'

'Their own wine,' said Freddie, 'is very nasty. I won't disturb your digestion by telling you what they put into it to promote fermentation.'

Whenever Kate tried to mention the cruise he firmly steered the conversation away to some other topic. Unpleasant subjects, it seemed, were not discussed at Keritha during a meal. Kate began to find him a little formidable. She thought that she had never seen a man so unquestionably master in his own house.

After fruit and cheese they went out to a shady corner of the terrace for coffee. As soon as Kate had got her Kümmel he said:

'Now! Tell us how you got here.'

'This cruise,' Kate assured them, 'is very unlikely ever to come again. It's appallingly organized. Everybody is most discontented. I should think the firm will go bankrupt quite soon.'

'What sort of people are they?' asked Edith unhappily. 'What do they want to find out?'

'Nothing. There's nothing here to find out, is there?'

'So what are they doing?' asked Freddie.

'Some of them are climbing the mountain and some are bathing.'

'Where are they bathing?'

When she described the bathing beach the Challoners exchanged glances.

'What a good thing you didn't bathe,' murmured Edith.

'Yes. Isn't it? I was strongly tempted, it looked such a nice place. But if I had I shouldn't have come up here. I'd have gone away without ever knowing you lived here. Whatever you may say about chance, Edith, it's very strange.'

'What,' asked Freddie, 'did Edith say about chance?'

'She says most things happen by chance. I don't agree.'

'You don't? Since when?'

'I've always thought we make things happen.'

'No. Not always.'

He got up and went into the house.

'When you go back,' said Edith, 'Freddie will take you

79

in our boat. It will be better than walking. We have a little quay and a boat house just down below here.'

'Oh, he mustn't bother. It's a very pleasant walk, and nothing when it's down hill.'

'It mightn't be so pleasant going back. I'm sure he'll say you must.'

'Edith! Is there anything against the bathing here?'

'That depends.'

'On what?'

'On chance,' said Edith, with one of her sudden, disconcerting fits of laughter.

'I can't help feeling it wasn't chance that brought me up here. I hadn't in the least expected to see you, yet when I did I wasn't all that surprised. Perhaps the name Keritha registered subconsciously. You must have talked about Keritha in the old days, although I've quite forgotten whether you did. I don't say that we make things happen, but something in ourselves is always pushing us along a certain path, whether we know it or not. Part of me remembered and came looking for you. My coming today was settled fifty years ago, when we were children in London!'

'The people here,' said Edith, 'would say that it was all written on your face when you were only three days old. On the third night after a baby is born they leave the door open and tie the dogs up and put food and drink on the table. Three of Them come. One gives good luck and the other bad luck, and the third decides how long the child is to live. So it's not much use worrying about anything.'

'But, Edith! Who on earth are They supposed to be? Surely . . .'

'Ssh! There's Freddie coming back.'

Freddie returned with a large notebook.

'Listen,' he said. 'Here's a poem about Chance. It's meant to make you think of a wheel going round, and some spokes coming up before the others are gone.'

He read:

'The turning earth
Is my domain,
And human gain
Is little worth,
Nor any pain
Endured for long,
Nor any wrong
In full repaid.
My wheel is stayed
To cheat the strong,
By me betrayed.
My wheel I turn
So cities burn,
And lizards sleep
Mid stubborn fern
On tower and keep.
The starveling sheep
A peasant calls
To flee the cold
In nameless halls,
Where royal walls
Provide a fold
O'er buried gold
That's nothing worth –
Since I ordain
Or halt the pain
Of turning earth.'

'I seem to remember that,' said Kate slowly. 'But I can't place it. Didn't we read it long ago when we were children?'

'Why, Kate,' cried Edith, 'you and Freddie made it up! There was a prize offered in a newspaper for a poem on Chance, and you competed for it. Have you quite forgotten?'

'I remember that Freddie used to write poetry.'

'You made up that one together. He thought of the wheel shape. You thought of a lot of the words. He put: *Stop* the pain. And you said: No. *Halt* the pain. It didn't get the prize though.'

'You sat on the garden wall,' said Freddie, 'with all your red hair flying down your back, and said: Not stop . . . halt.'

'I remember,' said Kate, and began suddenly to cry, greatly to her own surprise.

Her hosts observed her with calm compassion. Freddie gave her some more Kümmel.

'I'm so sorry,' she apologized, mopping her eyes. 'I don't know what's the matter with me.'

'You feel sad,' observed Edith. 'One often does when one thinks of old times. It's natural to cry when one feels sad.'

'I believe it's this abominable cruise,' declared Kate. 'I'm so tired. So exhausted.'

At her description of it they both exclaimed in horror. Edith immediately urged her to abandon it and to stay with them on Keritha. This invitation was seconded by Freddie, after a moment of almost imperceptible hesitation. Kate explained that she could not afford to lose her cruise passage home, upon which they asked if the *Latona* was going south again immediately. If not, could she not stay with them for a few days and rejoin the cruise at some later point?

'It's going up through the Dardanelles to the Black Sea

next,' said Kate. 'And on the way back it's calling at an island called Thasos. We collect mail there.'

'Thasos,' Freddie assured her, 'is quite an easy trip from here. We'll run over in time to catch your horrid ship again.'

After a formal demur she accepted, unable to reject the chance of escape from the garlic, the crowds, the noise, and the endemic bad temper on the *Latona*. Two or three days in this tranquil, uninquisitive company, lying in hot baths and eating delicious food, might steady her nerves. She finished her Kümmel and Freddie took her down to the boat below the house. He would run her round to the *Latona*, where she might pack a suitcase and explain her plans to the cruise office, and then he would bring her back again.

'I want to take Edith over to Thasos soon, in any case,' he said as they sped westward. 'She hasn't been well lately. I think she should see a doctor.'

'Is there no doctor nearer than Thasos? What happens to people on Keritha if they get ill?'

'They get better or they die.'

'They must die rather often.'

'Not oftener than people on the mainland. Everybody dies just the once.'

'They must die sooner than they need.'

'How soon need people die?'

'I understand,' she said smiling, 'that it might have been written on our faces when we were three days old.'

At his startled look she added:

'Edith was telling me about it. Is it only on Keritha they believe it?'

'Oh no,' he said frowning. 'There's the same ceremony on Zagros. Only there they have names: Christ, his Mother, and John the Baptist. Here we just call them The Visitors.'

'It looks rather dull, Zagros. No trees. This is much prettier.'

'Zagros had plenty of trees once. So had a lot of the islands. They weren't always so bare. There used to be springs and groves. But nothing will grow where the Turks have been.'

'I knew they deforested most of the land. But they didn't dry up the springs, surely?'

'Maybe not. Perhaps the springs dried up at the mere sight of them.'

She remembered that Freddie and Edith had always spoken of the Turks as though the very word might have some malign and blasting influence. It would be of no use to argue, or to suggest that some volcanic or geographical change might also be responsible for this prevailing aridity.

'Then Keritha,' she said, 'is a sort of survival of the older landscape? What has saved it? How did it escape?'

'Foreigners never come here.'

'Why not? When it's so pretty?'

He did not answer. They were running in under a rickety companionway slung over the side of the *Latona*. She scrambled up to the deck. The island, when she turned to survey it, seemed to be no longer ant infested. Nobody was to be seen on the bathing beach or on the mountain slope. The ship was full of noise and agitation as though most of the passengers had re-embarked. Miss Shepheard, who seldom bothered to land anywhere, lay somnolent in a deck-chair.

'Back safely?' she said. 'Are you all right?'

'Yes. Why shouldn't I be?'

'Nobody else is. They're all lining up for the doctor.'

'What happened?'

'What didn't happen! Bees! This island is swarming with

them. Stinging like mad. And sea urchins! Hardly any of the bathers can walk. Some can't sit. Doctor is digging out the prickles. Thank goodness I didn't go ashore. But what about you?'

Kate's story, and her decision to stay, were received with dismay.

'I wouldn't if I were you. They say these things are chance . . . but . . . Keritha doesn't seem to like strangers.'

Edith's laughter, Edith's warning that the walk home might not be pleasant, recurred to Kate. There had been, moreover, that atmosphere of uneasiness beside the waterfall.

'Mrs Carter,' said Miss Shepheard, 'says there's an Influence. She's psychic, you know.'

'Oh rubbish! She says she's psychic.'

'She can't be very,' agreed Miss Shepheard, 'or she'd have spotted the Influence before she sat on a sea urchin. But honestly, I wouldn't spend a night here for any money.'

And what, wondered Kate, had Yorgos been up to, when he ran off grinning with a message from Freddie?

'I shall be all right,' she said. 'I've been invited.'

5

For thirty-six hours she dawdled on the terrace, ate, slept, listened to Freddie's gramophone, slept, ate, and dawdled on the terrace. Never in her life had she come so near to complete relaxation. The misery in which she had arrived was not, of course, dispelled; it had merely moved away to an endurable distance. Still aware of it in the offing she was able to ignore it. Life on Keritha provided a powerful anodyne.

Sometime the struggle must be resumed. She must scan and control her bitterness, and consider whether anything at all could be done to rescue Andrew from his latest folly. She must credit Douglas with a genuine wish to spare her on her holiday, mixed though his motives might have been. She must laugh off Bridie's dramatic fantasy and Brian's criticisms. She must believe that even Pamela might have been actuated by kindly, if mistaken, intentions. Everybody concerned must be permitted to behave very naturally; she herself must soar to unnatural heights of selfless tolerance, and there would be time enough to do all this when she got back to the *Latona*.

On the second day Edith took her up the hill to the home-farm where a new-born baby, great-nephew to Eugenia apparently, was holding court. They carried presents with them: spiced cakes, honey, a holy medal and a knitted shawl.

'Don't look at the baby too much,' warned Edith. 'And of course don't praise it. But you needn't spit. Some people do, but we've never relied much on spitting here. Zagros! You should see a christening on Zagros. Everybody spitting at everybody else and shouting and dancing round the font. The baby gets the best of it because it's under water. They're very religious on Zagros.'

'But this isn't a christening?'

'Oh no. The priest won't bring the font over here if he can help it. He thinks we're heathens. Keritha babies generally get christened on Zagros, at some friend's house, when they go over to be vaccinated. Freddie says they take out two insurance policies on the same trip.'

'Oh? They've got round to being vaccinated?'

'Certainly,' said Edith, rather offended. 'They're still very much afraid of small-pox. It used to be terrible. Even on Zagros they call it by the old name: *Eulogia*.'

'*Eu* . . . good? Good talk?'

'Well yes. It's polite. When you're frightened of anything it's wise to speak politely about it. Like calling the Furies the Eumenides.'

Meditating upon these polite words Kate was reminded of a riddle as yet unsolved in the Challoner household. She ventured upon a tentative inquiry about Eugenia.

'She's Freddie's really,' said Edith.

'Mm?' murmured Kate, uncertain how to take this.

'When we came here, thirty-five years ago, Freddie was a young man. Mama didn't think it right for him to live all alone so she sent for Eugenia, who is a sort of cousin.'

'I see. And . . . er . . . it was a success?'

'Oh yes. If it hadn't been, Mama would have got her a husband and found him someone else.'

'And she . . . just came trotting along when summoned?'

'She was very pleased and proud to be chosen. She wasn't pretty, but Mama said she was *une bonne affaire* and it takes more than a pretty face to satisfy a man.'

Foreigners! thought Kate, and reproved herself for insularity.

'Of course,' continued Edith, 'Mama taught her some things before she gave her to Freddie. Eugenia thought a hot bath unhealthy. She thought the water might soak through her skin and give her dropsy. But when Mama threatened to send her home again she gave in.'

'And they never thought of getting married?'

'Oh no. That would have upset everybody. Mama was the Lady here. When she died I was.'

'How old is she? Eugenia?'

'I don't know. Not as old as she looks. All the women here are old crones by the time they're thirty.'

These revelations cast quite a new light upon Freddie, whom Kate had always supposed to be mouldering away in some secluded retreat, slightly abnormal, a mere shadow of a man. Poor Freddie indeed! thought she, as she panted up the hill. He doesn't seem to have been poor Freddie at all.

'But you, Edith,' she said. 'Hasn't it been rather a lonely life for you here? Did you never want to get married?'

'There was nobody here for me to marry, and I couldn't have endured to go away. I've been very happy, really. The children . . . I loved the children so much.'

'Children? You mean . . . Freddie and Eugenia . . .?'

'Three. They had a little girl who died. It was very sad. Such a dear little girl. And two boys.'

Edith sighed and paused.

'Rest a little,' suggested Kate. 'You're tired.'

'I am. I don't know why. Perhaps I have some illness that makes me tired.'

They sat down under a tree and Kate, eyeing her friend uneasily, thought that the sooner the doctor in Thasos was consulted the better. These sudden spasms of exhaustion were disquieting.

'And the sons?' she asked. 'Where are they?'

'Dead too. They went away to fight and the foreigners killed them.'

'Both? Oh, Edith, how dreadful! How terribly sad!'

'They were the Flowers of the Forest,' said Edith.

Her tone, a trifle cold, suggested that this calamity must be dissociated from Keritha. The sacrifice of youth was a foreign custom which had been imposed upon the world for centuries.

'The prime of our land is cold in the clay,' murmured Kate in sad agreement, thinking for an instant of a boy whom she had loved long before she met Douglas, poor gay Michael, killed in the spring of 1918. 'That's true everywhere.'

'In any case,' continued Edith, 'they would have gone away and left us. War or no war. They were *dromokopi* – travellers. That was chosen when they were born. It would have been far sadder if they had been chosen to stay and been forced to go, and be buried far away from the earth where they belong. But we all knew they'd have to go. They grew up knowing it.'

'Why should they? Who chose? Freddie?'

'No. They chose for themselves really. It's always done here. You see, Keritha is so small. Only very few people can live on it, or they'd starve. More children are born than can ever be allowed to stay. So it's found out at once if a child is *dromokopos*, and then it's brought up knowing it will have to go.'

'How? How is it found out?'

'Any time after the third night they take it and put it on a stone, up on the mountain. Naked. Freddie says the stone was an altar once. He thinks that once they just left it there for a night . . . two nights? And if it was still alive when they came back then it could stay of course. But now, if it cries they say it's *dromokopos*. The ones who don't cry are *klisouriasmeni*. That means stay-at-homes.'

'I should think any child would cry, put suddenly on a cold stone.'

'Most do. But then, most must go.'

'Those who don't can't be very quick in the uptake.'

'Yes, but it's the *dromokopi* who've got to be quick in the uptake, fending for themselves in savage countries.'

'Why? What countries do they go to?'

'Oh, all over. England and America and places.'

'Edith! Those aren't savage countries.'

Edith said nothing, and Kate reflected that the Challoners had been given no strong reasons for thinking England civilized.

'And what happens,' she asked, 'if a stay-at-home, when it grows up, wants to travel, and a traveller wants to stay put?'

'I never heard of a traveller who wanted to stay. Some go who ought to have stayed. Mama did. She should never have left Keritha. And I think that Freddie and I are *klisouriasmeni*, even though we were born in London.'

'In any case, why can't the children decide a thing like that when they reach the age of reason?'

'When is the age of reason?' marvelled Edith.

'Or the child's I Q could be taken.'

Edith, it appeared, had never heard of I Q nor was she impressed by Kate's elucidation.

'You might just as well put a child on a stone to see if it has the sense to squall,' she protested. 'Freddie thinks the stone is a very good idea. He says most of the trouble in the world is caused by people who don't like the place they're in and can't or won't go away. So they try to change it and upset everybody.'

'I must argue that point with Freddie.'

'Oh no, you mustn't.'

'Mustn't argue with Freddie?'

'Nobody does. And he'll say I oughtn't to have told you about the stone or the Visitors or anything. He doesn't want people to come here interfering and bringing changes.'

'But, Edith! Change is necessary. It's right. We shouldn't resist it.'

'Why not?'

'It's inevitable. Bound to come.'

'I dare say. But that doesn't mean it's right or nice. So is death inevitable.'

'Without change there can be no progress.'

'Anyone here who likes progress will yell as soon as they get onto that stone. Then they go away and look for it somewhere else. The people who stay don't want it. I'm rested now. Let's go on.'

As they toiled up the hill again Kate said:

'But are they Christians? The people here?'

'Certainly they are. They're more Christian than the people in England are anyway. They don't think Christ is somebody who was born and died ever so long ago. They think He's here. They can't see Him, but He's good. The best person they can imagine. He's born every year and He dies every year, but He is so good that He's stronger than death.'

They were not the only guests at the farm. Baskets of little cakes were scattered everywhere amidst pecking poultry and ikons. The three-day-old baby lay swaddled on a cushion and his buxom mother darted about serving refreshments.

Edith was received with respect and with an ease which Kate found unfamiliar. She was obviously the Lady of Keritha but nobody was awkward or shy with her. The scene flowed on, without flurry or bustle, like a well-rehearsed play. The actors said and did the expected things, harassed by no alternatives. People likely to introduce innovations, in the way of business or lines, had probably been eliminated by the rite of the stone.

Maroulla, the baby's mother, bowed low and handed glasses of brown liquid. Kate took one, wondering what island brew this might be. It tasted unfamiliar but agreeable.

'What's this?' she whispered to Edith.

'Coca-Cola.'

6

Freddie, for thirty-five years, had taken no orders from anybody. As she came to perceive this Kate began to see Keritha as a stronghold rather than an asylum.

His manner was so mild, his voice so quiet, and his taste, in all the refinements of life, so pronounced that she found him hard to reconcile with her notion of a manly man, a type hitherto associated with loud noises, bluff manners, and no taste at all. Fanny had always contemptuously referred to him as 'that born pansy'. His schoolmates had made life hell for him because he was so unlike themselves. Yet, speculating upon their lot, compared with his, she reached some surprising conclusions. They were now, in all probability, picking their cautious way through middle age, agreeing with their wives, contradicted by their children, and bullied by their servants, supposing them to have any. At home or abroad, they were continually taking orders, continually receiving instructions, set up for their guidance in public places. They were commanded to keep Britain tidy, their dogs on a lead, and death off the roads; to shut gates and to exterminate the Colorado beetle; to travel by rail, avoid the rush hour, and tender the exact fare; to fill up and return the enclosed form, to be immunized against diphtheria, to sneeze into a pocket handkerchief, and to wash their hands.

She had become inured to this civilized regimentation. She believed it to be necessary, yet a short sojourn on Keritha led her to wonder whether it might not, in some degree, diminish the manliness of a man. For his own good, perhaps, he must be forced to shrink a little – to forgo his natural stature. This, certainly, had been the creed of all the Mortimers and all the Naylers. She had never quite accepted it, and it now struck her that a world full of little notices and printed commands might indicate a world increasingly dominated by women.

Some facts about Freddie quite shocked her. His ethical code, though strict, was dismayingly unfamiliar. He observed duties towards other people, and considered their rights, but these were not rights and duties of which he could have heard very much at his English Public School. One day, when teasing Edith over the Challoner habit of giving a bath and a meal to any newcomer before asking why he came, she inquired whether a German, turning up during the war, would have received this ritual welcome.

'Oh yes,' said Edith. 'One came, actually. He'd been landed here secretly . . . but he was caught and brought here. Freddie gave him a bath and supper and next day invited him to fight it out with knives. Freddie won. He's quick with a knife. We buried the German in the orchard.'

'Freddie *killed him*?'

'He was an enemy.'

'Supposing he'd killed Freddie?'

'That wouldn't have been so nice for him. Our people would have killed him then, in some very cruel way.'

'Then what was the point of fighting it out?'

'He deserved it. He was a brave boy, even if he was an

enemy. He deserved to get a chance of taking Freddie along with him.'

'I suppose he was a spy really. Was he in uniform?'

'No. He was disguised to look like somebody from the islands. He talked Greek quite well.'

'Then he could have been shot by a firing squad.'

'Unarmed? That would have been very disgusting.'

'What did he come for? There's nothing here.'

'Oh, just to make sure there was nothing, I suppose.'

By the end of her visit Kate had thoroughly accepted the fact that Freddie must not be gainsaid, although she strongly disapproved of his plan to take Edith with them to Thasos. A doctor should be summoned to Keritha; Freddie's prejudice against strangers amounted almost to mania. Poor Edith was in no condition to set off on a sea trip in an open boat at five o'clock in the morning.

'I'm only so thankful he doesn't say I must go to Athens,' said Edith. 'I know he'd rather, and it would be much more tiring. The doctor on Thasos is a very inquisitive man. He's always asking stupid questions.'

'Doctors have to ask questions.'

'Oh, not about illness. Just impertinent curiosity; about the stone and things like that. Anyway, I shall be quite all right. Eugenia is coming. After I've seen the doctor she'll take me to rest at a house there, a friend of hers, before we start back.'

At dawn next day they all set off. Edith, who seemed to be quite exhausted, lay with her head in Eugenia's lap.

'The *Latona*,' murmured Kate to Freddie, 'won't be sailing till this afternoon. I shall be able to hear what the doctor thinks of Edith before I go. Is there a hospital on Thasos, supposing . . .?'

'If she needs hospital treatment immediately,' said Freddie, 'I shall hire a fast boat and rush her off to some place where she can get first-rate attention. I know where I can get a boat on Thasos if necessary.'

'Where is the nearest? Athens or Istanbul?'

'Istanbul is in Turkey,' said Freddie coldly.

'But the Turks are quite good doctors, aren't they?'

'I haven't the least idea.'

They were interrupted by an exclamation from Eugenia. She was smiling and pointing out to sea. Yorgos, who was running the engine, also pointed. About fifty yards away a silver wheel turned amidst the glittering waves. It turned again . . . and again . . .

'Dolphins,' explained Freddie.

'Lovely,' said Kate. 'And look! There are some more on the other side of us. We're all in the middle of them.'

Dolphins leapt and turned all round them, as though escorting them on their journey. Edith raised a wan face to smile at them. Eugenia leant over her and whispered something.

'She says this is a lucky journey,' reported Edith. 'We shall all five get back safely.'

'Tell her I wish I *was* coming back,' said Kate.

Edith translated and then reported again:

'She says you must come back. You'll be in danger if you don't.'

'How on earth does she know that?'

'The hens say so,' observed Freddie impatiently. 'It all depends on the way they turn their heads when they cluck in the morning.'

'What useful hens!'

'They are indeed. Quite a third of what they say comes true.'

96

Once they were round Zagros the dolphin escort fell away. Keritha dwindled to a mountain peak, sticking up behind the lower island.

Kate felt sleepy and reluctant to relinquish the repose of the last few days. Now nothing but the bright sea lay between herself and Thasos and the *Latona* and . . . the anodyne of Keritha was wearing off. The world would soon be with her. She could hear its voice already in the hum of a plane flying low on the horizon.

'That's one of the best things about Keritha,' said she. 'You never hear planes, not even in the distance. There's hardly any place now in Europe where you can get away from them. No spot so lonely.'

'They never fly very near to us,' said Freddie.

'I suppose it's not on the direct route to anywhere. But that's a rare thing now, an absolutely empty sky.'

As she said this she was struck by the thought that empty was not a good adjective for the benign sky over Keritha. She added:

'As empty as it always used to be, I mean.'

'Used it to be always empty?' asked Freddie.

'Well . . . there were no men in it.'

'No. No men. In other respects it might now be thought emptier than it used to be.'

Thasos rose out of the sea. It took on colour and detail. She scanned a pretty, hilly island, a little town, a harbour. Of the *Latona* there was no sign. If the wretched boat failed to turn up on the appointed day a night might, perforce, be spent on Thasos. There was enough currency in the bucket bag for that, although all the maids on Keritha had received lavish tips. A present for Eugenia was not quite so simple. When the *Latona* put in at Athens Kate meant to buy, and post, a nice leather purse.

They reached port and moored. Freddie cast an imperious eye round the harbour upon which a decrepit kind of taxi appeared. The Challoners and Eugenia drove off in it to the doctor's house, leaving Yorgos in charge of Kate's suitcase. There were ruins upon the hill, which she was advised to inspect, and Freddie recommended a winged horse in the museum.

The hill walk was pretty. She might have thought Thasos a delightful place had she not come from Keritha. Picking her way down the steep hill back to the town, she decided that the smaller island had something more alive about it. This one, in comparison, was comatose – a mere collection of animate and semi-animate objects, trees, earth, stones, dust, sea, and sky, amidst which human beings went listlessly about their tasks.

'Getting and spending,' she thought impatiently, as she paused to look at the Holy Bird outside the museum. It struck her as, in a way, an appropriate monument; once it might have breathed life and meaning; now it was so worn away that it meant nothing at all. Keritha, she felt, had not been worn away.

The winged horse was better and had a faint look of Edith. The lower part of the nose was gone and the short-ened head, gracefully bowed on a long neck with a stylized mane, caught the pose of Edith, 'the statue', sitting patiently in class. A pang of affection and anxiety assailed Kate. What had the doctor said? Freddie had agreed to meet her in the museum garden as soon as he had deposited Edith for her siesta in the house of Eugenia's friend. She hurried out and found him standing by the Holy Bird. He looked as calm as ever. It was impossible to tell, from his face, whether the news was good or bad.

'Well?' said Kate. 'Well?'

'Diabetes.'

'Oh? Oh yes. I never thought of that. Insulin . . .'

'He's given her an injection.'

'How bad is it? Can he get her right?'

'He hopes so. She must be careful what she eats.'

'I know. No sugar.'

'He has explained all that to Eugenia. The trouble will be to find someone who can give her injections in future. We have nobody on Keritha who can.'

'But surely . . . somebody here? This isn't such a very small place.'

'I doubt if anyone from here would come. There's a prejudice against Keritha; our fault perhaps – we're not very polite to strangers. We shall have to get a nurse from Athens.'

'It isn't very difficult. Any sensible person can learn. I can give injections. I'd have thought . . .'

'*You* can?'

He said no more but his look was eloquent. Never before in his life, perhaps, had he stood as a suppliant.

'Oh, Freddie! I wish I could stay. I wish I could! Just till Eugenia learns, or till you get somebody.'

'It wouldn't be for long, Kate. Then I'd arrange to fly you home from Athens.'

Strongly tempted, she shook her head.

'I'm very, very sorry. I must get back . . . to . . .'

Freddie gave her a hard look. She had scarcely mentioned her family during her stay on Keritha and her hosts had asked no questions. Then he nodded and turned to go out of the garden.

'Yorgos has taken your suitcase on board the *Latona*,' he said.

'Oh? Is it in?'

'It came in about twenty minutes ago.'

'When can I see Edith to say good-bye?'

'She's resting now. We shall start back at one o'clock. Come along, if you can, to our boat and say good-bye.'

The harbour was now crawling with a very disconsolate-looking ant heap. One cruiser, recognizing Kate, told her that a lot of people had got food poisoning in the Black Sea, nor were they receiving any treatment since the ship's doctor had been the first to succumb to it.

On board she encountered the familiar *Latona* smell – a rich mixture of oil, garlic, rancid fat, sweat, and inadequate privies. She asked for her mail at the Cruise Office and was handed one letter.

It was from Andrew and her first impulse was to leave it unopened until the ship had sailed, lest it might inflict further pain. In the museum garden she had been strongly tempted to change her mind; a return to Keritha must be put quite out of her power as quickly as possible.

The idea then occurred to her that this might, after all, turn out to be a reassuring letter. The whole prospect might have altered; if the girls had flown into a needless panic, if Andrew had changed his mind, she could forgive them all in a very few minutes.

Turning into the lounge, she sank into the nearest chair and read the letter:

My dear Mother,

I find that the girls have taken it upon themselves to inform you of my decision to change my profession. It's no business of theirs, and I didn't intend you to be worried about it on your holiday. But, since they've written, you may as well hear my side of it.

I can't stand life with Mortimer and Tyndale. It's routine work and entirely uncreative. You can't want me to spend my whole life doing work which I detest? I'm joining a firm which offers me work which I prefer. It's financially sound. Father has been into all that. As far as income goes I shall be rather better off than I am with M. & T. and the prospects are infinitely better. I shan't risk any chance of coming down on my parents for more money. I know what sacrifices you've already made, and I'm grateful, though they were mistaken.

The new flat will be better for Hazel. She'll be more in her proper element. You've all tried to be nice to her, no doubt, but it's quite obvious that you criticize her. She'll never make a good little suburban housewife, on the Benson pattern. She'll do much better being decorative and Bohemian and getting our meals from the delicatessen round the corner. That's the way we want to live and I fail to see why we mayn't.

To be quite frank, she's terrified of you, Mother. You may not mean to bully her, but you do. It appears that the last time you came here you got it all out of her about the new flat, though she'd been warned not to say a word about it, and never would have, if you hadn't scared the daylights out of her. I resent this very much, and I'd really rather you didn't come to see her when I'm not there to back her up.

She sends you her love and a long message, which I can't make head or tail of, about something which has gone wrong with your sewing machine. One of Hazel's virtues is that any machine is too much for her. She doesn't know which end of a vacuum cleaner sucks and which blows. She's divinely undomestic, and I like her that way, so please leave her alone.

I hope you are having a pleasant holiday.

Your loving son: Andrew

For some minutes Kate sat wondering what Hazel could possibly have done to the sewing machine. She then went down to her cabin. The suitcase, which she had brought from Keritha, was already there. Smiling to herself, riding high on the exhilaration of rage released, she began to pack up all the rest of her possessions. This accomplished, she sat down with a writing block and a Biro pen. Her words flowed smoothly for she had been rehearsing them in her mind while she packed and no doubts, no fears, no scruples checked their course.

Dear Douglas,

I got your letter on Skiathos. Also birthday (?) letters from the girls. Today, at Thasos, I've even had one from Andrew. I enclose them all by way of reply. Read them over and compare them.

I'm staying out here longer than I originally intended. I've left the cruise and shall be staying for a bit on an island called Keritha, with some old friends I ran into there. I think I may have mentioned them – the Challoners, a half-Greek family who used to live in the Addison Road. I'll put the address at the bottom of this letter.

An interruption here occurred since Miss Shepheard came in, full of news and inquiries. Upon learning that Kate meant to leave the *Latona* for good she looked doubtful.

'I don't wonder,' she said. 'It gets worse and worse here. But I wish you weren't staying on that horrid island.'

'It's not horrid.'

'We've heard stories since . . . it's supposed to be dangerous. No planes can fly aver it. They get struck by lightning. Some people say they have a secret weapon there.'

'Oh, rubbish.'

'Some people say it's supernatural. They . . .'

A hideous din, continuing for nearly a minute, made further conversation impossible. It was the gong for the first lunch. Kate had not realized that it was so late; the boat for Keritha would be off in half an hour. She went on with her letter:

Of course I'll come home at once if there's anything I can really do for any of you. But I shan't write again unless you can manage, amongst you, to send me nicer letters than these. I don't think I've deserved them, whatever my sins have been. Just now I'm rather tired of being a wife and mother, and anyway, I seem to have been a failure. The Challoners hardly realize that I am one, which is a bracing change. I think it would do you all no harm to pretend that you are a widower and orphans for a while. Yours ever: K.B.

This broadside she enclosed in a large envelope with all the letters which she had received. She stamped and addressed it, picturing, in high glee, the shock which Bridie's letter would give to Douglas. Then she rang the bell.

'No use ringing for a steward on this ship,' Miss Shepheard reminded her.

'I've got to get my suitcase taken along the quay. My friend's boat will be starting back any minute.'

'Then you must go to that black hole where the stewards play shove-halfpenny all day, and wave a lot of money about. Shall I post your letter? You'd better give it to me. That box upstairs never gets cleared. And what about your big white tweed coat? It's still hanging up in the wardrobe.'

'Oh bother! I forgot . . . I shan't need it. It's too thick. I can't think why I brought it.'

'I ought to confess I took the liberty of wearing it in the Black Sea. The wind was Arctic and my clothes aren't nearly thick enough.'

'Well, then, you keep it for the rest of the trip. Why not? Return it to Edwardes Square when you get home. I shan't need it till the winter. And if you *would* post that letter . . . I think you're right about that box upstairs. Post it on shore somewhere. I'd do it on my way now if I had more time.'

Kate rushed off to wave money at the surly stewards and to notify the Cruise Office of her intentions. It was just one o'clock when she got herself and her luggage on to the jetty. The Challoner boat was already putting out but came back when she waved.

'I've changed my mind,' she panted, as soon as she was within earshot. 'I'm coming back with you.'

Freddie nodded, handed her into the boat, and directed the disposal of her luggage with a fluency which startled the *Latona* stewards.

'It's only diabetes,' announced Edith happily. 'And he's stopped it.'

Eugenia beamed and offered obvious congratulations.

'She's so glad you're safe.'

'The hens,' explained Freddie, steering out of the harbour, 'say that the *Latona* is an unlucky ship.'

It looked like an unlucky ship, she thought, turning to

bid it farewell as they sped away. Nor was she sorry to miss the horrible meal now being eaten on board by those passengers who had escaped food poisoning.

I'm not sorry, she told herself. I'm glad. I shall never be sorry I wrote . . . they deserve it . . . they need a bombshell. 'then he can marry Mrs S.' . . . that'll make him jump! The very last thing . . . of course as soon as they write and say they're sorry I shan't be angry any more. But they've got to . . . how soon will they . . . what did I say exactly? That I shouldn't write until they . . . I wish I'd taken a copy. There wasn't time. How soon? How soon? Of course they'll write at once, but posts are slow on Keritha, coming by Zagros. I wish I . . . but I'm not sorry.

Thasos sank below the horizon and with it that unlucky ship.

PART THREE

BEATITUDE

There's many a strong farmer
Whose heart would break in two,
If he could see the townland
That we are riding to;

An old man plays the bagpipes
In a golden and silver wood;
Queens, their eyes blue like the ice,
Are dancing in a crowd.

The little fox he murmured,
'O what of the world's bane?'
The sun was laughing sweetly,
The moon plucked at my rein;
But the little red fox murmured,
'O do not pluck at his rein,
He is riding to the townland
That is the world's bane.'

W. B. YEATS

At the time when Selwyn Potter broke a table in Edwardes Square he was losing, although he did not know it, most of his university acquaintance. He had never possessed any friends. Nobody thought of him with warmth or affection, although few people actually disliked him. No malice lay behind his clumsiness and he harboured less ill-will than many who know how to make themselves superficially agreeable.

In his undergraduate days he was tolerated for his energy and his animation. He was ready to join in any spree. He could be summoned to fetch beer, run errands, or propel punts. For a dismal performance of the Antigone in the garden of a women's college, he had contrived a stage so ingenious that the occasion was almost a success. He drew masks for a domino party which were long treasured for their charm and originality. He was generous with the very few pennies in his pocket. He gave himself so few airs that the Glanville and other scholastic trophies were generally forgotten.

On the other hand he seldom stopped talking, always arrived too early, always stayed too long, and never knew when he was not wanted. If he found a caterpillar in his salad he would say so at the top of his voice. A hint had no effect on him at all although he never resented a plain request to shut up, or to go away. He was completely insensitive to social atmosphere but free from the egotism which often accompanies a thick skin.

In appearance he was not more unprepossessing than many of his contemporaries, but his blemishes were more conspicuous. Spots and dandruff might have been overlooked; greasy curls and a paunch were not. He might be invited to many parties but no girl would accept him as her official escort if she could secure anybody else. To arrive with Selwyn was a misfortune.

His origin and background remained obscure. At a spree to which he had not been invited speculation on this point gave rise to a paper game: *The Early Life of Selwyn Potter.* Amongst many diverting suggestions one became proverbial in his circle: he had been found in the Umbrella Room of the British Museum and sent to the zoo by mistake, where he was reared. Eventually Dr Challoner, arguing with a colleague in the monkey house, was set right in a quotation from Crinagoras by this creature behind the bars.

Upon leaving the university he found employment in a publishing house famous for its classical editions. Since many of his former cronies were also working in London he had expected the old sprees to continue. For two years he waited hopefully for invitations. None materialized. He had been dropped, not of set purpose but because nobody needed him any more. These cronies had formed new friendships and developed other interests. They married, and the news reached him months later, since he did not read the social announcements in the newspapers and was never invited to their weddings.

This evaporation of the past saddened him but he

supposed it to be a general affliction. Since he never now saw his old friends it never occurred to him that they might still be seeing one another. He was therefore as much surprised as delighted when he received, one morning, a document forwarded from his old college. His name was written at the top of it, and, below that, he read:

Lady Myers
Requests the pleasure of your company
At the marriage of her daughter
Rosemary
to
Mr Peter Hosegood
At St Paul's Church
Sloane Terrace
On Saturday, April 29th
At two-thirty
And afterwards at the Rockford Hotel.

R.S.V.P.
69 *Glastonbury Court*
S.W.

A Society Wedding! He was filled with pleased excitement, for he had never been to one although he had heard of them. He had never, in fact, been to any wedding at all. Lady Myers was a stranger, and so was her daughter Rosemary, but Peter Hosegood had always been reckoned by Selwyn as an intimate friend. They had gone, with two other men, to the Orkneys, during their first long vacation.

There were three things to be done. The invitation must be answered, a present bought, and suitable raiment hired for Saturday, 29 April. The last task was the simplest; he knew where one hired clothes. Upon the other two points he consulted a Mrs Gray, an elderly woman, who worked in his firm and who was very good-natured. She told him how to word his answer and regretted that the invitation had not been printed in silver. As for a present, she suggested a lampshade and offered to choose it for him. It cost more than he could afford and seemed to be made of an old parchment Will. He thought it awful but trusted Mrs Gray to know what might be suitable for a Society Wedding Present.

It was dispatched and created considerable dismay in the Hosegood household. Mrs Hosegood, a very inefficient woman, had sent an outdated list of Peter's friends to Lady Myers. Now the harm was done and poor old Selwyn could not be forbidden to come. The lampshade was, in any case, no worse than some of the presents received by Rosemary.

In very good time, on the appointed day, Selwyn set off for Sloane Terrace. His hired suit was a tight fit and a top hat perched uneasily on his curly pate. The sight of several familiar faces clustered on the church steps astonished him not at all; the sight of him astonished everybody. To some it was evidence that Peter had not, after all, turned into a crashing snob. To others it was obviously one of Mrs Hosegood's boners. Since they had all of them, by now, completely disengaged themselves from Selwyn they were able to greet him cordially, although they took care not to be photographed whilst talking to him.

'I've never been to a Society Wedding before,' he told everybody. 'What do we do now?'

A man called Michael Brewster, who had been one of that party to the Orkneys, and who thought that this reunion had gone on for long enough, told him at last to go into the church. He did so, admiring the red carpet, and gave his name with aplomb to a reporter. Some tactful usher put him into a pew very far down the church; it was not a good place, he decided, and removed himself to a better one almost at the top.

The organ was playing a nice piece of Bach. He looked round him with the pleased curiosity which was his unconscious defence against the inclement solitude of his life. All the women, he observed, were wearing hats. There were flowers put about in unexpected places. Suddenly everyone rose. Some clergy were going down to the porch; one of them had odd-looking sleeves. Lawn sleeves? A bishop? No mitre? Everybody sat down again. A harassed woman in tight shoes titupped up the aisle to the top pew on the left-hand side. She looked quite exhausted and was making grimaces of desperation. Whispers informed him that she must be Lady Myers. What could she have been doing? Peter and another man popped out from behind a pillar and stood at attention, facing the altar. Everybody else turned to look the other way. The choir broke into full cry and all surged to their feet. The bishop and his retinue were coming back. After them came a red-faced man with a bride on his arm, all in white, with a veil frothing about, just like the brides one saw in shop windows.

Peter still stood stolidly with his back turned. Did he have to? Must he, until the very last minute, pretend to be unaware of what was creeping up behind him? A kind of marriage by capture, reflected Selwyn, only the other way round. A toddling assortment of children now held the scene, so nearly stepping on the bride's train that a ripple of anxiety went through the onlookers.

Then the sun rose in splendour upon the chilly twilit world of Selwyn Potter.

A shock ran through all his nerves and his flesh tingled, as it had when he first caught sight of Aphrodite rising from the waves in the Terme Museum at Rome. When in collision with some great work of art this shock was familiar enough. Now all light, joy, and beauty had come to life. It was floating up the aisle.

How she came to be there was a mystery. She could have nothing to do with all these odd capers, although she wore the same long green dress that the children wore, and the same flat little wreath of roses. Some girls, walking two and two behind her, were all got up to look like her. She floated past, and Selwyn turned to watch her.

At the chancel steps rearrangements had taken place. Peter must, at last, have acknowledged the arrival of his bride. She now stood between him and the red-faced man. The singing had stopped. The children formed two ragged lines, leaving a clear space up the centre of the aisle. A clergyman said something. Presently she floated forward to take the bride's bouquet. The bridesmaid! perceived Selwyn. They have them!

She stood just in front of him, her young head lifted, gravely watching the ceremony. He decided that she was a girl, as though he had never seen one before. She was watching her friend being married. What was she thinking?

To imagine the thoughts of another person was an unfamiliar exercise. He had done so very seldom, and then only because his compassion had been aroused. Beholding extreme pain, grief, or fear, he had been aware that these were experiences unknown to him, and had made efforts to comprehend them. Of the multiple preoccupations, the contentments, satisfactions, felicities, anxieties, resentments, and grievances felt by others he had little idea, supposing everybody, normally, to be exactly like himself. Now a mysterious truth burst upon him. People think, privately and secretly, all the time, nor is there any sure way of guessing what they think, since each of them is an isolated world.

Is She hoping Her friend will be happy? he wondered, casting a softened look at the foaming white veil, now elevated to a place in Her thoughts. *Happy*? What does happy mean really? What does She think it means? Why does She bow Her head?

She had bowed her head in prayer. Everybody in the pews now crouched devoutly. Selwyn alone remained erect until a woman beside him poked his leg. He dived down hastily, upsetting a prayer book from a pew ledge with a bang. She was praying for Her friend, he decided. She believed in God. Did he believe in God? Might he not have been taking far too many things for granted? He must start again at the beginning and think everything out afresh.

As the congregation squatted the choir began to sing, in English, a hymn of which he knew the Latin version. She, probably, he surmised, might think it was written by St Gregory. A lot of people did. He would have known no better himself if he had not begun to poke about in mediaeval poetry, just to annoy old Challoner. She might not have heard all the arguments in favour of Rabanus, although there was reputed to be a recent pamphlet by St Quentin, which Selwyn had not read, casting doubt on them.

The hymn ended. The lawn sleeves blessed the squatting faithful. Everybody sat up again and the bridal party went off through a door under the organ pipes. Lady Myers and some people in the pew just in front of Selwyn scurried after them. A rustle of discreet conversation broke out. A child in the aisle began to eat its bouquet. The nearest adult interfered. Not all those girls in green dresses had gone away, although She had. They stood in a group, smiling and nodding to their friends and whispering to one another. They were now to him a touching sight since they had something in common with Her, which made of them a dedicated bevy. The female creatures with whom he had romped, when amorous romping was on the programme, were girls too, but not quite the same species of girl.

Now She must be coming back again, since the organ was making trumpet noises, and everybody was jumping up. Ta-ta-ta-TA! Ta-ta-ta-TA! Peter, Rosemary and the rabble of children got themselves down the church and out of the way. Chords of joy crashed from the organ. Chords of joy thrilled through Selwyn as he tasted for the first time the exquisite felicity of knowing that the Beloved was coming. He would see Her again.

She was there. She was gone. Where? To the Rockford Hotel. He tried to rush out after Her but was informed that the bridal party must be allowed to get away first.

The April sunshine was full of pealing bells. Happy people poured out of the church and set off in little groups towards Knightsbridge. Marvellous! Everything was marvellous! Champagne! They had it at Society Weddings. Had they drunk it already? No. Not yet.

'She shouldn't have worn dead white,' said somebody.

They were crackers. She wore green.

He followed the gay throng, absorbed by this impression that he had been taking too much for granted and that life, life, and people, were more astonishing than he had thought. It seemed to him that he had been walking all his days down a narrow bare corridor and had emerged, during the past hour, into a trackless but enchanting forest. Still dazed by surprise, he reached the Rockford Hotel and joined a long line of people which crept slowly across a lobby towards a large room with a chandelier. A great hubbub and chatter went on and an irritating voice kept bawling unlikely sounding names.

'DOCTOR . . . and . . . MRS TONKS.'

So happy? What does it really mean? Must come from *hap*. Chance.

'MR . . . and MRS . . . and MISS . . . SLUGG.'

A happy man . . . a man who has had a lot of good luck? Is that all it means?

'MR . . . CYRIL . . . BRAGGE.'

No. We say somebody *ought* to be happy. Meaning he's had good luck but isn't enjoying it. It's something in himself that he hasn't got.

'LADY . . . COTTON.'

Have I got it? I've always thought so. But I never was happy like this before. Because I've seen . . . and that was luck. I happed to be here. So why . . .

'MRS . . . GURNEY.'

It makes a difference to the future. 'They say that hope is happiness.' That's what that means. Who said it? If it's true, it turns on luck again. Who did say it?

'Byron,' he murmured as he passed into the room with the chandelier.

'Beg pardon, sir?' said a voice at his elbow.

'Byron. Lord Byron. . . .'

'LORD . . . BYRON.'

He found himself looking into the startled eyes of his hostess. There were two lords at this Society Wedding and both were feathers in the Myers' cap. The Hosegoods could rise no higher than a baronet. Now a third had turned up.

'Thank you for asking me,' he said, shaking her heartily by the hand. 'I hope you aren't too tired?'

With a dazed look she passed him on to Mrs Hosegood who quavered miserably:

'Nice to see you.'

'Isn't it?' he agreed. 'Thank you for asking me.'

Dr Hosegood, next in line, had long ceased to know or care who anybody was. Peter thanked Selwyn very earnestly before anything had been said at all. The bride, finally, gave him a radiant smile.

'I'm glad you are so happy,' he told her.

'Sweet of you,' she murmured, turning the radiant smile elsewhere.

At liberty again, he looked round in eager hope. The room was sprinkled with girls in green dresses, but none of them was the right one. Somebody gave him a glass of champagne. A voice at his elbow said:

'Hullo, Lord Byron. What a good bad-taste joke!'

It was Michael Brewster, discreetly snickering.

'It's going the rounds. You really are rather like Byron, you know. In the last stage, when he got fat. But what a thing to do to poor Lady M.!'

'I don't know what you're . . . Oh!'

There She was! Surrounded, the centre of an animated group, talking and laughing, She looked more beautiful than ever.

'Who is she?' demanded Selwyn.

'Who . . . Oh! That's Liz Colleoni. Quite a puss, isn't she?'

'You know her?'

'Everybody knows her. She's a very, very prominent Deb. The daughter of Amanda Kreutzer. You know! The tragic millionairess.'

'Could you introduce me?'

'No, old man, I couldn't,' said Michael, who had never spoken to her in his life. 'She's not your style of puss.'

'How did she . . . get to be here?'

'Ah!' Michael looked sage. 'A lot of people are wondering about that. Lady M. is a remarkable woman. Definitely on the up and up.'

In the Orkneys, five years earlier, Michael had been a fanatical bird watcher. His transformation into a man about town did not impress Selwyn, who made his way obstinately to the group surrounding the Beloved. There he stood for many minutes, glass in hand, edging a little way towards the centre whenever he got a chance. Her voice, when audible, matched the rest of her; it was sweet, low, and clear. At last he gained a position at her elbow. As if aware of his unflagging attention, she shot him sundry little glances of inquiry while she listened to, and answered, other people. Finally, she turned to face him, allowing him an opportunity to say something.

'I saw you in church,' he told her.

She gave him a mirthful glance and agreed that she had been there. Since it appeared that she might be going to turn away again he added hastily:

'Who do you think wrote that hymn: *Veni Creator Spiritus*? Rabanus?'

She stared. Her face clouded and she gave him a sharp, almost a suspicious look. Sinking her voice to a whisper, she said:

'Yes. I don't think anything of St Quentin's red herring.

Or anyway, it must have been some pupil of Alcium. It's the scansion of Paracletus. . . .'

Selwyn leapt into the air and did a sort of *pas de chat*. This habit of his, when excited, had been known to bring down ceilings.

'Exactly! *Exactly*! *Qui ParaCLEtus dicitur* . . . . Anywhere else in Europe, anywhere else, it would have been *dicitur ParACletus*. Their Latin by that time was all sweet . . . only those boys from l'Ecole Palatine would have known enough to get it right. But have you read St Quentin? Where?'

His voice rang through the room. The group immediately surrounding them had fallen into a kind of gaping stupor at *ParaCLEtus dicitur* and the silence had spread. She, aware perhaps that they had by now a large audience, sank to an even lower murmur:

'In the Sorbonne Library. But we can't very well talk about it here, can we?'

'Then where can we talk about it?' boomed Selwyn. 'When can I see you again?'

She hesitated. Somebody tittered. At that she flushed and spoke up.

'Thursday afternoon? Three o'clock?'

'Yes! Yes! Where?'

'Five Mount Square.'

'Elizabeth! Elizabeth dear! Rosemary wants you.'

Lady Myers, pushing her way through the listeners, had come to rescue her prize exhibit from this terrible person. She had been making inquiries about him and a few unpleasant words had passed between her and poor Mrs Hosegood. Seizing the girl by the arm, she marched her away.

Selwyn blissfully finished his champagne and walked out

of the Society Wedding just as the bride's health was being proposed. He spent the rest of the afternoon wandering about in Hyde Park. His top hat had been left in the pew at St Paul's Church. He did not discover this until it was time to return his hired plumage whence it came.

at the Society. Walking just like the people hardly was being recognised. The single she, out of the allowance, would find again to study that. He was has had been out in the new state. Billy looked. He saw his dark eyes this smart it was now to wish he hired plunge wound it thing.

2

Mrs Gray, who bought the lampshade for Selwyn, had been a good scholar in her day. In the early 1930s she had been mainly responsible for a new edition of a classical dictionary for which the firm of Richardson had been famous for more than a century. During and after the war, owing to the paper shortage, this work had, for a time, gone out of print. Now another, considerably enlarged, edition was to be brought out. In recognition of her past services she was again put in charge of this exacting work, but, without Selwyn's help, she would have found it a good deal too much for her. She was growing old. Her memory was uncertain; when tired she was liable to stupid blunders. Everybody in Richardson knew this and most were anxious to cover up for her, since she had still a year to go before qualifying for a full pension. Recent changes in the firm, and the influence of a new partner bent on economy, made it unlikely that she would be treated with any particular generosity, in spite of her past record.

Selwyn was soon doing two-thirds of her work as well as his own. He found it necessary to look over proofs corrected by her, before sending them to press. Obvious misprints, which she had failed to detect, he corrected on his own responsibility, but he was occasionally obliged to send the proofs back with a query.

On the Monday after the wedding she found a batch of them waiting on her desk. Not for the first time she was horrified at her own carelessness and grateful for the trouble that he had taken. To her room mate, Ruth Thomas, she remarked that Selwyn Potter was really very nice.

'It's all on the surface, his annoying ways. If only someone would take him in hand, drop him a few hints, he would get on so much better.'

Ruth pursed her lips. She had no liking for Selwyn. She intended to marry, if she could, a man called Eric Tipton, also in Richardson, who would have got that work on the dictionary if Selwyn had not been promoted over his head.

'So who is likely to take him in hand?' she asked coldly. 'Why should they?'

'It would do him a lot of good to get married.'

'Then tell him so. Why don't you? Tell him the world is full of poor girls who'd sooner marry him than nobody. It's a wonder he's dodged the altar for so long.'

'I don't believe he's ever had a home of his own – anybody of his own. We must find him a girl.'

'There's Dillon.'

'Poor Jean? Oh no! She's too plain and dreary.'

'She might do something for her catarrh. You can hear her sneezing from here to St Paul's. But Selwyn can't afford to be choosey. Really he can't.'

'He's got a very good brain. Really he's brilliant.'

'So some people seem to think,' agreed Ruth bitterly.

'I don't believe he's ever forgotten a single thing. Generally people who come up with a fact or a date are rather boring;

they have minds like card indexes. But Selwyn remembers things because he's always been so intensely interested.'

'So how will that get him a wife?'

'Some girl with intellectual tastes . . .'

'Even intellectual girls like to hear their own voices once in a while. They wouldn't want to hear Selwyn talking all day and all night into the bargain.'

'I wonder . . .' speculated Mrs Gray.

'You needn't. He's got a love life of sorts. Pretty crude.'

'And who is your authority for that, pray?'

'Eric'.

It would be, thought Mrs Gray, who loathed Tipton.

Later in the day she took the proofs back to Selwyn, thanked him, and asked if the wedding had been fun.

'Oh, it was wonderful!'

'Very pretty?'

'Quite beautiful. I didn't know they were so beautiful. I've been trying to remember what picture . . . couldn't place it at first. You've been to Florence, haven't you? Remember the Gozzoli Frescoes in the Medici Chapel? They're rather in a corner. Three girls. Daughters of Piero. On horseback, with little wreaths. They're dressed like pages because they're on a pilgrimage and riding astride. Of course, he wasn't really a very good painter, but the wedding made me think of those girls. Only she wore green.'

'What? The bride wore green?'

'Oh no. The bridesmaid.'

'Only one bridesmaid?'

'No. There were some more. They all had the same clothes.'

'Oh?' said Mrs Gray. 'I see.'

'There was a bishop. But he only wore sleeves. Nice

music. At the end they played that bit out of *Midsummer Night's Dream* when Theseus and Hippolyta come in. Lah! Lah! La-lah! Lah! Lah! . . .'

'Mendelssohn? They always have that.'

'And there was a nice eighth-century hymn with, I think, a Gregorian tune. But a poor translation. She . . . the bridesmaid . . . told me that she'd got hold of a pamphlet in the Sorbonne Library . . .'

'You know her?'

'I got to know her at the party.'

'You did? How nice.'

'I'm going to see her on Thursday afternoon. Which reminds me. If anybody asks where I am on Thursday afternoon can you say I've gone to have a tooth pulled out?'

'Well . . . all right. I will. What's her name?'

He hesitated. It was the first time that he had said it to anyone.

'Elizabeth.'

'A pretty name. The Sorbonne Library? Does she teach?'

'No. She's a prominent Deb.'

It was delightful to see him so much in love, but she went back to her room in two minds about it. Poor sneezing Dillon might not be good enough for him, but a prominent Deb must surely be quite out of his reach. She was sorry that she had undertaken to cover up for him if he played truant on Thursday, since he was probably setting out to break his heart.

3

Five Mount Square was such a very large house that Selwyn wasted a few minutes in a vain search for Elizabeth's doorbell. There should be, he thought, a row of doorbells with cards beside them and he would have been glad of some such guide to her surname, of which he was not quite sure. Eventually he rang the only bell to be seen.

The manservant who opened the door seemed to recognize his errand. They shot up in a lift to the top of the house. A maid, waiting in a corridor, took charge of him. He was shown into a pleasant room full of books, pictures and flowers. The Contessina, he learnt, would be with him shortly. Before he could explain that he had not come to see a Contessina the woman went away.

He looked eagerly round the room. A large photograph of a starving lady caught his eye. Why was she starving? The hair, the clothes and the pearls were incompatible with such a hungry face. That face was the only ugly thing in the room. The pictures on the walls were delightful. A drawing over the fireplace, a woman and a child sketched in a few firm lines, quite charmed him. He was still busy with it when Elizabeth came in, wearing the wrong clothes. She had exchanged the green dress which he had expected for some kind of grey suit. Her aspect, also, was a little chilly.

'Is this,' he asked, pointing to the drawing, 'a Tiepolo?'

'Yes.'

'It's marvellous. It might be the real thing. I've never seen a reproduction that gets what the artist does with empty space so well. That woman's face is just an empty space inside a curved line. But it's so round you could poke your finger into her cheek.'

'It's not a reproduction.'

'What? It's a genuine Tiepolo?'

She nodded, her severity a trifle relaxed.

'That explains . . . But is it yours, then?'

'Oh no. It was downstairs, and very badly hung. I took a fancy to it and brought it up here. When I go away it will go downstairs again, I suppose.'

'You're going away? Soon?'

His heart took a downward plunge.

'I've never lived in the same place for long.'

'Isn't this your house, then?'

'No. It belongs, I believe, to some people called Cohen. My mother rents it.'

'Er . . . Mrs Colleoni?'

'Her name, now, is Mrs Blaney.'

'I see. I'm sorry. There was so little time at the wedding. I don't think I told you my name.'

'I know it,' she said, more sternly than ever. 'Mr Potter.'

'How did you know?'

'Lady Myers told me.'

'Are you angry with me?'

'Why did you say you were Lord Byron at the wedding?'

'I didn't. That announcer must have been a lunatic.'

'You must have said *something*.'

'I suppose I must. I was thinking about Byron just as I

came into that room, I must have muttered his name in an absent-minded sort of way.'

'It wasn't meant to be a joke?'

'Good heavens no! Why? It would be an idiotic joke.'

'I agree. But some people thought it amusing. They thought you were making fun of your hostess.'

'But why should I? It would have been a cad's trick. I thought it very nice of her to ask me. I didn't even know I was going to be announced. I'd never been to a Society Wedding before.'

Suddenly she smiled.

'At a Society Wedding,' she said, 'you must never be absent-minded. There's often a lot of caddishness about.'

'But this is awful! Did she think I'd done it on purpose? Should I write to her? Explain? Apologize?'

'No. Don't worry. It was rather a nasty wedding. Nothing you did could have made it much worse. I only asked because, if you had done it for a joke, I don't think we should get on very well.'

'I should think not! You must have been sorry you said I could come here today.'

'I'm glad I did because now we've cleared it up. Let's talk about something nicer. Go on about Tiepolo.'

He gazed at her miserably, his bright mood shattered.

'There's nothing to go on about,' he muttered. 'I ought to have known the genuine thing when I saw it.'

'So ought I. Take me for a walk. I haven't had a breath of fresh air for weeks and weeks.'

He followed her out of the room, giving a last glance at the starving woman.

'That's my mother,' she told him. 'Just now she's in the States.'

This information raised his spirits a little. Such misery ought not to be sharing a roof with Elizabeth. Also, unworldly though he was, he had a faint suspicion that he might never have got into Mount Square if Mrs Blaney had not been in the States.

They went into Hyde Park and strolled by the Serpentine. He felt better in the air and the sunshine but he still remained unwontedly silent. Elizabeth had to do the talking. She told him that she had a hobby for Charlemagne, and everything to do with Charlemagne. A curiosity about the revival of Latin ordained by him had led her to look up St Quentin's pamphlet in the Sorbonne Library. Had he been to Paris? She had lived there for some years. Had he been to Rome?

Normally he would have had a good deal to say about both, but he was earthbound, still brooding over poor Lady Myers. At last, when they had found themselves two chairs, he burst out:

'I can't get over it. That poor woman! She looked so terribly tired. I noticed it in church. She must have worked herself to death over that wedding. And then to have it rather ruined because I was a blockhead! It's too cruel.'

'Lots of things are cruel. Tell me . . . how did you get to be a blockhead?'

'Me? I just am one.'

'I don't think so. Not really.'

'Don't you? Don't you?'

'No. But who *are* you? I mean tell me the story of your life.'

'There isn't one. A story . . . it must have a beginning and a development and a climax and a conclusion.'

'Perhaps. But I don't expect all that. I'd like the first

chapter. You must have been born somewhere, sometime, to somebody.'

He admitted as much and explained that he could remember neither of his parents. His mother had been Greek. Her father, according to Mrs Blackett, had kept a restaurant. He offered a few sparse details about the Blackett household. His childhood had left no impression on him at all; he remembered it as a frog might recall its tadpole existence. He had really been born when he learnt to read. He had always believed himself to be happy. Why should he be otherwise? He had enjoyed himself a great deal and had made many friends of whom he had lately seen nothing at all. He had gone abroad whenever he could, hitch-hiking and singing for his supper in various ways. He had managed to get a month in Athens by taking a job as night porter in a hotel. He liked working for Richardson but regretted the loss of opportunities for travel, since he would now have only a fortnight's holiday in the year.

'About as eventful, all this, as a piece of string?' he suggested after a while.

'I must say I should have liked a little more about early struggles. Why do you work for a publisher?'

'One must have a job. And I like books.'

'Too much. You've used them instead of people. I believe you ought to get a job that has nothing to do with them. What sort of birthday presents did they give you? These Blacketts?'

He tried to remember and realized that he had never got any.

'I never expected them,' he explained. 'And what you don't expect you don't miss.'

'Exactly. Blessed is he that expecteth nothing. I believe they call that the Eighth Beatitude. And that's how you got to be a blockhead.'

Her smile robbed the word of its harshness. Beatitude! he thought. There was no other term for his condition at the moment. It seemed hard that this bliss should be entirely one-sided.

The willows in their spring green were exquisite. She would do much better to enjoy them than to inquire why he was a blockhead. He said so, and she agreed that they were very lovely.

'You're looking at the wrong ones. I mean those ones behind the bridge.'

'Why those? They're all lovely.'

'The curve of the bridge and the curve of the willows – they cut across each other in just the right place. And there's the hardness of the stone against their softness.'

He pulled a pencil out of his pocket, looked about for paper, fished a sandwich bag out of a near-by litter basket, and drew a line or two to show her.

'That's very good,' she said. 'You've got the hardness and the softness. I can't think how. Why aren't you an artist?'

'Because I can't draw pictures.'

'Yes, you can. This is a picture.'

'No, it's not. You couldn't put it in a frame and hang it on a wall.'

'I see what you mean. But if you did rather more to it. . . .'

'I couldn't. That's just it. Anything I do, it needs something more and I don't know what. Sometimes that makes it into a thing.'

'I think it might look nice on a bowl. No! Don't tear it

up.' She took it from him, adding: 'I'd like to show it to a man I know.'

'A *man*?'

'Quite quite bald,' she told him soothingly. 'One of his fourteen children went to school with me in Stockholm.'

'Oh!' He felt better. 'Very well. But that bag is a bit smelly.'

'I must go home. No, we haven't been here only five minutes. It's been two hours. What is your telephone number?'

This inquiry made up for her determination to go home alone. He gave her the number of the house where he lodged. She did not promise to ring him up, but he took her request as an assurance. Without much diminution of beatitude he watched her walk away until she vanished among the crowds at the eastern end of the Serpentine. Then he went home to await, in complete confidence, a telephone call.

After a week she rang him up to ask if he had any more sketches which might look nice on bowls. If so, would he post them to her immediately? He rummaged through his papers and found several. Two suggested wind: the last leaves of autumn whirled away from tree-tops blowing, and a flock of birds raising from a stubble field, shaped by a gale into a half-circle against a cloudy sky. Another showed London roof-tops and chimney-pots under long shafts of light from a hidden sun. He posted them all to Mount Square.

At Richardson he was admonished by Mrs Gray, who took a proprietary interest in the whole business. He should be the one to ring up, she said; he should do so, suggesting dinner and a theatre.

'I think,' he explained, 'she goes out as much as she wants.'

'Very popular, is she?'

Mrs Gray's hopes sank again. Any serious competition would be fatal to poor Selwyn.

He, however, had no misgivings. Every morning he awoke to fresh hope. No night quenched his faith. Moreover, he was much preoccupied with a new idea for a bowl. The design, on the inside surface, was to show, upside down, a water-front, hills, trees, and houses, reflections in some land-locked harbour. The conception excited him, but, whenever he imagined it inside a bowl, it lacked the limpidity which might suggest reflections. He feared that it would all look too solid.

After another week he got a note from her. Her bald-headed friend from Sweden was in England and had asked them both to lunch on Sunday, at the Barchester Hotel. His name was Hagstrom, and his line was glass.

Glass! thought Selwyn. *Glass!* Of course!

4

'Swedish?' said Mrs Gray, when he reported this latest development. 'Oh, but Swedish glass is lovely. You remember that vase we all gave to Miss Skinner for a wedding present? That was Swedish.'

'Umph!' said Selwyn.

The vase given to Miss Skinner had thick white lumpy figures on it. Great skill was doubtless needed to put them there but he had wondered why they should have been put there at all.

'And I had a bowl from Sweden. Only it was bombed. A lovely blue-green, with mermaids in very high relief swimming round it. I wish you could have seen it.'

'Umph!'

He was glad that he had not. By some ill chance he was continually confronted by nasty pieces of glass. They caught his eye in shop windows. He had never thought about the stuff before. Now that he had begun to do so it was only to conclude that a great deal of it had been a ghastly mistake. 'All these colours and lumps and curls and twirls would never serve for anything that he wanted to do.

Sunday, however, was rushing towards him. He had not many hours in which to ponder upon glass. He must take his other suit to the cleaners.

Elizabeth had told him to call for her at half past twelve in Mount Square. He duly presented himself and was shown into a room on the ground floor. It seemed to be some kind of ante-room; a larger, brighter expanse was visible through an arch. After waiting for a few seconds he became aware that there were people in there. He heard mutterings, gigglings and scufflings.

He took a couple of paces towards the arch and then paused, recalling some advice that Elizabeth had given him. At the wedding he had behaved like a blockhead partly because he had not been prepared to encounter a lot of caddishness. The noises now audible sounded uncommonly like a romp in the hay. Had this been a barn he might have gone to investigate. Since it was Mount Square he had better not stick his neck out.

The romp gathered impetus. There were thumps, squeaks, and a crash. The squeaks became squeals. A well-built blonde rushed through the arch. Her pursuer, thudding close behind, caught her half-way down the room, up-ended her on one of the chairs, threw her dress over her head, and smacked her with mounting zest until Selwyn gave a squawk of protest.

Silence fell. Two faces peered at him in amazement. The nymph rolled off the chair and pulled her dress down. The satyr asked Selwyn who in hell he was.

'I'm waiting for Miss Colleoni.'

'Liz, d'you mean? She hangs out upstairs. You should have gone up in the lift.'

'I was told to wait here.'

'Bloody fools . . .'

'Who's Liz?' demanded the girl, as her companion went back into the other room.

Selwyn turned away and looked out of the window at Mount Square. A voice through the arch, obviously telephoning, said:

'Liz? A boy-friend of yours has been let loose down here. Come and remove him, will you?'

The stranger returned. He was a handsome fellow of indeterminate age, wearing an artificial boyishness just as he wore an expensive suit and an Irish brogue.

'Who's this Liz?' repeated the blonde.

He grinned at her, pondered, and said:

'She's me stepdaughter.'

'Your *what*?'

'I said stepdaughter. You knew I had one, didn't you?'

There was a long pause.

'And she lives here?'

'Of course. Why wouldn't she?'

'Not gone back to America with her mother?'

'Gone back? Amanda has only gone to the States for a few weeks. She'll be in England for my Première.'

The door opened. Elizabeth sailed in, bringing with her a breath from the North Pole. The atmosphere became glacial. Taking no notice of the other two, she said to Selwyn:

'I'm so sorry you were kept waiting. Let's go.'

A moment later they were in the Square. He choked back a number of questions which, a month ago, would have been asked forthwith. Was that heel really her stepfather? Had she been abandoned to his guardianship while her mother went to the States?

He must not be a blockhead, and he was feeling a little frightened of her. That so sweet and gentle a creature could feel, and convey, such a degree of icy contempt was disturbing; nor was it pleasant to reflect that she might have a good deal of practice.

After a while she said:

'Don't worry. I'm leaving Mount Square on 14 June.'

His heart rose. His heart sank. If she was going to America he might never see her again.

'On 14 June I'll be twenty-one and I can live where I like. The world is all before me.'

'Which . . . which bit of it?'

'I haven't decided. I want to get a job.'

'You?'

'I couldn't hold down a job, you think?'

'I shouldn't have thought you'd need one.'

'Why not?'

He spied barbed wire ahead. It would be indelicate to say that he had thought her very rich.

'Did you think I'm very rich?' she asked, so nicely that they were over that fence without a scratch.

'That house . . . those pictures . . . all those servants . . .'

'Did anyone tell you I was rich before you saw the house?'

'One of the . . . at the wedding . . . one of the . . .'

More barbed wire! She took over.

'One of the cads at the wedding told you I'm Amanda Kreutzer's daughter. Had you ever heard of her before?'

'No. But he seemed to think I would have. He said she was a millionairess.'

'She was. I don't think she is now. What else did he say?'

'That you were a . . . a . . . very prominent Deb.'

'Ex-Deb. I came out last year. Now I've gone in again. His dentist must only keep very, very old *Tatlers* in his waiting-room.'

'I didn't know they went in again, Debs.'

'They don't generally. They go on, or up, or off. Not in. But I like to be different. I want to consult you, as a matter of fact. I think you might help me.'

'Could I? Oh, could I?'

'Yes. I'll explain some other time. Listen now while I tell you about Olaf Hagstrom. He and all his family were very kind to me when I lived in Stockholm. His glass-house is ten miles out of Stockholm, on the lake. Do you know anything about glass?'

Selwyn declared that he knew nothing and had, in the course of the past week, taken a dislike to a great deal of it.

'Oh, colours and lumps. I know what you mean. It's engraving on white glass that you ought to think about. Just lines, like you draw. Olaf is making a great drive . . . he's looking for designs. He's got some people who are first-class at wheel engravings, but rather commonplace when it comes to ideas for designs. And he has nobody really good at diamond point. Did you never take a look at diamond point?'

'I've always given glass a miss in galleries and museums. One can't look at everything. I've seen it being blown, at Murano, of course. Very good fun to watch. But I never had the slightest wish to know more about it.'

'I can't understand that, when you're so quick to spot things. That Tiepolo . . . Oh well! I mightn't have got to know anything about it myself if I hadn't made friends with Linda Hagstrom.'

'This diamond point . . . in Amsterdam I saw some, I think. Mostly fine lettering. Remarks in Dutch.'

'After lunch you must go to the Victoria and Albert and

look at some things they've got there. Now try to let Olaf Hagstrom say a word or two. He's worth listening to and he's the best friend I've got, I think.'

They had reached the Barchester Hotel. Selwyn entered it with very warm feelings towards Olaf Hagstrom and was able to see a kind of halo round a huge bald head which waited for them in the vestibule. It was extremely pleasant to know that Elizabeth's best friend was so well up in years. He got through the introduction with credit and survived a good deal of critical observation during the first fifteen minutes over olives and cocktails. His natural friendliness had never appeared to better advantage, tempered, as it was, by respect.

Hagstrom looked at his hands rather than his face. A woman, pushing past their table, shook it and a glass fell off. Selwyn caught it neatly and put it back, as he listened to an account of Linda Hagstrom's wedding. Elizabeth was eager for news of all her Swedish friends and spoke of Stockholm as though it had once been her home. From something said, as they made a move to the dining-room, Selwyn got the impression that she might have had more than one stepfather.

In the dining-room his success was maintained. Unaware that he had been brought here to sell anything, he regarded this as Elizabeth's party. She sat, bathed in radiance, while her two friends saw to it that she enjoyed herself. Enormous menus, spread in front of them, dazzled him with the number of things she might eat. He listened until she had made her choice, and automatically chose the same for himself.

When the talk turned to his sketches he was surprised, for he had forgotten them. He explained that the medium of glass had never occurred to him, but that he now realized the importance of translucence in most of them; it had been the missing element.

'A pity,' he said mournfully. 'Glass! I could never handle stuff like that. It would break if I looked at it. Most things do.'

'Most things perhaps,' agreed Hagstrom, with another glance at Selwyn's hands. 'But tell me . . . have you ever, in your whole life, actually broken a glass?'

'Oh, I must have. I break everything . . .'

'Try to remember an occasion.'

He tried, without success, very much to his own surprise. His path through life had been strewn with wreckage of all sorts, but he could not remember so much as a smashed tooth-glass.

'I should have been surprised if you had,' said Hagstrom. 'You may not know it, but glass is your material, I think. You would never handle it clumsily. I have seen that already. I think that you might learn very quickly.'

He then offered to buy the sketches, which Selwyn had sent to Elizabeth, and to pay for them in notes, taken then and there out of a wallet. Selwyn, who badly needed new socks and shirts, pocketed the notes hastily before this lunatic should change his mind. What, he wondered, could anybody else do with them?

'We are needing designs of this kind very badly,' explained Hagstrom. 'It will not be so good, of course, as it might be: my people must use them. It will be better when you can do your own work yourself. But until you have learnt . . .'

That he should learn had become, at some point, a settled thing between the three of them. Elizabeth, as he discovered later, had made up her mind that he was a glass man when sitting beside the Serpentine. Hagstrom was taking a chance.

For Selwyn, the vision of that reflected water-front was decisive. It could only be realized by fine lines drawn on white glass. He must, therefore, learn how to draw fine lines on white glass.

'Where?' he demanded. 'How?'

Details sprang into his mind which he had not recognized before. He knew exactly how they must be. Could he ever contrive to transfer them to that limpid, transparent surface? With a tenth of his mind he listened to Hagstrom; with the rest of it he wrestled with some new problems of perspective.

A tenth of his mind was enough to tell him that he was being offered a start in the Hagstrom glass-house; he would be given every opportunity to learn his craft and would pay for it, at first, by supplying designs which could be used by wheel engravers. Should he prove as apt a pupil as Hagstrom hoped, he might soon be earning a good deal. There was no knowing, of course, how soon he would be able to engrave his own designs, but if he liked to take the chance there was but one stipulation; an option on all his work for the next ten years.

Clouds at the bottom, he thought, and said:

'Thank you, sir. I'd like to. When?'

'At once, if possible. I should like to take you back with me. How are you situated with this publisher?'

'Oh, they'll let me go any time. People who can do what I'm doing there are two a penny.'

Then his face fell. He remembered Mrs Gray. If he left before the last pages of that dictionary had gone to press she would be sunk. Tipton would certainly take over his job and Tipton would never cover up for the poor old dear. If she dropped a brick he would give the fact the widest possible publicity and would take care that it sounded like a cart-load.

'Oh dear!' he said. 'It's not as easy as I thought. I couldn't get away for . . . say six weeks, to be on the safe side.'

He explained the case. Richardson would not suffer if he left tomorrow, but he did not feel able to desert Mrs Gray.

'Six weeks?' said Hagstrom, with a glance at Elizabeth. 'Very well. Stay in London for six weeks and then come to us. You will not, I think, waste your time.'

'Oh, I won't,' said Selwyn, with the Victoria and Albert in mind and wondering why Elizabeth had blushed.

5

In Park Lane, outside the Barchester, he reminded her that she had wished to consult him about something. She declared that this could wait; he ought now to make use of a Sunday afternoon by visiting the Victoria and Albert. He had promised Hagstrom not to waste his time. When he grew obstinate she offered a compromise: she would come with him. There was an exhibition of water-colours which she wanted to see. At half past four she would meet him in the tea-room.

'We shall be hungry again by then,' she said, 'and we can talk about me while we're eating.'

'All right. We'll take a taxi.'

'No, we won't. We'll take a bus.'

'I'm rich. Think of all that money he's given me! I can treat myself to a taxi.'

'Taxis are no treat to me. Give your Mrs Gray a ride home one night if you're in a hurry to get rid of that money. Bus!'

'You know, I think you're rather bossy.'

'Has it taken you all this time to find that out?'

Selwyn signalled to a taxi and opened the door for her. After a second's hesitation she got into it quite meekly. Something between them seemed to solidify. They drove to the museum. She told him more about Stockholm and the Hagstrom family. The man Blaney, it appeared, was only one of a series of stepfathers. She had a little brother in Sweden of whom she had been very fond; she had not seen him for six years.

When they got to the museum he allowed himself to be dispatched to the glass gallery, although he was much tempted to assert his independence by wasting his time amongst water-colours. She might be bossy but, in this matter, she was quite right, and she had given in about the taxi very sweetly. The pleasure of forcing her to do as he wished would lose its edge if demanded too often.

He went upstairs to contemplate his own future, arranged in long ranks of cases and shelves. But he could not concentrate upon those objects. Too much was happening to him, too quickly. First Elizabeth and now this! In less than a month he had been transported to a new planet where everything was unfamiliar and unexplored. He had today pledged himself to a vocation concerning which he knew almost nothing. He had become a new person. Perhaps he had only just become a person, and had been in the past merely an assembly of ingredients.

Yet I must have been me all the time, he thought, staring vacantly at a masterpiece by Laurence Whistler, or she wouldn't have known who I was.

He felt that he was setting out, had already set out, upon a fantastic journey in search of some better place than any yet known to man. He might never find it, but go he must, since this beatitude, this comprehension of happiness which had burst upon him, carried him like an irresistible current.

At four o'clock he went down to the tea-room, having learnt nothing whatever about diamond point. Half an hour later she joined him there, deploring the fact that they had eaten too much at lunch. How could they have supposed that they would ever want tea? He insisted that they should patronize the waitress enclosure, to which she agreed, observing that he had better not be let loose with all that money and a tray.

'So now,' he said, as soon as they had found a table, 'so now, do please consult me!'

She nodded, but did not immediately begin, as though considering what to say first. In the dim light of the tea-room people came and went. Trays rattled and urns hissed at a self-service counter behind a partition. For all he saw and heard of his surroundings he might have been alone with her in the Gobi desert.

'I must get away from my mother,' she began at last. 'I ought to be sorry for her. I expect I shall be, when I've got away. It's not all her fault. But I can do nothing for her and I can't bear it any more.'

'She looked very unhappy in that photograph.'

'She is. She's never learnt how to look after herself. Rich people have to learn that, just as much as poor people. They ought to stick together like a little nation, and only marry each other, if they want to be sure of any real love and affection. Everybody else thinks of them as nothing but a great big dollar sign, and either cadges on them, or keeps away from them for fear of cadging.'

'How on earth did she come to marry that man?'

'He's the fourth. She'll never learn. It's partly her own fault. She doesn't just want ordinary love and friendship. She wants something hardly anybody ever gets and if they do they get it for free. She wants to be worshipped. Like Helen of Troy. Who launched a thousand ships and never had sixpence, that I know of. My poor mother will launch ten thousand ships out of her own pocket if only somebody will worship her. She has. That's what has happened to the Kreutzer millions.'

These millions recurred, like some sinister *leitmotif*, in the story which she now unfolded. There had always been, perhaps, fewer of them than was generally supposed and the recession in the 1930s had depleted them before Amanda had even begun to launch her more disastrous ships.

Colleoni had been extremely expensive. The Kreutzer millions had rebuilt his villa near Rome and restored the frescoes in his Venetian Palazzo. Neither of these could Amanda remove to the United States when she discovered that he did not really worship. He was now dead, shot in some anti-fascist demonstration at the end of the war. His daughter could remember nothing of him; the marriage had collapsed when she was three years old.

Nor was her first stepfather more than a vague memory. He was a virile American to whom Amanda, sick of European aristocrats, gave an enormous ranch stocked with costly animals. He had looked like a cowboy to eclipse all cowboys, so long as he was not on a horse. Amanda expected him to live in the saddle, when not worshipping. After nearly breaking his neck on several occasions he bowed himself out, preferring a whole skin to the Kreutzer millions.

Europe was forgiven. The Swedish stepfather appeared when Elizabeth was ten years old, and he had been much the best of poor Amanda's bargains. In Sweden there had been five years of something like tranquil domestic life. A boy was born upon whom a considerable portion of the Kreutzer millions were settled. In return for this generosity Amanda received kindness, affection, and fidelity. They were not enough. She wanted worship. To dismiss so good a husband was not easy; his price, which she eventually had to pay, was the boy and the boy's fortune. She relinquished both and fled to Paris, taking Elizabeth with her. She was through with marriage and said so, to the newspaper reporters, thus earning the title of the Tragic Millionairess. Elizabeth never forgave her.

In Paris more ships were launched on behalf of innumerable toadies and protégées, all of them ready to worship the Kreutzer millions. Racing stables were financed, plays were produced, an expedition was sent up the Amazon in search of a lost civilization, and another to the Himalayas in search of an orchid. There were also large donations to Moral Rearmament; these were Amanda's defence against the accusation that she expected too much of human nature.

Elizabeth merely waited for the day when they should wake up to find themselves in the bread line. She insisted upon a good Lycée education and a course at the Sorbonne in case she should some day be obliged to support herself. Even Amanda began to do sums and to decide that a husband who could support Elizabeth might be a sensible investment.

They must, she said, remove to London if they were ever to find him. A début in Paris would be a waste of money. French families are too sharp about money and would expect unreasonably large *dot*. A début in New York would be ignominious. Too many people there had been laughing at Amanda for years. The English seldom laugh at anything and are unpractical about money. The house in Mount Square was taken, a much advertised ball was given and Elizabeth became a prominent Deb. She was glad to get her mother away from Paris on any terms.

The experiment paid no dividends. The English might not be sharp about money but none of them seemed to have any. Elizabeth danced through a season with penniless young men and was never obliged to vex her mother by refusing an eligible suitor. Amanda, disappointed, went to the Dublin races and came back with a fourth husband.

A new ship was launched. Sian Blaney only needed financial backing to become a film star. A remnant of the Kreutzer millions got him an impressive contract in a picture where he would have little to do save lie down, in unlikely places, with the female star in his arms. His shortcomings, as a worshipper, became apparent as soon as the picture went on the floor.

Long experience in disillusionment had given Amanda some skill in retaliation. She knew how to withdraw support at a moment, and in a manner likely to embarrass those who had exploited her. Elizabeth suspected that some such gale was blowing up now, and that Blaney might shortly find himself out on his ear. These suspicions were strengthened by her mother's last letter which bade her quit Mount Square immediately and seek shelter with a Mrs Pinkerton, in Tite Street, to whom Amanda had been very kind twenty years ago and from whom gratitude was now expected.

'Mrs Pinkerton happens to be dead,' finished Elizabeth. 'And I shouldn't go to Tite Street if she wasn't. But I'm leaving Mount Square. I've had enough. I'm going to get myself a job. And while I'm looking for one I thought perhaps I might find a home with some nice family, where I'd get board and lodging in return for helping in the house. I can cook quite well. I had lessons. The kind of family that takes a foreign student. And I thought you might know of a family like that. You're the only person I can think of to ask. The only person I can trust. I know people who might produce a family, but they would make a tale of it and laugh at my poor mother. Do you know of anyone?'

This story had so much horrified Selwyn that he did not immediately answer her question.

'I'd thought,' he protested, 'I'd imagined, that you must always have had a nice time. That you must have had a very happy life, with everybody looking after you.'

'Oh? Why?'

'Because . . . because you behave as if you had. Well, I mean . . . when I first saw you coming up the aisle . . . and when you were laughing and talking to all those people . . . nobody would have thought!'

'It wouldn't have done much good to come up the aisle screaming blue murder. Do you know of a family?'

'Yes, I do. Some people called Benson in Edwardes Square. I think they're exactly the kind of people you'd like. And Mrs Benson would look after you. She looks after everybody.'

He described the Benson household with enthusiasm.

'They certainly sound very nice,' she said. 'Do you go there a lot?'

'Actually I've only been there once.'

'Quite lately?'

'Well . . . no. It was just after I'd come down. I'd have gone again if they'd asked me. I wish they had. I rang up Judith once or twice but I never could get her.'

'Perhaps,' said Elizabeth sadly, 'we'd better not bother them. Can you think of anybody else?'

'There's Mrs Gray. I could ask her. She knows about you.'

'Oh? What does she know about me?'

'I told her about the wedding. And what you wore. And

about Rabanus. And that I've been seeing you. And that you have a Swedish friend who makes glass.'

'Quite a lot really! I dare say she knows more about me than you do.'

They fixed upon a discreet version of the case, which might satisfy Mrs Gray. The Kreutzer millions could be suppressed, nor was it necessary to mention more than one stepfather. Amanda's prolonged absence and Blaney's behaviour provided quite enough of a dilemma.

'She sounds like a very sensible girl,' said Mrs Gray approvingly. 'I'm sure I can find a family. But we'd better meet. Then I should know better what would suit her.'

This struck Selwyn as a pleasant way of spending all that money. He took them both out in style, to dinner and to the Opera. They all enjoyed themselves very much.

Mrs Gray sought him out next day and went to the point at once.

'Why are you going to Stockholm and leaving that girl behind?'

'I don't like to leave her. I must get her settled before I go.'

'Why not marry her and take her with you?'

'*Marry* her?'

'Why not? You're very much in love with her. That's obvious.'

'Oh yes. The first moment I saw her . . . she's so beautiful. But that's not to say she . . . I'm not . . .'

He shook his head. He was no phantom of delight, green gowned, rose wreathed, to gleam upon the sight of an enraptured maiden.

'You must have thought about it.'

'I did think that perhaps . . . sometime . . . when I'd got a little farther . . .'

Marriage with Elizabeth did play some part in this fantastic pilgrimage to which he was pledged.

'She can't feel about me as I feel about her. Not yet.'

'A woman's feelings for a man aren't quite the same as a man's feelings for a woman. But they're just as strong. I think she loves you. And you've given her very good reasons for supposing that you love her. It would be cruel to go away to Sweden without saying a single word.'

Paradise opened before him. He scrutinized it doubtfully.

'What makes you think that she . . . that she . . .'

'It's obvious, when one watches the two of you.'

'But if you are mistaken . . .'

'No harm in asking. She can but turn you down.'

'That might upset her. I'm the only friend she's got, just now. The only person she can trust. She can always call on me and rely on me and tell me things. If she had to turn me down . . . she's a very kind girl. She'd feel she ought to let me get over it; not see me so much. She wouldn't like to be always asking me to do things for her. She needs a friend so badly.'

'And how long do you mean to go on being so very very considerate?'

'I hadn't thought . . .'

'Selwyn! I could box your ears! You don't know your luck. She's the sweetest girl I ever saw; so pretty and

152

intelligent and good mannered. You behave as if you adore her. And then you rush off, without ever explaining yourself, leaving her to cook and wash up for some nice family. If you don't take care you'll break her heart.'

'She can't have got to love me as quickly as this. I don't see why she ever should, only I hope she will, because I want it so much. But there's nothing wonderful about me!'

'She doesn't have to think so. We women . . . we were put into this world to make men happy. Which is rather a waste because they never are. But they'd be unhappier without us. When a woman loves a man she knows his happiness is her job. She doesn't have to tell herself fairy tales about him. He's her man and that's enough. It's you men who thrive on fairy tales. You have to believe a woman is wonderful before you'll let her boil an egg for you. On an equal footing anyway.'

Here they were interrupted, but he thought that he saw her point. One or two girls had boiled eggs for him. He had thought them exciting, perhaps, but not wonderful. On balance they had struck him as rather silly. The footing had not been equal.

Mrs Gray might be romantic. He rushed out of Richardson vowing to place little reliance on her judgement. Yet she might conceivably be right. He must observe Elizabeth keenly for signs of emotional response. He must not be such a blockhead as to miss Paradise by an oversight.

Elizabeth had been remarkably friendly, he remembered, as he put pennies into the telephone box to which his steps had led him. Why should she have been so kind?

'Yes?' said that adorable voice.

'Elizabeth?'

'Hullo? Who is it?'

'Elizabeth! It's me! Selwyn!'

'Who is speaking, please?'

'Can't you hear me?'

'Hullo! Are you somebody who's forgotten to press Button A?'

He pressed Button A and began again.

'Elizabeth! It's Selwyn. How are you?'

'Hoarse as a crow, yelling at you. I liked your Mrs Gray.'

'She likes you. She says so.'

'She'd better.'

'Elizabeth!'

'Yes?'

'What are you doing just now?'

'Telephoning.'

'I mean, can I come and see you?'

'Where are you?'

'Hold on a minute and I'll find out ... I'm at Chancery Lane Station. Could I come right along now?'

'Yes, if you can manage to take a westbound train.'

He hung up and rushed out of the booth. On his way westwards he planned his course. Should she show any trace of anxiety or depression over his departure to Sweden he would, with extreme tact, hint at his own feelings. Should the hint appear to be distasteful to her, he would sheer off so light-heartedly that she need not distress herself at the thought of giving him pain.

The need for delicacy made him very solemn. He rang the bell and went up in the lift looking like an undertaker come to take measurements for a coffin. When he found himself face to face with her he could say nothing at all. He gazed at her, dumb with suspense, until she broke the silence.

'The answer is . . . *yes*.'

'Oh!' gasped Selwyn. 'Oh! Oh! O-o-oh!'

He caught her up and wandered about the room, carrying her in his arms, unable to put her down because no place in the world was quite good enough for her.

7

They were married on Elizabeth's birthday in St John's Church at the corner of the road where Selwyn lived. Her national status had given them a little trouble, but this was the only obstacle in their path.

Mrs Blaney was unexpectedly amenable. When they rang her up in New York she gave them her blessing. A formal wedding, she said, would have been very inconvenient at the moment, and this scheme would dispose of Elizabeth until her own plans were more settled. If the marriage did not work out, it could be dissolved later on. Meanwhile she was sending some money to Stockholm – enough to pay for Elizabeth's trousseau, a paltry sum she feared, but all that she could afford at the moment. Elizabeth reckoned that, with care, they could live on it for a couple of years.

The only objection to these hasty espousals came from Selwyn who thought that this sort of thing should be done in style. He wanted pealing anthems and rejoicing friends. Elizabeth pointed out that they had no friends save Mrs Gray. This he would not at first allow. He had a host of friends. With some difficulty she induced him to believe that he had been dropped by most of them. Even that wedding invitation had been sent by mistake; Lady Myers had told her so.

At any other time this would have been hard to bear,

but he was so happy that he accepted the truth without much pain.

'Blockhead again,' he sighed. 'Though I still don't see what it has to do with not getting birthday presents.'

'You've grown up thinking it was a feast when people gave you scraps.'

'I'm learning. But I still think we ought to give a party.'

'*L'Hymen n'est pas toujours entouré de flambeaux*. That's what Hippolyte says in *Phèdre*, when he's trying to persuade his girl to a runaway match.'

'A dreary type. Never managed to get married after all. Couldn't hold his horses. And you've got friends! Won't the Hagstroms be surprised to see you turn up in Stockholm!'

'I think not. I believe Olaf suspected me of craftily providing for my own future when I brought you along to lunch.'

He still hankered for a party. When some of his colleagues at Richardson presented him with a travelling clock he longed to offer them unlimited champagne.

Elizabeth, though extremely happy, was more distrustful of felicity. She had suffered too many anxieties and disillusionments. Despite her outward composure, she was sure of nobody save herself and him. Life terrified her. Bliss, she thought, should be enjoyed as inconspicuously as possible lest fate should observe and blast it.

Happiness was an undiscovered territory for both of them. He took it over, without a moment's hesitation, as his natural habitat. The very word alarmed her slightly. She had seen too much misery brewed in pursuit of it.

'That's two churches we've been in now,' he said, as they drove to catch the Stockholm plane. 'St Paul's and St John's. What church-goers we are!'

'Look! It's raining.'

'You'd rather it did, wouldn't you? They mightn't notice what we're up to, if there's a nice lot of thick clouds about.'

'Do you mind if it rains?'

'I want to see what it's like flying.'

'It couldn't be duller.'

'Nothing in this world is dull and I've never flown before.'

'One gets there too soon, somehow.'

'We can't get there too soon.'

He looked about him eagerly while they were waiting, with a little group of passengers, for the Stockholm flight to be called.

'Just look at all these people! Do people who fly always look like this?'

She had to agree that their travelling companions looked exotic. The party included a nun with a string bag full of onions, a girl in a sari with a cricket bat and a blue-haired lady with a mink coat in a plastic cover.

A disembodied voice announced their flight. They went down a ramp to a bus which was to take them across the rainy field to their plane.

'Now they're all different,' whispered Selwyn.

They were. The nun was now wearing the coif of the Order of St Vincent de Paul. The girl with the cricket bat had changed into a small black boy with a pineapple. The blue-haired lady clutched a tiara case.

'Thinking it over,' she whispered back, 'one never does see the same person twice on a flight.'

'The children are the oddest. Quite, quite international.'

'Our children will be completely international. A quarter English, a quarter Greek, a quarter Italian, and a quarter American.'

Selwyn pictured these intruders without much enthusiasm. He thought of them as all aged about ten and very noisy.

'I don't believe I'm a bit philoprogenitive,' he declared.

'I should hope not. Nice men never are.'

'What? Nice men don't like children?'

'Not until they've got them.'

They boarded the plane and found their seats.

'Oh, look at the lovely air hostess! Does she ever sit in that skirt? Elizabeth! *There's no nun now on this plane at all.* Look! Maps! They've given us lovely maps. Do we have to study them? What would happen if we didn't? Oh listen! We must fasten our safety belts.'

'A good thing, too, or you'll start your ballet jumps.'

The plane began to vibrate; it taxied a little way and then stopped.

'What's wrong?' he asked anxiously. 'Won't it work?'

'It always does this.'

'Don't be blasée.'

The vibration increased to a roar. They were moving. Grass and tarmac sped past them in a molten stream. It vanished. In a second they were quite high up, looking down on wet fields and a road with a little bus crawling along.

'Too quick,' he complained. 'I couldn't follow it.'

After a few minutes she said:

'Go on.'

'Go on what?'

'Being excited. I like it.'

'I will when we get out of these clouds. How nice and private these high seat backs make it for us.'

'The man across the aisle can see us.'

'He's leering at the air hostess. Oh listen! We can unfasten our belts and smoke.'

'Never a dull moment.'

'We're married. We're off. Up in the sky. Ever so high.'

When the clouds thinned they were over the sea. They caught glimpses of it, in dark wrinkled patches, far below. All about them were towering banks of vapour slashed through with sunlight. A meal was brought to them on plastic trays.

Suddenly she started and nearly upset her pork chops.

'Oh! Oh! Look! A whole rainbow!'

It blazed upon the clouds, a perfect circle.

'I never saw one before,' he said, 'though I'd heard of them. I believe you can see one from a mountain, if you're high enough.'

'It's the first quite new thing we've seen together.'

They gazed at it and marvelled.

'I'm not sure that I like it,' she said. 'The half is more mysterious.'

In a flick it was gone.

'*Brevis in perfecto mora*,' said Selwyn sententiously.

'Even the half,' she murmured, 'never stays for long.'

PART FOUR

THE NUMEN OF KERITHA

But how could I forget thee? Through what power,
Even for the least division of an hour
Have I been so beguiled as to be blind
To my most grievous loss? – That thought's return
Was the worst pang that sorrow ever bore. . . .

WORDSWORTH

1

> 'L'oiseau qui vole en gazouillant
> Vers les demeures éternelles . . .'

A voice, sweet as honey, tearing at the heartstrings, floated out into the moonlight over Keritha. Dr Challoner had no use for Freddie's collection of gramophone records. The orchestral music was to be sent to the schoolmaster on Zagros, who had put in a request for it. The songs and the gramophone itself were to be given to the islanders who had often, in the old days, gathered in the shadows of the garden to listen when Freddie had a musical evening. A recital was now being held for their benefit, so that they might choose which songs they liked best.

> '. . . Est venu fracasser les ailes!
> Voilà ce que je suis sans toi!'

Sentimental, this one, thought Kate, as she sorted her embroidery wools. Very lush!

Dr Challoner turned from his examination of Freddie's papers to observe that it was rather pretty.

> 'Un frêle esquif parmi les flots

Pendant une nuit ténébreuse;
Sans gouvernail, sans matelots,
Au sein de la mer orageuse.

Voilà ce que je suis sans toi!'

There was an outburst of applause on the terrace. A voice shouted a question. What was all that about? Selwyn translated. Puzzled silence was followed by a bellow of laughter. Even Eugenia, sitting by the window, smiled in a stately way.

'They think it's funny?' marvelled Kate.

'Enough to make anybody laugh their head off,' said Selwyn savagely. 'Somebody liable to turn into a bird or a boat if somebody else isn't there.'

He held up the record inquiringly. There was some discussion.

'They've decided it's a Voice, anyway,' he reported. 'And they seem to know of somebody who'd like it, because she sings very well herself. They'll take it to her on their way home. Let's try them with *Batti! Batti!*'

He wound the gramophone, which was old-fashioned since there was no electricity on Keritha. *Batti! Batti!* won unqualified approval and his translation was applauded too. But nobody liked *O Wusst Ich Doch Den Weg Zurück* enough to ask what it was about.

'The wrong intervals,' he commented. 'They don't like unexpected yawps.'

'Freddie didn't care for that one much,' remembered Kate. 'He only got it because he admired Schumann.'

'Schumann?' said Dr Challoner. 'I thought it was Brahms.'

'Not the composer. The singer. Elisabeth.'

Selwyn threw down the record with a loud clatter.

'Don't break it,' she said. 'If nobody wants it, my husband would. He has a good gramophone,' she added, turning to Dr Challoner. 'There are several records here, that the people don't want, which I'd like to take back to him, if you don't mind?'

'Not in the least. Take any you want,' said Dr Challoner, pulling out another drawer in Freddie's desk.

'We'll try *An die Musik*,' said Selwyn. 'I believe that would go down better.'

He began to hunt for it among the albums. Conversation broke out on the terrace, grew louder, and sank again at a stern look from Eugenia. Dr Challoner gave a snort of amazement.

'What's this? A letter to me! From Alfred! Mrs Benson, did you know this was here?'

'No. I left all the papers in the desk for you. He once told me that nothing there was very important. The deed box in his room I sent at once to the lawyers.'

'I'd better read it, I suppose.'

'Here's *An die Musik*,' said Selwyn, turning to wind the gramophone again.

Dr Challoner, rather reluctantly, began to read:

Dear Percival,

If you ever read this it will be because I have died before carrying out certain arrangements which will, I hope, save you the trouble of coming to Keritha.

I want to transfer to you immediately some property which should in justice be yours – some valuable ornaments belonging to your grandmother, which your father ought to have had. There may be some difficulty about export licences, with which I must deal. I should have seen to it long ago. You are my heir and next of kin, and I want to save you the trouble of coming here to enquire after your inheritance. When I have taken the necessary steps I shall tear this letter up, as I am sure you will never come willingly.

Yet the idea haunts me that you may come. I may die suddenly and lie helpless, buried beside my dear sister . . .

Poor Alfred! Poor Edith! Buried under that absurd stone! Dr Challoner took off his glasses and wiped them as the gramophone sang:

Hast mich in eine bessere Welt entdrukt!

A pretty song! A better world. . . . I'm not a religious man, but I don't discount the possibility of . . . poor souls! They were quite at sea in this one. He writes very justly about the jewellery. A cross! I'll put a cross. And a suitable . . . 'The bright day is finished' or whatever it is . . . that's not what one wants on a gravestone . . . a suitable text. May they rest in peace!

In that case there are certain things which I must say.

As boys we disliked one another intensely . . .

Disliked? He disliked me? I never knew that. I couldn't stand him, of course. Boys are intolerant creatures. But I'd have thought him too spiritless. . . . Well! Well!

Now we are old men, but not, probably, more reasonable.

Speak for yourself, my dear Alfred! I was always pretty reasonable. You never were.

Unless you have changed very much, our points of view, our attitude to life, must be diametrically opposed.

Got an attitude to life, have you? Oh my God! The row these people make!

The applause at the end of *An die Musik* was so distracting that he fled upstairs to his room. At a nod from Eugenia a maid tripped up with him, lit a lamp on his desk, bowed and withdrew. He sat down and read on:

Since I am doing my best to restore to you what should be yours, I implore you to respect my wishes in certain matters which cannot affect your interests.

I hope that you will allow Eugenia to remain in my house for the rest of her life. I have already made over an income to her but this is her home and here she should remain. My sons are dead, but she was their mother.

What? That woman? Alfred? Sleeping with the servants! The old goat! Foreigners! Mrs Benson? Does she know he went on like this?

Secondly I am anxious for the future of my friends and neighbours on Keritha. I have always envied them a little. They strike me as better able to endure the human lot than people elsewhere in what is called the civilized world. They take a view of life which is now very rare, although at one time it was universal. They have been protected by various circumstances from change.

At one time nobody supposed man's lot to be happy. It was wretched. He was born only to die. A long life meant that time would inevitably change and take from him all that he held most precious. He lived at the mercy of chance; was certain of no good fortune. All that he knew for certain was evil. Men called themselves wretched mortals and made no bones about it.

What earthly grounds has he for saying all this? *Deiloi Brotoi?* Homer never meant that seriously. A conventional epithet, like Gentle Reader or The Fair Sex.

Yet men were often very happy. They persisted in being happy because it is their nature, not their lot, which commands them. And this capacity to rejoice was strengthened by the fact that they saw their own nature reflected in the landscape round them. The sun was a person. The moon and the dawn and the winds and the sea were people. Every spring had its naiad, every tree its dryad.

Dryads! Naiads! Does he take them literally? Poetic imagery! Nobody believed . . . peasants, of course . . . folklore . . . imagery is based on folklore, but peasants are not responsible for literature.

I believe this is why our ancestors, who never supposed themselves destined for felicity, have left so many memorials, in this part of the world, to human happiness and to the spectacle of men rejoicing. In the earliest sculpture they are smiling. It is this forgotten smile, sometimes called 'mysterious', which I have sometimes seen on Keritha. We have preserved it because, in the eyes of the world, for many centuries, there has been nothing of note to be sought on our island.

Does he mean the archaic smile? Another convention.

Elsewhere the opposite view prevails. Men believe that they ought to be happy and that their own destiny should be within their power to determine. Chance is still a nuisance, but can be countered by efficiency, organization and scientific discovery. Human misery springs from human nature which is evil and perverse. It must be subdued, ignored or altered.

For nature man has no respect. He is sole lord of the universe and does what he pleases with mindless, senseless matter. He wreaks his will upon it down to the very atoms which he splits. He fears no gods. He fears nobody save himself, of whom he is more terrified than anybody had been, in the past, of any god. However frightening he might be, there was always a chance that a god might be propitiated. How can man propitiate himself? He dares not represent himself as smiling. He prefers to contemplate his own image in some violently distorted form. As a purely natural object he feels himself to be too horrible.

My friends on Keritha cannot for ever be protected from taking this view of themselves. Your world will overtake them. Yet I hope that they may be allowed to smile for a few years longer.

Leave them alone. I charge you – *leave them alone*! Discourage any form of inquiry concerning their lives and ways. No effective research can be made into our landscape and our smile. Both would vanish before any findings could be published. A.C.

Mad as a hatter! thought Dr Challoner, tearing up the letter. He needn't have worried. I'm not likely to encourage inquiries into a peasant's grin.

Most of the letter was negligible nonsense but the facts about Eugenia were disquieting. She had already puzzled him a little. Her assiduous attentions suggested that she regarded herself as a sort of legacy, along with the house and furniture. He hardly felt able to face her again until he had got over the shock.

Some dignified manner of dealing with the problem must be devised. He debated this as he went downstairs again, and out into the moonlight along the track which led to the waterfall. She must, of course, stay. He was bound to observe Alfred's wishes, but he shrank from appearing to take any cognizance of her former position in his house. Mrs Benson might be called in to act as go-between; she probably knew the truth, since she had lived for so long with the Challoners. He need not acknowledge that he knew it; he could merely say that Eugenia might stay on as caretaker if she wished to do so.

The tramp of many feet behind him proclaimed that the gramophone recital was over. The people were going home. He dodged behind a tree close to the waterfall. Whooping, laughing, chattering, they trooped past, carrying amongst them the gramophone and the records. When they had all gone over the bridge he returned to the house.

To his relief Eugenia had disappeared. She had, in fact, gone to prepare the Ovaltine which had always been Freddie's nightcap, and which was now brought in state to the new Lord of Keritha. Kate and Selwyn were stacking the discarded records.

'Completely wasted on those people,' announced Dr Challoner. 'They're throwing them away already.'

'Oh no!' said Kate. 'They wouldn't do that.'

'I saw them do it. They threw one over the bridge.'

There was an odd silence. Kate looked flustered. Selwyn grinned. Eugenia brought in the Ovaltine which she presented to her lord with a proprietary air. The mere sight of her covered him with confusion.

'That bridge,' he said, 'looks new. How long has it been there?'

Kate said that it had been put there in place of the old rough track which led down to some kind of ford and up again. She asked Eugenia exactly when. Eugenia replied at some length.

'What's all that?' asked Dr Challoner.

'My Greek,' said Kate reluctantly, 'is pretty patchy.'

'The first day they used the new bridge,' said Selwyn, 'a man fell off it and broke his neck. No wonder! Very rude to go making a bridge without asking leave.'

Dr Challoner gulped down his Ovaltine and took flight, in vain. Eugenia attended him upstairs and stood beside his bed until, by signs, he induced her to go away.

'You shouldn't have said that,' scolded Kate, when left alone with Selwyn. 'You might put ideas into his head.'

'Nobody could. If they'd sacrificed a virgin on the bridge he'd merely think it was foreigners being funny. Is sugar the usual tip? I gather She only gets a goat when somebody breaks his neck.'

'Yes. A pinch of sugar or a sweet. I can't think why they thought she'd like a gramophone record.'

Selwyn began to laugh.

'Know what we gave her? Bicarbonate of soda. She took it all right, though. But why was Freddie so anxious to keep it all dark?'

'I'm not sure. He used to quote some old poem that said: Once the dead used to leave a living city behind them.

Now the living hold a funeral for their city. I think he meant by a city the mysterious power which turns a lot of people into a single creature . . . a city . . . or . . . or . . .'

'A procession?' suggested Selwyn thoughtfully.

'Yes, yes! A procession. He thought there was a lot of it here and very little anywhere else. They certainly can turn themselves into a procession. When we buried Edith . . . oh it was as if the island itself was mourning, not only the people. I said so to Freddie. And he said: Yes. Keritha weeps for its dead. As long as it knows how to do that, the living will never have to weep for Keritha.'

'I shouldn't have thought they go in for weeping much here.'

'Oh, they do for the dead. You never saw people cry so much. They're very sorry for them. They think the next world is a terribly dreary place. They have a lot of songs, folk songs really . . . so sad! Freddie translated some of their songs for me into English verse. There's one . . . it always wrings my heart when the women sing it. Freddie's version was:

> Uncounted gifts did God bestow
> On men, yet two He has denied:
> A bridge to span the ocean wide,
> A ladder to the world below.
>
> We cannot seek them out, nor guess
> What exile young and old must share,
> Nor ask how little children fare,
> Lost in the shadows – motherless.

Selwyn gave her a blank look, turned his back, and went

on stacking records. She remembered that he was, and always had been, a lout. Freddie's little translation might not be up to much, but anybody save a lout would have made some comment.

2

On the following day Kate and Dr Challoner went over to Zagros to collect the mail for Keritha, delivered by the bi-weekly post boat. They took with them the records for the schoolmaster, and Kate had a long shopping list. The larger island had a sort of general store where it was possible to buy soap, darning needles and other essential commodities.

'Is there a chemist?' asked Dr Challoner as they ran in to the Zagros jetty.

'No. Did you want something from a chemist?'

'Harrumph! It doesn't matter.'

There was a well-stocked cupboard, said Kate, in the bathroom formerly belonging to Edith. It was supplied, from time to time, with extensive orders from Athens, and it was now his. She did not specifically mention aperients or pile ointment, but thought it probable that one or the other was in question.

They landed. Yorgos took the records up to the school house. Kate departed with her shopping bag. Dr Challoner strolled round the village which seemed to be a mouldy little place although a distinct improvement upon Keritha.

An antagonism to Keritha had been growing on him ever since his arrival and the ridiculous figure which he had been forced to cut at the grave. The place overwhelmed him with uneasiness, as though some invisible creature were continually thumbing its nose at him. Alfred's letter, in spite of its nonsense, strengthened the impression of some unidentified foe. 'Every tree its dryad, every spring its naiad.' Those words, in particular, nagged at him, as though dryads and naiads, safely immunized as poetic imagery, imprisoned between the covers of books, had been snatched from durance by a lot of foreign oafs who were not even, according to Alfred, dead. This insane rubbish was a menace. Alfred was in his grave, the letter was torn up, but the Thing on Keritha continued to thumb its nose and would do so until he had succeeded in proving, to himself and to the world, that Nothing was there.

Zagros, dry, dusty, and treeless, was infinitely preferable. He surveyed it with an eye which was almost benign until the post boat came hooting in. Amidst the usual babel of shouts, greetings, and exhortations, a cargo and a few passengers were brought ashore. The mail bags were carried away. The people scattered to their homes, all save two, one of whom Challoner recognized. It was Tipton of Richardson, with whom he published; most of his work was handled by Tipton and they had always got on pretty well. A chat would have been quite pleasant had Tipton been alone; he had a woman with him, which might entail introductions, pleasant faces and tedious civilities. The two stood arguing on the jetty with a ferocity which stamped them as man and wife. At length the woman went off by herself towards the village and Tipton made for the *taverna*. Dr Challoner approached. He turned. They agreed that Zagros was an odd place in which to meet.

'We've come over from Thasos for the day,' explained

Tipton, as they sat down outside the *taverna*. 'We're going back on the post boat. My wife thinks she can buy those boring peasant embroideries here, bags and things. They cost the earth in Athens and they're all supposed to be made in places like this. She thought she might get them cheaper from the women who actually do them. But why are you here? It seems a dreary place.'

He looked startled at hearing that Dr Challoner had come from Keritha. As soon as they had ordered their drinks he said:

'You're actually staying on Mystery Island? You were allowed to land?'

'Of course. Why not?'

'I'd heard there was some old ruffian living there who never lets anybody land. He sent Spaulding off last summer, with a flea in his ear.'

'Spaulding? Really?'

This was good news. A flea in Spaulding's ear was well placed since that frivolous mountebank was reputed to be in the running for a Chair which should, by rights, be the reward of pure scholarship. Spaulding was no scholar, although accepted as such by the ignorant herd. He was a jack of all trades – classicist, archaeologist, anthropologist, historian, and aesthete by turns, dabbling here, dabbling there, and stealing the thunder of his betters.

'What did he want on Keritha?'

'To investigate the rumours, I suppose. You've heard of them, haven't you? No? It all sounds pretty cock-eyed to me – mutterings about a survival of some sort. You've never come across them?'

'No,' said Challoner, and then remembered Alfred's letter. He had an impression that some such claim had been made for a landscape and a smile. The smile was, of course, pure rubbish, but the landscape could not be completely ignored.

'Trees,' he conceded. 'There are more trees than you often see in these parts. It's much greener than Zagros, for instance. I suppose that some natural features might have survived on Keritha which were more common on all the islands before the Turks came.'

'Spaulding, it seems, met some joker – a waiter in Soho I think – who claims to have been born on Keritha, and spun some lovely yarns. He said they still keep down the population by exposing redundant babies on a sacred stone, and leaving them to the crows. And they bury the dead with five lepta under the tongue as Charon's fee. They call it *pieratikion*.'

'Oh!'

This word startled Dr Challoner.

'If this Soho oracle meant to pull our learned friend's leg, he succeeded. Off goes Spaulding. He talks like a native, as you know. The story is that he ran into this old party, who has quite a house there. Some kind of local squire. Poor Spaulding thinks he's found a friend. He's given a very good meal. Very good wine. Plenty of cultured conversation. So out he comes with his mission. A stone? Oh yes, certainly there's a stone but he'll get to it best by boat, as it's on the far side of the island. A fast motor launch is put at his disposal. In he gets. Next thing he knows he's back at Thasos.'

Tipton paused to guffaw and Dr Challoner contributed a few dry chuckles.

'But is it all a myth? Is there no old party of that sort on Keritha?'

177

Dr Challoner explained that the old party must have been his uncle, outlined his present errand, and declared positively that there was *nothing whatever* upon Keritha. He was obliged, however, to admit that his knowledge of modern Greek went no farther than a single word of apology.

'But there's a man who went with me who talks it very well. He's a bit of an ass, but he helped me to get a boat. He's always jabbering with the natives. If he'd heard anything of that sort he'd have mentioned it, I imagine. Used to be a pupil of mine; a man called Potter.'

'Not Selwyn Potter?'

'Yes. You know him?'

'He used to be in Richardson. We called him Lucky Potter. As you say, a bit of an ass. And then became a super-success. Married an incredibly beautiful wife and fell into a pipe dream of a job in a Swedish glass-house. My wife used to be in Richardson too, and she was always hearing about Lucky Potter from an old woman there, who was rather fond of him for some reason. I never quite believed in the gorgeous wife till I met them both, by chance, at the Opera in Paris one night. She really was gorgeous. And he looked intolerably prosperous and pleased with himself. Dress clothes that fitted, and on chummy terms with all sorts of important people. Beaming at everyone, as if going up the ladder had been no trouble at all; he might have been an important person himself. She'd made a wonderful job of him. What she could have seen in him . . .'

Tipton broke off to observe, without much enthusiasm, the reappearance of his own wife, who was now wandering about the waterfront in search of him. Picking up a newspaper which had been left on their table, he held it in front of his face and continued:

'However, now that she's dead, we can't call him Lucky Potter any more, poor chap.'

'I knew nothing of all this,' said Dr Challoner. 'Dead, is she?'

'Very sudden, so I heard. Must be a couple of years ago. Upon which he completely cracked up. Went all to pieces and lost his job. What's he doing now, do you know?'

'Teaching, so he says.'

'One might have guessed that.'

Mrs Tipton was a determined woman. She made for the *taverna* in order to discover what manner of man was hiding behind that newspaper. Dr Challoner was obliged to get up, but he did not have to make pleasant faces for long, since she merely wanted an audience for her grievance against Zagros. No peasant embroideries were going at bargain prices, although she had seen a woman actually at work beside her cottage door. The sum asked was rather higher than that demanded in Athens.

'Yet I'm sure the shops there don't pay her what I offered. They must make a profit. If only I could talk Greek I'd have told her what a fool she is.'

'Pity Potter isn't along. He could have told her for you. Know what, Ruth? Selwyn Potter is on Keritha, just over there.'

'Really? Old Mrs Gray would be interested. She's always saying she's quite lost touch with him. Oh, I do feel mad about that embroidery.'

'I told you it was a wild-goose chase. A day completely wasted.'

'Must you say that *again*? Am I to be allowed to drink or not?'

Tipton ordered some *retzina* for her and turned to Dr Challoner.

'Then anybody can go to Keritha now? They won't be thrown out?'

'Not if they're fools enough to go. But you needn't pass that on to Spaulding.'

'I won't,' promised Tipton. 'But there's somebody else who'd like to go. Garland Becker. Know him?'

'Slightly. Quite sound in his own field, I believe. Why on earth should he want to go?'

'I think he wouldn't mind taking the wind out of Spaulding's sails. He was foaming at the mouth over Spaulding's last book.'

'Oh that. I haven't read it. Don't intend to. I can't think why your people publish him.'

'He . . . er . . . sells quite well.'

'He would!'

'Anyway Becker is of your opinion. He says Spaulding's two and two always come out as seven. If there's anything worth investigation on Keritha he wants to dispose of it before Spaulding gets to work. I think I'll drop him a hint that there'd be no difficulties now about his going. You wouldn't object, would you? He can be trusted to take sensible people along.'

'Eric! The steamer is hooting!'

'I heard.'

'Tell him from me,' said Dr Challoner, 'that he'll waste his time. Keritha is a hopelessly dull little place. As soon as my business is finished I'm off and I shan't come back.'

'We shall be left behind.'

'Leaving that house empty? What a waste! Becker is going with a party to the Dodecanese this summer. He could slip over to Keritha . . .'

'Well, get left behind if you like. I'm starting.'

Mrs Tipton jumped up, bared her teeth in a farewell grimace, and bustled off towards a boat which was taking passengers off for the steamer.

'Your house!' said Tipton. 'From what you say, very comfortable. Left empty! Why not let it to Becker? He . . .'

Another long hoot from the steamer drowned Tipton's voice. His wife, in the boat, was waving and shouting.

'Oh God! I must go, I suppose. Think about it. Drop me a line if you like the idea. I shall be in Athens till the end of next week. The Acropolis Hotel . . .'

He set off for the jetty at a lumbering run and jumped into the boat just as it was putting off. This last-minute gallop and the shrieks of Mrs Tipton greatly diverted Zagros.

The steamer sailed away. Dr Challoner watched it go and turned over Tipton's proposition in his mind. That the house might be let was a perfectly new idea. He had thought of it as completely valueless, since no person in his senses could want to stay on Keritha and he did not care to deal with imbeciles. Tipton's offer to arrange everything had been a trifle officious, as though two such Mandarins as Challoner and Becker could not communicate with one another directly, should they wish to do so. It might, however, be more diplomatic, on this occasion, to act through a third party. Any direct approach might look like an admission that Keritha was worth a visit. It was not, and Becker could be trusted to discover, and to proclaim, that it was not.

There was, on the other hand, that gravestone. It must be removed and replaced by something more seemly if any civilized visitors were likely to set eyes on it. The cost and the trouble must be set against the advantages to be gained by letting the house. Dr Challoner hated trouble, and had pretty well decided that, so long as nobody ever came at all, the thing could be left as it was. Alfred's silly letter had inclined him to feel that much distress over it was needless.

Moreover there was Eugenia. Her presence in the house would create difficulties and might entail awkward explanations.

Best let it go, he thought sadly, as he worked out a proper tip for the girl at the *taverna*. I can't turn her out. Must do what he asked me. He's been very just about the jewellery and the money, and only asked for one thing in return: that I'd let her stay on. Pity! Becker! He'd make short work of that stupid island. Dryads! Naiads! Give Becker a week and there'd be precious little left of *them* on Keritha or anywhere else.

3

Selwyn would have liked to go to Zagros but was not invited by the other two, who were endeavouring, by sundry snubs, to make him understand that he had outstayed his welcome.

He understood that perfectly but meant to remain until told outright to go away. The situation on Keritha amused him, especially now that old Challoner had obviously tumbled to the truth about Eugenia. He wanted to see what would happen next.

Having watched the boat start for Zagros he got the maids to cut him some sandwiches and set off to explore the island. The highest point of it was barred by rocks only to be scaled by the agile. Turning aside, he crossed a shoulder of the mountain to a point where he had a fine view of the sea to the south. Here he sat down, ate his sandwiches, and chuckled over the memory of Dr Challoner last night, bolting upstairs to bed with Eugenia in pursuit. After a while, having exhausted this diversion, he began to count. A lizard, sunning itself on a stone by his foot, caught his attention when he had got as far as 753. Its palpitations fascinated him. They were so regular that he did not need to count. Presently he fell asleep.

The lizard was still there when he awoke, although he

felt as if he had been submerged in nothingness for hundreds of years. Strangely relaxed, at peace, he floated out of some dark tunnel into the breath of bright air on Keritha, the glitter of sea and sky. There was his little friend, gently vibrating on the hot stone. He could watch it and not think; he could almost be the lizard, placidly vibrating with it, feeling the spring warmth in all his limbs.

Suddenly he sneezed. The lizard shot into a crevice of the stone; it was amazing that so sleepy a creature could move so quickly. He bent down and murmured:

'Sorry, old man! Couldn't help it.'

Later he made his way over the shoulder until the western side came into view, the scattered homesteads, the fruit blossom, the jetty, the boats, and a man ploughing yellow earth under the olive trees. As a landscape it was familiar enough; he had met with it before in many parts of Greece. But this one struck him as completely satisfying, as though he had been famished and was making a meal as he looked at it. How long he gazed he scarcely knew; some time later he pursued the track which led him eventually to the bridge in the shady ravine. The faint tinkle of water could be heard before he got there. Sugar! He had none, but he had not eaten all the little sweet cakes which the maids had packed with the sandwiches. He threw one over, as he crossed the bridge, and paused to listen in case She said thank you.

Then he turned to look at the laughter of the sea below. He was waiting for something. A few moments later it happened. Cosmos turned a somersault. The scene steadied and took on an extreme actuality, as though loudly asserting itself.

This had happened to him before, on his first visit to the islands. He had once watched the sun rise over Delos, supposing the sun to exist because he saw it, and had suddenly become aware that he existed because the sun saw him, that he was perceived by some such mind as the sun might have, in no sense anthropomorphic, but charged with intelligent cognition.

The dizzy shock of this escape from solitary confinement, from the cramped cell of *cogito ergo sum* to the wide latitude of *cogitat ergo* . . . lasted but for a couple of seconds. He was back in his cell before he could grasp its import, nor could he, upon reflection, call it an intellectual experience. Yet it produced a vital sharpening of all his faculties – intellectual, sensory, and imaginative – which lasted for several months. Mentally he defined it as 'that time at Delos when I got out'.

Now, as before, he was out and in again between one breath and another. The trees, the sun, the sea, and the stream had all taken a look at him, made him a target of life, before his prison walls closed again, leaving him with keener eyes and ears to make what he could of them.

The song of the water continued without end but not, as he thought after listening for some minutes, without form. There was perhaps a cadence, a succession of notes, which might be scored for some instrument never yet devised by man. This waterfall might have its own voice. If he listened often enough, got to know it well enough, he might be able to recognize it. Hearing a variety of records, taken from a number of little streams and cascades, he might be able to pick out one and to say positively: That's Keritha! Each would be different. The length of a drop could in no two cases be quite the same. Some particular stone, or obstacle, must cause a unique cadenza, bound to recur. He lingered and listened to Keritha until he felt that he had got it by heart.

On his return to the house he sat down at Freddie's desk, with a pencil and paper, trying to score it. He managed about a dozen bars which were, he was sure, constantly repeated. The intervals were wrong; no musical scoring known to him could convey them. The rhythm was right.

There was, besides, another rhythm going on in his mind which had nothing to do with the waterfall. A slow contented pulse was beating. That also was Keritha. He remembered the lizard on the stone – its quiescence, its immense vitality. Smiling slightly he took his pencil again and sketched it, sprawling across the sunny rock amidst a pattern thrown by thistle shadows.

So now what? he wondered when he had finished.

So now what?

He was sunk. He had forgotten to keep on keeping on, and now had no defence at all against the return of thought. For one hour, two hours, he had been living heedlessly, at peace in a world without her. He tore the drawing in half and stumbled away.

The truth could only be endured if he never, never, lost sight of it. He must live with it hour by hour, minute by minute, second by second, through each heavy day, never forgetting why he had to count, why he had to behave like a man to whom nothing much can happen. To come back to his loss, to scan it afresh, after some brief treacherous reprieve, was more than he could bear. Keep on keeping on! Count!

Kate, on her return from Zagros, found the torn drawing on Freddie's desk. During the trip home Challoner had passed on Tipton's story. They both felt a little remorseful at the cold shoulder which they had given to Selwyn, now that his wretchedness, and the cause of it, had been revealed. She went out at once and found him sitting on his usual bench in the garden. Her face told him that she knew. He said quickly:

'Don't! Don't talk about it.'

'I won't,' she promised, sitting down beside him. 'I came to give you those cigarettes you asked me to get.'

'Oh, thanks!'

She handed them over, glad to do him some small service although, that morning, she had thought it rather cool of him to expect it of her.

'Did you,' he asked, 'make whoopee on Zagros, you and Challoner?'

'He did. I shopped. But he met a kindred spirit. A man called Tipton.'

'Oh, him? He was in Richardson. So that's . . .'

He did not finish. The meaning was plain: that was how his story had come to light.

'If it wasn't for the children . . .' he said suddenly.

'Children?'

'Didn't Tipton mention that? We had two boys.'

He thought this over and added:

'I have two boys.'

'No. I didn't know that. How old are they?'

'Paul is five. John is three. I mean they *were* . . . Paul is seven now and John is five.'

'Paul and John?'

'They were called after . . . two churches.'

'Where are they now?'

'In a sort of home.'

He opened the packet of cigarettes, lit one, and continued:

'I had to go to Sweden. I left them with a person who

didn't look after them properly. The neighbours complained to the NSPCC and they were put into this home because they needed care and protection. I knew nothing about it till I got back to England. Everybody was very kind when I explained. They said they'd keep the boys for a bit and I said I'd pay for them. It's near Guildford, where they are.'

'And are they happy?'

He looked at her as if asking what that word meant.

'They look after them all right. I live in, at the school where I teach. In Suffolk.'

'But you see them pretty often?'

'Sometimes. It doesn't do, really. They cry, when they see me. I don't think John remembers. He was only three when . . . when . . . but he cries when Paul cries.'

He took out a wallet, adding in an explanatory tone:

'It's very sad . . . Matron sent me this the other day.'

He handed her a photograph. Kate thought that Matron might have managed better. A dozen children were posed on some uncompromising steps. They were well clothed. They looked well nourished. Some were smiling. Yet, despite the toys they all clutched, they faced the camera bleakly. There was an elderly wariness about them which reminded her of the little Challoners next door. Perhaps it was not Matron's fault. Poor Matron! What could she do for children who knew too much, too soon. *Lost in the shadows — motherless.* That mother must have been fair-haired. There was no look of Selwyn about either child.

'This one's Paul,' he said. 'And that's John.'

It was not very easy to imagine the mother. Dr Challoner had not repeated Tipton's description of her. Kate pictured some dim, plain creature, glad to get a husband, who had been able to love Selwyn because her love had never been sought elsewhere.

'But must they be in this home?' she asked. 'Have you no relations who would take them?'

'I haven't. They've a grandmother. Mrs Blaney. She went to America ages ago and never came back. I've never seen her. She's quite cracked. Founded some new religion and given it all her money.'

'But had you no friends? Where did you live?'

'We had a flat in Stockholm. For the first years we were there pretty well all the time. I worked for Hagstrom. You know? The glass people. Later on we were in France and Italy a good deal. Hagstrom has premises in Paris and Florence. They're showrooms really. He sells a lot to Americans. But they had a work-room for me, and I could meet customers personally. People who wanted to order special things. Do you know Hagstrom glass?'

'I've heard of it, of course. And I saw a lovely thing in an exhibition that was theirs, I think. It was called the Marigny bowl, I don't know why. All the work was inside, upside down, as if the top edge was the rim of a lake and these were reflections, and the bottom was a cloudy sky. Yes, and I saw a picture of another: fountains playing and spray blowing and people faintly suggested in the spray – hardly more than shadows.'

'The Nereids. That was one of mine. So was the Marigny. It was called that because it was commissioned by the Marigny Institute. It was one of the last things I did, though I'd had it in mind for years. I didn't dare tackle it before.'

'Selwyn! One of yours? What do you mean? You did that engraving?'

'Yes. I told you. I worked for them.'

She had supposed him to have been some kind of salesman and even so she had wondered that Hagstrom should trust him within a mile of their wares.

'But . . . but how did you do it?' she stammered.

'Diamond point. They both are.'

'You did those lovely things with your own hands?'

'I couldn't have done them with anybody else's hands, could I?'

In stupefaction she stared at his ungainly hands.

'I thought . . . it's very stupid of me . . . I thought somebody drew it out and then somebody else, specially skilled, put it into the glass.'

'They do that sometimes with copperwheel. While I was learning, another man adapted some designs I'd made. But diamond point . . . you might as well draw a picture and give it to somebody else and say: Now! Draw that picture for me.'

'But what a dolt I am! Not to have noticed your name. It must have been on the label in that exhibition, but I never took it in. I just thought: Hagstrom.'

'A lot of people do. A lot of people don't know the difference between blowing and engraving.'

The Tipton-Challoner rumour of some mysterious remarkable success was now explained. She was astonished, but less so than she would have expected. She had always thought of Selwyn as possessing capacity and liable to do something or other very well indeed. The wonder was that he should have done it with his hands. Then the end of the story recurred to her: cracked up . . . lost his job . . . went to pieces . . . teaching somewhere.

'Selwyn! You've not given it up?'

'It's given me up.'

A finality in his tone warned her against protest or argument. She remembered the torn drawing on Freddie's desk and came very near to guessing the reason. *It* had not given him up, but he could only acknowledge *It* by some surrender which he refused to make. Sighing, she studied the wan faces of Paul and John once more.

'I still don't see ... why Guildford?'

'Well, some nuns in Florence looked after them at first.'

'Oh? It was in Italy ... that ... that ...?'

'In the Apennines. In a little village beyond Vallombrosa. We thought it was indigestion. Till too late. Appendicitis. When we got her down to Florence it was too ... They were very kind, those nuns. But Mrs Blaney cabled from America that I'd better take the boys to a friend of hers in London; she'd arranged it. So I brought them to England. But the friend was furious; she said she'd never been very intimate with Mrs Blaney, and oughtn't to be asked to cope with it. She knew of a person, though, who could take the boys while I went to Stockholm. Some woman who had worked for her.'

'Who didn't take proper care of them? How monstrous!'

'I expect it was a bit of a shock our turning up like that. She'd only just got the letter from Mrs Blaney to say we were coming; hadn't had a chance to protest. And we arrived late at night, in the middle of a big party she was giving. It was more than she need have done to find anybody at all.'

'Still ... in her shoes I'd have ...'

Kate drew her breath sharply, picturing this forlorn trio upon her own doorstep. She would have taken them in until satisfactory arrangements could be made.

'I did go to you, as a matter of fact. Only you'd gone.'

'Where? To Edwardes Square?'

'I told you I'd called there once, the summer before last.

That was why. I was at my wits' end. I didn't much like the look of this person Mrs Blaney's friend had found . . . I didn't know anyone to consult. I used to have a friend, Mrs Gray, but she'd left London. You were the only person I could think of. I'd always thought you so very good at being a mother. Your family . . . that time I was there . . . you all seemed so happy and so fond of one another. I used to talk about it to . . . to Elizabeth.'

So that had been her name. Kate had an impression that he had not uttered it to anyone for a long time.

'She never had much of a home herself,' he said. 'Her mother . . . oh well! We wanted our children to be . . . we hadn't either of us much idea how to set about it. When she was in a spot about how to manage them, or if they had a temperature, she used to say: so what would Mrs Benson do, I wonder?'

Since she had recently decided to dislike him, Kate was embarrassed at these tokens of regard; she must be, she thought, an ungenerous, cold-hearted creature to have felt no warmth where she had inspired it. She sat staring unhappily over the sea at Zagros while Selwyn sought in his wallet for another photograph, which he handed to her. At a first amazed glance she exclaimed:

'But . . . how *lovely!*'

'She was very beautiful. Everybody said so.'

A longer study convinced her of something else.

'I'm sure,' she said at last, 'that I must have met her somewhere. I can't think where. But I've seen this face before.'

'You might have seen her picture in the newspapers when she had her big coming-out ball. She was photographed a lot that year.'

Not immediately did Kate take this in. She was struggling to remember, was sure that it had not been a photograph. They had met. They had spoken to one another.

'She was the Contessina Colleoni,' explained Selwyn.

Kate gave a faint squeak of astonishment. She sat stunned while he, after two years of frozen silence, poured out the story of his strange marriage, his flawless happiness, loving and beloved by a creature who had given him all that one human being can bestow upon another. As he spoke the lost Elizabeth emerged: her beauty, her wit, her constancy, her courage, her sweet temper and her warm heart. Every hour of their seven years together had been steeped in felicity; it had irradiated the commonest things and lent a zest to the dullest exertions.

He had been, she perceived, too happy for safety. No refuge was left to him in a world which had completely disintegrated. For the bereaved, who must nourish existence without joy, commonplace tasks and uncongenial company offer a kind of refuge; they provide a territory where lost happiness is least missed. For Selwyn there was no such harsh protection. The sun had shone full upon him wherever he had gone, whatever he had done. Now he was so totally severed from all contact with life that he had not even learnt how to be miserable.

She tried to tell him so, when he had finished his story.

'You don't mourn for her,' she said gently. 'That's the first part of learning to live without her.'

'I am living without her.'

'Not really living.'

'I keep on keeping on. I must do that, for the children.'

'You drew something today. A lizard. Then you tore it

up. I found it in the house. I think you tore it up because, when you were drawing, you forgot, for a little while, and lived without her. Then you remembered. Dear Selwyn . . . you've got to face it! That dreadful moment of having to remember. Face it again and again. That's life. Is this the first time you've drawn anything since . . .?'

'Yes. And if Keritha does that to me, I'm off.'

'You should stay, if Keritha does that to you. And draw. And then you might get your job with Hagstrom back.'

'No.'

'You must. You must live in this world and know that it's a changed world because she isn't here any more. So you have to change. The more we love people the more we have to change when they die. If the dead could come back, those who loved them most would seem to them the most changed. Only those who cared nothing would be just the same, because nothing would have happened to them.'

'If she came back she wouldn't find me changed.'

'She would. You are. Don't tell me you're *now* the man she loved. Are you?'

He thought it over, remembered the man she had loved, the man who had fashioned the Marigny bowl, scanned the shrunken, aimless creature who had replaced him, and muttered:

'No.'

They said no more, and sat on together in silence, while the shadows lengthened. He, aghast, acknowledged the change in himself. She, with a resignation born of long practice, thought of those who had once loved her and who, mourning, had consigned her to Lethe.

PART FIVE

'DE MORTUIS . . .'

Crossing alone the nighted ferry
With the one coin for fee,
Whom on the wharf of Lethe waiting
Count you to find?

HOUSMAN

1

The island hens had been well informed about the *Latona*. That unlucky ship, after many mishaps, had reached Venice thirty-six hours behind schedule. The *Wanderers* missed the train which should have taken them home. Some braved a rail journey without seats or reservations. Many waited for a day and took a plane from Milan which crashed in the Alps. There were no survivors.

Douglas never received Kate's broadside. When she did not turn up by train the Benson family could only assume that she must have taken the alternative route. Miss Shepheard, and the Cruise Officer, with records which might have inspired a doubt, were both dead.

Newspapers seldom reached Keritha. Freddie habitually listened to a world news bulletin on the radio; mention of the disaster in that quarter gave him no grounds for connecting it with Kate, since it occurred three days after she should have been back in London.

She waited with impatience, with anxiety, with mounting bitterness, with a broken heart, for some word from her family. As time went on she hardened. She would not be the first to break this cruel silence. Had they loved her they would have written. There was no excuse for them, even if her letter had gone astray. They would, in that case, have been surprised when she did not return and would have made inquiries of *Wanderers Ltd*. She had not trusted entirely to Miss Shepheard. The Cruise Officer could have told them where she was. There could only be one explanation for their silence: they had got her broadside and were going to ignore it.

Thus she fed her own resentment until the prospect of Christmas broke it down. She had only to recall other Christmas days to know that, whatever they did, they were still very dear to her. In a burst of agony she wrote. She took the blame upon herself and offered no excuses as she implored them to write, to tell her that they were all well and happy.

She was still reminding herself that it was far too early to hope for a reply when a maid came knocking at her door one morning. Two lords, the husband and the son, were in the hall. Douglas and Andrew had lost not a moment when her letter arrived. They flew to Istanbul and chartered a fast launch to Keritha. They arrived while telegrams from them and from everybody else dallied in the post office on Zagros.

Down she ran and fell upon their necks. They snatched her from Keritha in a tempest of questions, answers and confused explanations. They had come to take her home, home, home as fast as ever they could. No, they had not been angry with her. Why should they? No. They had had no letter from her. No letter at all. They had thought her dead, *dead*, thanks to that arch idiot, Brian Loder.

He had been the only person to blame. It was he who flew out to Switzerland, to the little village where charred bodies, brought down from the still-smouldering wreck on the mountain side, were laid out for identification. Had he made any real attempt to carry out his mission efficiently some doubt might have arisen as to Kate's presence on the flight. There would have been further inquiries. The scattered travellers who had returned by rail might have been rounded up and questioned. Although she had not mixed much with her fellow cruisers, one of them might have remembered that she left the *Latona* long before it reached Venice.

That Brian had volunteered for the errand was now remembered against him, as an instance of his cocksure officiousness, although Douglas and Andrew had been thankful at the time to escape such an ordeal. He had declared it to be necessary and had overruled any inclination to accept Kate's failure to return by train as certain evidence of her death. Having checked at the Malpensa Airport the names of passengers taking the flight, and failing to find any record of her, he had insisted upon further investigation. He bustled off to the scene of the disaster, spent five minutes in that grim morgue, hastily identified something in a familiar white tweed coat as his mother-in-law, and rushed out to vomit.

It was all, complained Andrew and Douglas, typical of Brian. After a blustering display of thoroughness and efficiency he had, when it came to the point, made a spectacular fool of himself. Little was said, save abuse of him, during the first part of their flight back to London. Kate was at last driven to take his part and declared that she would, probably, have been sick herself. Moreover, the coat had been hers, since she had lent it to poor Miss Shepheard.

'If you can forgive him,' said Andrew, 'I suppose we must.'

He gave her arm an affectionate squeeze. Ever since their reunion they had been catching hold of her and squeezing her as though to make sure that she was quite solid. Their manner, awestruck, almost reverent, made her wonder if she had changed very much.

'But you always were an angel,' he murmured.

Nobody in the world had ever called Kate an angel before, except Bridie when she wanted a blouse pressed in a hurry. Now the word matched those solemn looks. She supposed that it would wear off when they grew calmer.

'Stop abusing poor Brian,' she commanded, 'and tell me some news. What have you all been doing?'

There was a pause, as though they could not remember what they had been doing, or could not decide which of their doings would be likely to interest an angel. Andrew then recollected that Hazel was expecting a baby in March. She was, he declared, very well but had had a tough time of it, getting out of the flat when she was feeling very sick. The move had been a nightmare without Kate to help and advise. They had missed her dreadfully. Hazel's Mummy, who came to lend a hand, fell off a step ladder and got concussion.

'And will your new flat,' she asked, 'be large enough for a baby?'

'A flat? We're not in a flat. It's a house . . . in Chiswick. That house, you know, that you always wanted us to take. Chiswick. Where you're coming to stay with us now.'

'Oh? We're going to Chiswick?'

'Yes, Mother! We told you. Father and you are coming to stay with us for a bit. We told you.'

Perhaps they had. She could not remember much of those first bewildered moments. They had said they came to take her home, and home, for her, was Edwardes Square.

'Then,' she ventured, 'you gave up the Bruton Street flat?'

'Bruton Street?'

He stared as though he had never heard of it. Then he remembered and flushed.

'Oh, *that*! No. That job fell through. I'm still with Mortimer and Tyndale.'

And what had become of Pamela? wondered Kate, but did not ask. It was safer to say how nice it was that they had gone to Chiswick.

'But why didn't you and Hazel stay in Edwardes Square while the move was going on?'

Andrew looked accusingly at his father. Douglas cleared his throat.

'I'm afraid this will be rather a shock for you, Kate. Edwardes Square is sold.'

Sold? They had lost no time! Ah well . . . six months . . . it was her own fault that it had been six months.

'I had a very good offer for it,' said Douglas, 'in August. It was much too big for me. I'm . . . I mean I've been sharing a flat in Chelsea with Ronnie Sinclair. It seemed a good idea . . . the two of us . . .'

'Yes. Yes, I see. A very sensible idea. I hope you have somebody capable looking after you?'

'Oh yes, indeed. Mrs McKintosh. Cook housekeeper. A wonderful woman. I never . . .'

If he had been about to say that he had never lived so well before, he remembered in time not to say it. There was a light in his eye which Kate recognized. This Mrs McKintosh appealed to the sentimental streak in him. She might not be another Pamela but was probably quite as bogus.

'Yes,' he repeated happily, 'we've been in luck, getting Mrs McKintosh.'

She glanced at Andrew, who made a face at her and then looked hurriedly out of the window at the clouds.

'Edwardes Square was too large for us anyway,' she commented. 'I suppose you've stored most of the furniture?'

'No. Well . . . there wasn't anything to store. We've got Ronnie's stuff at the flat. The children took anything they wanted from Edwardes Square, and I sold the rest and got rid of all the junk.'

She nodded and tried to smile as she envisaged this complete evaporation of her home. The *junk* must have included all those worthless little possessions, those pathetic oddments, which a human being accumulates as part of his existence. Such things, she reflected, are always thrown away when people die. Old letters and photographs are burnt. Much goes to the Parish Jumble Sale.

There had been a shabby dog-eared Shakespeare, which she had won at school as a prize. She could not imagine reading Shakespeare save in that old book, but now she would probably never see it again. Why should they preserve it? They all had their own Shakespeares. That scuffed object meant nothing to anybody save herself. It was a fragment of the living Kate, now for ever discarded. How much else was gone?

She must foresee these shocks and be ready for them, since the whole distressing business had been her own fault. Needless discomfort must be avoided. Since they thought her dead they had acted very sensibly; they had not been callous. Upon the whole the news was good, and she need not have suffered so much anxiety in the summer. Pamela seemed to be mysteriously out of the picture. Andrew was in the house she would herself have chosen for him and was still with Mortimer and Tyndale. No sooner did they believe her dead than they behaved, it seemed, exactly as she would have wished.

Changing the subject she asked cautiously about Andrew's work. He talked readily and pleasantly; he had shed the sulkiness which formerly attended any reference to Mortimer and Tyndale. He volunteered the information that the firm had treated them very well. His resignation in June had been overlooked when the Bruton Street plan fell through. He had got a small community centre to design, on a new housing estate, and found it an interesting piece of work.

'They mightn't have been quite so nice about it,' he added, 'if they hadn't been sorry. . . . I mean we were all in such trouble . . . thought we were, I mean, at the time.'

He was changed, and changed for the better. A certain chronic resentment against life had vanished. He had grown up. That peevish letter which she had received on Thasos was the last she would ever get from the Andrew she used to know. The umbilical cord was cut. *Bonsoir, petit . . . Bonjour, Monsieur!* she thought, recalling some lines in a French film which had once moved her. She sighed.

'Are you all right?' he asked anxiously, with another of those awestruck looks. 'You seem to be tired.'

'I am rather. It's all been too exciting. I'm sleepy.'

Thankful to escape the pitfalls of further conversation, they settled to sleep. Little more was said until they were circling over the airport.

The mild damp of an English winter greeted them as they got out of the plane. They hurried through a light drizzle to the Customs hall. She had nothing to declare; she had brought nothing new back with her save some warm clothes which she had been obliged to buy when the cold winds of winter blew over the Aegean.

They passed through a doorway. She was seized, clutched, and hugged afresh. All the family were there – Hazel bathed in easy tears, Bridie as white as a sheet, and Judith with the stiff expression of one who is determined not to cry. Mother! Mother! they kept saying. Dear Mother! Darling Mother! Oh, Mother! Mother . . .

Brian was shuffling uneasily in the background. As soon as she could she went up to him, kissed him, and murmured:

'My poor Brian! You were perfectly right. It was my coat. I'm sure anybody would have thought it was me.'

He gave her a warm, grateful hug and echoed the universal cry:

'You're an angel.'

If she heard that word much oftener. . . . *De Mortuis*, she remembered. But that, surely, could not last for long? It pervades the first few months, when the bereaved are learning to get over it and faintly remorseful at doing so. Later they can revert, without embarrassment, to other memories. *Really he was an old devil!* . . . or . . . *She was always a very tiresome woman!* And later, much later, the final verdict: *He had his points* . . . or . . . *There was this to be said for her.*

The rest of the Bensons had their heads together. Andrew and Douglas were probably trying to explain to them why she had never written before. They must have forgotten by this time what had been said in those horrid birthday letters.

Then they came flocking round her again and carried her out to a waiting car. She was their angel, returned from Paradise, perforce a guest of the living, since she had, at the moment, no earthly habitation of her own at all.

2

They took her back to Chiswick for a late supper with champagne. The noise, the laughter, the inconsequent chatter, a dozen small, unexpected shocks, a flavour of hysteria in the atmosphere, made her feel quite giddy. At length this was noticed with concern; there seemed to be a tendency to suppose her in a delicate state of health. They declared that she must be exhausted and should go to bed.

Judith and Brian departed. Kate was conducted to a small spare room which she was to share with Douglas. Hazel bustled about with hot-water bottles while Bridie unpacked the overnight bag, and exploded into apologies as soon as she got her mother to herself.

'That *awful* letter I sent you! Did you get it? Oh, I could kill myself. I can't tell you how . . .'

'Darling, let's put the whole thing right out of our minds.'

'But I must, *must* say this: Of course I realize now what an utter fool I was. I don't quite remember what I said. But afterwards, when we all thought . . . when we believed . . . when I started remembering the past, and you, and our home, and all those happy days, and what it meant . . . to write about it as if it was something that could be tossed away. I mean I started thinking about the past quite differently.'

'I know. I know. But please . . .'

'You were always so wonderful,' murmured Bridie fondly.

No I wasn't, thought Kate, and nobody thought that I was. If they think it now it's because they don't quite believe in me.

'And that beast of a Pamela! Letting everybody down!'

'What happened exactly?'

'Didn't they tell you? The moment, the very moment she heard the news, she dropped Father and Andrew completely. Threw over the plan for the firm in Bruton Street. Went abroad. Now she's in Jamaica. Father couldn't believe it at first, that she'd behaved so badly.'

'Bridie! We'd better not talk about it. We've all been stupid. Let's forget it.'

'As long as you understand that we do appreciate what you *were*, what you *did* for us . . .'

Hazel here appeared with a hot-water bottle. After kissing them both good night Kate fell into one of the twin beds, which felt very small after her stately couch on Keritha. Presently Douglas came in and stood beside her. She said:

'What nice pyjamas!'

'The girls gave them to me for Christmas. They're called Dry-Drip. I wash them in a basin and hang them up.'

'Drip-Dry. Your Mrs Thing ought to wash them for you.'

'Mrs McKintosh? Oh, I couldn't ask her to do that. It's amazing all she manages to get through. She's a wonderful woman.'

He kissed her, climbed into his own narrow bed, and turned off the light.

Mrs McKintosh now, thought Kate sleepily. He had to sentimentalize over somebody. She had always thought that Pamela would fly the coop if ever in danger of having to marry him. Now it was this Mrs Thing. A small flat; only Ronnie and Douglas to look after, and she couldn't wash their pyjamas. Men! Silly creatures!

In the morning she woke up worrying over Edith, abandoned so suddenly on Keritha. Eugenia had now learnt to give the injections but Edith's sight had begun to fail and she depended upon Kate for many comforts. They read together a good deal. Reading aloud had been a standard Benson diversion. Kate read well. She and Edith had been in the middle of *Guy Mannering* when Douglas and Andrew snatched her away.

Day-time noises were going on in the little house and Douglas was no longer in the other bed. It must be quite late. Just as she came to this conclusion Hazel appeared with a breakfast tray, daintily set out like a tray in a women's magazine. There was no salt but the egg was concealed in a coy little cosy like a penguin, and there were snowdrops in a vase. Andrew might once have denounced good little suburban housewives on the Benson pattern, but no Benson, thought Kate, had ever been quite as suburban as this. Against the vase of snowdrops was propped a letter from Fanny.

'But you shouldn't,' protested Kate. 'I'm not an invalid. Why . . . Hazel dear . . . what's this?'

She held up a little string of pearls.

'Just something of yours I've been looking after,' said Hazel, with unusual finesse. 'It's so lovely to be giving them back.'

That string had originally belonged to Kate's mother-in-law, and she had never much cared for it. The Mortimers set little store by conventional jewellery. She had been aware that Hazel hankered after this class symbol and would have given it to the child long ago, had she not feared that Douglas might be hurt.

'Oh, but I always meant to give it to you sometime! You must keep it now. I'd like you to. Really!'

'Oh, I couldn't. I couldn't. I'd feel awful. Besides . . . Judith and Bridie . . .'

Hazel paused, embarrassed.

'You mean they've got things of mine too?'

'It seems so awful of us, now . . .'

'Not a bit. Very sensible. We mustn't let that kind of thing worry us. I think we'd better let most of it stand. Anything I specially want back, I'll ask for. My favourite things . . .'

Hazel still looked worried.

'Bridie has all those. That jade bracelet and the big opal. It would be hard on Bridie if all her share . . .'

'We needn't settle it now. Let's wait and see how things work out. You keep these, anyway. I'll see to it that Bridie doesn't suffer.'

'Angelic of you,' murmured Hazel, shamefacedly bearing off the pearls.

Trust Bridie to collar the really nice things, thought Kate as she opened Fanny's letter. No. That was unfair. Bridie and she were alike; their tastes often coincided. She read:

Dear Kate,

Just a line to welcome you home. I'd have come to the airport if I wasn't tied by the leg here. Bill has scarlet fever and can't go back to school! A lovely thing to happen in the Xmas holidays! Do write at once and tell me what really happened. Why didn't they find out sooner you were in this place in Greece? Didn't you write? Weren't you surprised they didn't write? Was there some sort of upset?

Anyway you've given us all an awful shock, so don't do it again. I could laugh, though, when I think of the Memorial Service and all the soppy things we said about you. And the letters! Stacks of them! From the most unexpected people. Judith and Bridie were weeks answering them. I hope they've kept them. You'll be surprised to discover what a wonderful woman you were. At the time it didn't seem so odd, somehow, but it does now.

Do you remember that awful Mrs Bucket who used to do loose covers for us? The one you always thought pinched your silver punch ladle? She wrote to me saying she'd 'read where I'd had an irrapable loss' and you'd been so kind getting *leegal ade* for her husband when he was in *trubble*.

Well, don't go dying again in a hurry. Nobody is going to call you irrapable twice. Yrs affecty Fanny.

This repulsive letter was, in its way, reassuring. Fanny did not think her an angel, or regard her with awestruck compunction. Fanny was, it seemed, quite unchanged; as insensitive and irritating as ever.

There was no reason, discovered Kate as she attacked her cold and saltless egg, why Fanny should be changed. They had never been fond of one another; the news of that plane crash had disturbed nothing in Fanny's world.

After re-reading the letter she unkindly hoped that Bill's scarlet fever would keep Fanny in Sussex for a very long time, so that they need not meet. Nobody else in the world would have been so coarse as to mention the Memorial Service and the letters. That such things must have been Kate now realized but she shrank from knowing any particulars. They must be forgotten as quickly as possible. Since they had been hers on false pretences, they had now become a parody of human sorrow and human loss, robbing natural words and ceremonies of their innate dignity. Delicacy, she was sure, would keep everyone else silent about them.

Douglas knocked at the door and came in with a newspaper. He glanced, with some alarm, at Fanny's letter on the quilt. Kate laughed and tore it up, saying:

'Fanny, as you might expect, says all the wrong things. How long are we going to stay with Andrew and Hazel?'

He looked at her helplessly. She realized that very seldom, in their life together, had she asked him that kind of question. Formerly she would have told him exactly how long they were going to stay with Andrew and Hazel.

'I think,' he said, 'that Andrew hopes you'll stay quite a while and look after Hazel a bit.'

'Of course . . . if I could be of any use. . . . But you wouldn't want to stay here? It's not very comfortable.'

'No. And the food is beastly. That poor girl can't cook. I don't wonder Andrew wants you to teach her.'

'Does he?'

'That's his idea.'

'She mightn't welcome it. We must see. I could stay for a bit till we can make definite plans. Why don't you go back to Ronnie and your Mrs Thing? You'd be much more comfortable.'

'Oh, it would look rather odd, don't you think?'

'Everything that we do will be apt to look odd for quite a while,' said Kate. 'So we might as well do what we like.'

He gave her a long speculative look and went away. He had been going to say something and then thought better of it, for which she was glad. The less said between them, the better, but she feared that he would not have the sense to leave well alone.

3

After another day in Chiswick, he fled to his widower's burrow. Kate gave a vague promise to visit him there as soon as she could. She must, he said, meet Mrs McKintosh and Ronnie would wish to pay his respects to her. This last she doubted. Ronnie despised women and had been so invariably rude to his friends' wives that he now had very few friends left. As for 'the Haggis Hag', as Andrew called her, all the children had hinted that their mother's first task must be to eliminate the creature.

It was a task which Kate felt inclined to postpone. She preferred to avoid Douglas as long as there was any danger that he might insist upon telling her that he now saw the past quite differently. They were all given to doing this, but his particular version of it was sure to be the most exasperating. Upon one excuse or another, she kept away from Chelsea.

She must, she declared, go to Blackheath as soon as possible, in order to kiss her grandchildren. She must make an expedition to an outer suburb where Bridie, who had finished her training, was playing a very small part in a very small theatre. She must teach poor Hazel to cook.

This activity was thrust upon her by Andrew who now saw the past quite differently and spoke of Edwardes Square as a domestic Paradise. Pamela's ill faith, the collapse of the Bruton Street fantasy, had made a strong impression upon him. He no longer demanded a decorative wife, elegant bohemianism, or meals from the delicatessen round the corner. Hazel was not merely expected to know the difference between the two ends of a vacuum cleaner. Since he had come, in retrospect, to overrate his mother's achievements, he now demanded an impossibly high standard in cookery and housecraft.

Hazel welcomed advice. The sweetness of her temper preserved her from any grievance against this Canonized Mother. She had, so Kate discovered, no idea at all of the many ways in which she could save herself trouble, or the number of occasions when the use of a tin opener is perfectly justified. The cooking lessons, after a day or two, took on a slightly cynical turn.

'If he gets what he likes,' Kate told Hazel, 'he'll think you a wonderful cook, however little trouble it's been. He likes ice-cream. You can get that anywhere, so why make pancakes? . . . Don't look as if you toil and moil. If you bring in a turkey with all the trimmings, looking as if you'd roasted yourself along with it, he'll think you inefficient, however perfectly it's cooked. If you trip in airily with a Heat 'n' Eat dish that's only taken you five minutes, he'll think you a *cordon bleu*. . . . Talk a lot about herbs. Everyone uses them, of course, but men think it's a magic word. They go about solemnly telling other men: *My* wife cooks with herbs . . . Ask him for the dregs of the sherry for the soup. That always sounds impressive . . .'

Bridie, dropping in one day, overheard these counsels and took her mother to task.

'You're not teaching Hazel cookery! Only artfulness.'

'Well? Why not?'

'You never used to be artful. You never put on an act with Father over herbs and sherry.'

This was true, since Kate had never striven to please Douglas as poor Hazel was now striving to please Andrew.

'Your father,' she said, 'never demanded as much as Andrew does.'

'Quite. Andrew is perfectly unreasonable. He expects far too much. She should tell him where he gets off.'

'I think it's only a phase,' pleaded Kate. 'It will wear off. It's a pity to have a quarrel over a phase. If she humours him a little, he'll settle down.'

Bridie gave her a look of profound disapprobation and said accusingly:

'You've changed!'

'Mayn't I? People do. *You've* changed. You used to say that nothing would induce you to go into a Provincial Repertory Company and now . . .'

'I've altered my opinions. I've been through a lot these last few months.'

'So have I.'

Bridie's silence suggested that people who have been dead for six months go through nothing, and have no excuse for changing their opinions.

The visit to Blackheath was wrecked by a violent cold which Kate had caught whilst sitting in a draught watching Bridie act. She was forbidden to kiss her grandchildren, or even to breathe over them. They showed no signs of remembering her, although the elder asked suddenly if Jesus had a lift in His House.

'We told them you'd gone to live with Jesus,' explained Judith, when they were washing up after lunch. 'At least, I did. Brian didn't approve. He said one should always tell children the truth. We ought to have said we didn't know where you'd gone. I said: "It's what my mother told us, when anybody died. What was good enough for her is good enough for me. I consider we had a perfect childhood."'

'You didn't always think so,' said Kate. 'When you married you told me you didn't mean to bring your children up as I'd brought you up. You said I'd been too domineering.'

'Did I? I was talking rot. You were wonderful!'

Judith's sharp face softened into the fond reminiscent smile which Kate had come to know so well and to detest so much.

'I was thinking the other day of that time when we got caught in a raid and Andrew suddenly panicked and clutched you and said: Oh, Mother! We're going to be killed! Don't let us be killed! Mother! Don't let us be killed! And you said: All right, I won't, but we'd better take the Duke of Wellington's advice, and told us what it was, and escorted poor Andrew to the loo, which he badly needed. So we all laughed and felt better.'

Oh, hell, thought Kate. I don't care what I *did*. What do I *do* now? Nobody thinks of that.

'Brian, of course,' continued Judith, her face sharpening again, 'would say it was deceiving a child to say you wouldn't let it be killed. His mother hasn't the faintest idea of managing children. You can't think what a nightmare it was at Freshwater this summer. If she's upset, she goes into a flat spin and lets the children see it. Fatal! No wonder Brian has no sense of security!'

'He strikes me,' said Kate, 'as being a good deal more self-confident and sure of himself than Andrew.'

'Oh, that's all on the surface. Underneath he's in a wild

panic about the state of the world. If I so much as murmur that life is much nicer nowadays for masses of people, he starts roaring at me: Do you realize? Do you REALIZE? And goes into ghastly statistics about radioactive fall-out. Although he says himself he can't think what's to be done about it.'

'I'm glad you've got a dish-washer,' said Kate hastily. 'I never regretted getting ours, though it was so expensive.'

'Well . . . this is yours, actually. Of course, as soon as you and Father . . . by the way, Hazel has your pearls. Did you know?'

The news that Hazel was to keep the pearls had a poor reception. Kate declared that she was past caring what she wore; none of her jewellery need be returned. This apparently raised a new problem. Most of the jewellery, said Judith, had gone to Bridie since she had taken none of the furniture, of which Andrew had secured the bulk, since he was at the moment moving into his Chiswick house. Judith and Brian had thrown out some shabby pieces and replaced them with better, brought from Edwardes Square. Much of this furniture would presumably be needed, when Kate and Douglas set up house together again. Bridie would therefore be the chief gainer by her mother's generosity.

'Not that we grudge returning the furniture for a minute, Mother. I'm sure you know that. Only I thought I ought just to mention it.'

'You deed't,' snapped Kate, whose cold was growing rapidly worse. 'I'b dot a borod.'

Judith, startled at this display of temper in a returned angel, became solicitous and talked about temperatures.

'I'b all right. Just a cobbod or garded cold.'

'It sounds awful. Perhaps, if you don't mind, you'd better keep right away from the children.'

This plea was reasonable. Kate, knowing that the children must shortly be given tea and baths, suggested that she return to Chiswick, but was not allowed to do so until Brian came home. He was coming early, on purpose to give her a drink and to drive her back. She was taken into the living-room, where a fire was lit for her by which she sat shivering while infant clamours echoed through the rest of the house. This room now contained a fine tallboy, and two small pictures, a Wilson and a Cox. All three were Mortimer property; they had originally come from the Addison Road.

There had been some spirited scenes at old Mrs Mortimer's death. Kate had been in bed with influenza on the day when Moira, Stephanie, Georgina, and Fanny descended upon their old home in order to strip it bare. Each had taken what she wanted and left the rest for Kate, as they blandly explained later. They thought the arrangement fair since the rest made up in bulk for what it lacked in quality. It included all the furniture from the servants' bedrooms, several fumed oak overmantels, a mammoth sideboard, a settee upon which nobody had ever sat, a harp without strings, innumerable chamber pots and some bound volumes of a magazine called *Good Words*. Kate's words, when she discovered this, had been forcible and fluent. They prized, after some lively wrangling, the tallboy and a Louis-Quinze table out of Stephanie, the pictures out of Georgina, and a Worcester dinner service out of Moira. Fanny had firmly stuck to what she had got.

The Bensons seemed to have survived this test of character with considerable credit. They had stripped Edwardes Square without quarrelling and with some consideration for one another's needs. Kate was glad to know it. Had she been smiling down upon them from heaven she could have felt that her efforts to bring them up as civilized beings were not entirely fruitless. She did not, however, want to feel pleased with herself at this particular moment. There were too many flattering obituaries in the air already.

Brian's cordiality, when he joined her, was more welcome. Her magnanimity over the white tweed coat was not again mentioned but she knew that he was grateful. That at least was something which she had managed to do in the present.

It seemed strange that she should now feel most at ease with him, among them all, for she had never liked him very much. As he mixed her a drink it occurred to her that he, perhaps, had never liked her very much. Her disappearance had given him so little distress that he could accept her reappearance as calmly as Fanny had done. He might have grieved for Judith, but that was probably the only pain that he had felt.

He now asked her about her life on Keritha, a topic in which nobody else took the slightest interest. He seemed actually to understand that it was a real place, not some shadowy limbo across the Styx. She eagerly described the Challoners, their strange history, their beautiful house, and the charm of an island completely unencumbered by admonitory little notices. So well did he seem to understand this that she ventured to put the point: that official litter baskets under every tree might have a more devitalizing effect upon men than upon women. He gave her a sharp look, as though a little surprised to hear such a reflection from his bossy mother-in-law. Then he said:

'I believe you've got something there. It must feel very odd to come back to the Welfare Kindergarten.'

'But why does it suit women better?'

'Women profit by it most. And they aren't law abiding,

you know. If a woman thinks a law is silly, she doesn't give a damn for it. She may keep it, to save herself trouble, but she has no respect for the law as such. A lot of little notices don't mean a thing to her. We men . . . even if we break the law, we do it more solemnly than you do. We've got all these bees in our bonnets about Law and Justice and Truth. *Truth!* Women couldn't care less about it. Once a woman gets into the saddle, the things she'll say! No man would dare. Why, if she thinks it's for our good, she'll announce, without turning a hair, that there's no difference between butter and margarine. A man might tell us we'd jolly well got to eat margarine. He might tell us the nutrition value is the same. But only a Mother Dia . . .'

Here Judith joined them, having put the children to bed. Brian mixed her a drink and demanded more details about Keritha.

'Oh yes,' said Judith vaguely. 'That place where you've been. Was it nice?'

'The people,' Kate told them, 'are very odd. They're all alike to look at and rather attractive. They remind me of a statue there is in the Acropolis Museum at Athens. A man carrying a little calf on his shoulders.'

'I know,' said Judith. 'Moschophoros. We've got a photograph of him in a book, I think.'

She hunted in the bookshelf while Brian said:

'The archaic doesn't photograph well. There's a kind of life breathing in the actual surface of the stone which doesn't come across. In a photograph it's too much simplified.'

'This man is smiling,' remembered Kate. 'I imagine Odysseus smiled like that when he was offered immortality and said: No thanks. I'd sooner be a man.'

'Here he is,' said Judith, bringing the book. 'He's nice.'

As they all studied the picture she added, a little aggressively:

'But he'd have been happier today. He was probably a slave. Owned by other people. Pushed about all his life.'

'And not even pushed about for his own good,' agreed Brian. 'Poor chap! No butter and no Holy Mum to tell him that it was just the same as margarine.'

He shut the book with a bang and put it down, adding:

'For all that, I agree we'd probably think him an awful brute. He's going to kill and eat that dear little calf. He's merely smiling to think of his nice dinner.'

'I suppose,' said Judith sharply, 'he ought to be scowling and saying: I kill and eat poor little calves. It's dreadful, but I can't help it. Oh, what a horrible man I am!'

'He'd have to, if he lived in the Welfare Kindergarten. We've all had it properly drilled into us that we're just naturally very naughty boys and girls.'

Kate brightly strove to allay the tension in the air by telling more stories. She described the horror of Freddie and Edith when the *Latona* put in, the rite of the stone, the legend of the Visitors, and the offerings to the waterfall. These last Brian maintained to be less fantastic than certain offerings made to the characters in a radio programme called *The People Next Door.*

'According to Bridie,' he said, 'one of these deities, these figments of the collective imagination, was recently compelled by the script writers, to give birth. Vanloads of offerings arrived at the BBC – nappies, shawls, bootees – all for a perfectly non-existent baby. What's the difference between that and offerings to some pagan god?'

Kate thought of the God of Keritha, whom nobody had

seen, but who was there, born every year, dying every year, yet stronger than death. More Christian than England, Edith had said.

'The gods were supposed to have power,' objected Judith. 'People were frightened of them. Nobody's frightened of the families on radio programmes. They're all supposed to be incredibly nice and ordinary. Just like us.'

'So who has power nowadays?' demanded Brian. 'Nice ordinary democratic people, just like us. And we're terrified of them, because they're all very busy making You-Know-What. No wonder we send them nappies.'

'I'm sorry,' said Judith in a tight voice. 'The tiny brain can't take that in.'

'I must go,' said Kate, jumping up.

On the drive home she felt tempted to scold Brian for talking about the Welfare Kindergarten, since the term obviously enraged Judith. He did so, just as he had talked of 'Holy Theophagy' to devout communicants, in order to elicit an emotional, rather than intellectual, response.

'Another thing I've come back to, that I'd rather forgotten,' she said, 'is this underlying anxiety, going on all the time, which affects everybody's temper.'

'You mean the shadow of the mushroom? They dodge it on Keritha? Plenty of people do that here, believe me. Judith, as you may have observed, is determined to take no notice of it whatever.'

'That's not such a bad line to take,' protested Kate, 'if we're really in for a kind of universal Thermophylae.

'The Spartans on the sea-wet rock
Sat down and combed their hair.

220

'Do you think there's anything very manly about self-righteous explosions of Angst?'

'Well! Well! That's the first time I've ever heard you quoting poetry.'

'Oh, for heaven's sake! Don't you start telling me I've changed and mustn't quote poetry because I never used to. I've not spent six months in a coffin. I've been in a place where people live and think thoughts.'

Brian laughed.

'Sorry. You have changed a bit. Why not? It must be quite a place, Keritha. But you know I'm afraid Freddie and Edith are fighting a losing battle. Someday somebody will publish a report on poor old Moschophoros.'

'What harm would that do? Very few people will read it.'

'Day trips,' he prophesied, 'to the Island of the Pixies. Boatloads, twice a week, to see Moschophoros doing his stuff. Some enterprising Tourist Company is sure to see how cute he is.'

'He won't oblige. He doesn't like foreigners.'

'He will, when he's learnt to cash in on his dignity. All the kids will be lined up at the waterfall, offering to be photographed throwing sugar to the naiad. Giggling like anything. No wonder Freddie and Edith are frightened.'

'I don't think either of them is vulgar enough to think of it.'

A moment later she shivered, no longer quite certain that Freddie had never foreseen some such squalid end for a harmless, defenceless little community. She had heard him quote a mysterious poem about the living who hold a funeral for their dead city. At the time she had associated the death of a city, or of any corporate existence, with violence and calamity; with war, plague, famine, fire, shattered masonry, terror, and lamentation. She now saw that none of these are inevitably involved. The ultimate, the most dire, obsequies are accomplished with a snigger.

She thought of advising Brian to try phenobarbitone but held her tongue, partly from prudence and partly because she felt too ill to talk any more.

4

Next morning she felt no better and would have given much to stay in bed. The thought of poor Hazel, nursing a sick mother-in-law, got her out of it. The head cold was better but she was weak and unsteady as though she walked on clouds of cotton wool. Very slowly she got into her clothes, wavered downstairs, and helped Hazel with the breakfast.

On the preceding night she had accepted an invitation to lunch with Douglas at the Chelsea flat. Andrew and Hazel had looked relieved when they heard of the engagement, as though they thought it high time that this inexplicable separation should cease. Permanent plans of some sort must soon be made. Perhaps she merely felt so ill because she wanted an excuse to dodge the visit. Later in the morning she crept off to Chelsea.

The flat was exactly what she had expected. It evoked, subtly, a prefect's study, preserving something of the cloistered school life in which the friendship of Douglas and Ronnie had taken root. There were no cricket or football groups on the walls, nor was there any clutter of toasting-forks, apples, boots, and textbooks. All was spare and neat, but the atmosphere was implacably masculine.

Mrs McKintosh was not, of course, the invaluable Scots

body they thought her to be. The rooms were not thoroughly cleaned nor was the lunch particularly good. They, however, clearly believed themselves in clover.

Ronnie greeted her with his customary distaste. He was a rangy creature with bushy eyebrows and a very long neck. He earned his dinner, efficiently but without enthusiasm, in a Government Office. His leisure was passionately dedicated to fishing, music, mountain-climbing, and chess.

During lunch he did nothing to help them out; he wolfed down his food while Kate and Douglas made strained conversation. To talk at all, or to swallow, had become an increasing effort for her. She braced herself to it and told them about Freddie's collection of gramophone records, hoping that this might interest Ronnie, who collected them himself. He did, indeed, display some animation upon learning that Freddie possessed a record of Adelina Patti. He spoke:

'Most improbable. That would be a museum piece.'

'I've heard it,' said Kate. 'He often plays it.'

'I doubt it. He wouldn't play valuable records often. They might get scratched.'

Douglas fidgeted uneasily although he might know by this time that she would not throw her pudding at Ronnie's head.

After lunch he left them, stumping out of the flat without leave-taking or apology. Kate, quite exhausted, lay back in her chair and tried to believe that a cognac was doing her good. Douglas sat waiting for her to say something.

'I suppose,' she murmured at last, 'you'd really rather go on living with Ronnie?'

'That's impossible, now.'

He rose and went to the window where he stood looking out at the wintry street while he said:

'Naturally we must set up house together again. What else can we do? But I believe it will be better to tell you, as well as I can, what's in my mind. How I feel about it.'

He need not. She knew perfectly well that he had for years nursed a grievance against her, believing that she had only married him because she wanted children.

'I quite realize I brought it on myself,' he allowed, when he had persisted in telling her all this. 'I had to ask you three times. Only a fool asks a woman more than once. If she loves him she takes him the first time. It was your mother who encouraged me to go on. She assured me that you really loved me. She was a great one, your mother, for getting her daughters to the altar.'

Kate nodded, wondering whether she should not tell him her side of it. Her mother had upbraided her for those two refusals, and had brushed aside her objection that Douglas, although sexually attractive, seemed to have a streak of silliness which might annoy her later. All men, said Mrs Mortimer, even the best of them, are incurably silly. A woman's happiness depends upon her ability to accept that fact.

To tell him this now would serve no purpose. His bitterness was, on the whole, justified. She had married him, suspecting him to be silly, because she wanted a home and children. On the other hand, she had put up with his silliness, during their life together, with more patience than another woman might have shown, who had expected better from him. The loneliness and disillusionment, upon which he was now dwelling with considerable gusto, might have been his, whoever he had married.

'But,' he concluded, 'all that is changed now. That's why I'm making a clean breast of it, before we start again. All the bitterness suddenly melted away when you . . . when I thought you were dead.'

'You saw the past quite differently?' suggested Kate.

'Well . . . yes . . .' He looked slightly disconcerted as though she had stolen one of his lines. 'You realize that? I thought of your life and asked myself what it had really been. I saw it suddenly as full of pathos . . . mysterious . . . unfinished . . .'

'One often does when people die,' said Kate.

He was going to get through it without having to mention Pamela, whom he had now probably managed to forget, save as a financial client.

'I'd always assumed,' he was saying, 'that you'd had exactly what you wanted out of life. Were a happy woman. But then, when I remembered you as you were when I first fell in love with you, I realized that long ago you were quite a different person. I looked through your papers and found a lot of relics of those years and the years, too, before I met you. Some queer little poems you must have written. And this, clipped together with some letters and a piece of bog myrtle.'

He handed her a faded snapshot. A very young Kate sat in a boat on a lake with a boy in white flannels.

'Michael!' she said, peering at it. 'He's dead.'

'I know.'

'I told you about him.'

'Yes. You loved him.'

'He was killed. I got over it. I've hardly thought of him for years.'

'If you'd married him you'd have been a different person. I suppose they were his letters, with the photograph. I didn't read them, I burnt them. I kept this, to remind myself of what you *really* are. Our marriage was as much of a mistake

226

for you as for me. Now we are getting old. We must finish our lives as best we can. But . . . I understand you better. Tell me what you'd like to do. Where you'd like to live.'

'I don't know,' she said vaguely. 'It's all very complicated. There's the dish-washer!'

'What?'

She stood up, swaying slightly.

'Judith has our dish-washer. I'll go home now . . . I mean, I'll go back to that house . . . Hazel's house . . . it's difficult to think when it's so cold. You've got everything mixed up. Those were Freddie's poems. I copied them out. And I think I'd have been exactly the same person whoever I'd married. What we really have to worry about is furniture.'

'I wish,' said Douglas bitterly, 'that you could ever manage for a moment to stop thinking of perfectly trivial things. I try to be frank with you . . .'

'It's not trivial. My coming back . . . it's going to mean sacrifice from everybody . . . everybody giving up something to make room for me again. All their ideas and their dish-washers. I shouldn't have come.'

'Kate! You're upset. You don't know what you're saying.'

'Not very well. My cold makes me stupid.'

'You should go to bed. I'll take you to the bus stop. You go to bed and nurse that cold.'

'Hazel would bring trays up. Too much for her . . .'

He hustled her along the street to the bus stop. As they waited there he said:

'You understand, don't you, that I've said all this because I feel that we can't start again without facing the truth?'

'Oh yes. I agree. So we can't start again, because I haven't t-told you what I think. It's t-too c-cold anyway. And you wouldn't like it a bit. Here's my b-bus.'

She jumped on to it meaning to get out at South Kensington Station. When next she roused herself she was a long way past that. A violent fit of shivering assailed her. She shook all over, and her teeth chattered so loudly that the other passengers heard it and looked round at her. At the next stop she got out again in a hurry because this was the Addison Road where Edith lived.

Edith ought to have an injection. She was late. She must hurry. It was not nearly so cold here as it had been in Chelsea, although a few snowflakes were drifting down from a leaden sky. It was unbearably hot. She would have liked to take off her coat as she panted along on cotton-wool clouds, past St Barnabas Church, past Oakwood Court, past many remembered houses, until she came to those two, side by side, the Mortimer house and the Challoner house.

There were a great many bicycles outside Edith's house. On such a very hot day, Edith would probably be out in the garden. The side door was not locked. She went through into a wintry expanse where it was growing very dark — very dark indeed, under the shadow of the mushroom. Down remembered paths, beneath leafless trees, she wandered, calling to Edith, until she came to the rustic bench at the far end.

There she sat to rest for a moment and took off her coat. She would explain everything when she gave that injection. Edith would be surprised that everybody had got so old. Even Michael had been young for forty years achtung! *Achtung!* ACHTUNG! YOU ARE VERY ILL SAVE YOURSELF YOU WILL DIE IF YOU STAY HERE ACHTUNG! . . . *Achtung!* . . . achtung . . . I must remember I must remember it's not true they are not all of them silly Freddie but we can't start again he would keep nagging at me to be that other that girl he made her up nagging like Menelaus long afterwards when the young war was forgotten and everybody was old and Michael . . . sleeps . . . upon Scamander side.

5

Events and sensations swirled into a merry-go-round, stridthe with anxiety, since there was something which she must, at all costs, insist upon doing. Only in snatches could she remember what it was. When the whirligig stopped for a moment, with a jolting bump, she thought of Edith's injection; she was off again before she could explain that to all the black men, rushing about in a snowstorm, and the policeman, and the men with a stretcher. They thought Edith was in a hospital. A kind black face came very close to hers, when she was on the stretcher, and said:

'Mayam! You don't have to worry. They're taking you to the hospital.'

She could not explain that Edith was on Keritha because of the bells ringing – *dinga-dinga-dinga-dinga* – like a fire engine can't you tell them to stop that noise she said to the policeman sitting beside her but he just wrote something down in a book – *dinga-dinga-dinga-dinga* fighting through the fiery snow sans gouvernail sans matelots Patti is in a museum – *dinga-dinga-dinga-dinga* – BUMP!

Edith's injection! She had not got to Keritha. She was in bed and the fire engine had gone away. She said to the chubby young man in a white coat:

'I don't need an injection. It's my friend, Miss Challoner . . .'

He took no notice and stuck the needle into her arm so that the whirligig began again. She spun through chaos and missed the boat.

There was dead silence in that no-light, as she stood on the bank and watched it slide away over the water.

'Wait! Wait!' she cried. 'I've paid. They paid my fare in June.'

The shadowy people stood turned away, gazing at the darkling shore ahead. Yet one of them heard her. A young anguished face, spotlighted like a face on the stage, looked back and a desolate wail rang over the water:

'The children . . . the children . . .'

'Where?' called Kate. 'Where?'

'The children . . .'

That cry continued long after the boat and the bank and the water had vanished. The children! The children! I must find the children. That's why I missed the boat.

So she searched and searched amidst the stalactites and the stalagmites and the caves and the waves. She fought stubbornly for her life against phantom hordes, and against cobwebs hanging like veils from the dead trees, and the brassy clamour of cobnobs which choked her with a bursting pain.

'How can I find any children with all these cobnobs about?' she complained to the man with a long nose. 'That Mrs McKintosh! A slut if ever I saw one.'

Chaos whirled her away again and brought her to a glowing emerald, hanging in mid air. Beneath it was an arrangement of white and blue and red. She thought it pretty. In a little while it came into focus. The emerald was a lampshade pulled low over a table where some girls sat. They had blue dresses, and little red cloaks, and white caps on their heads. Nurses. A hospital. She was ill. She shut her eyes to think about it and when she opened them next the emerald was gone. It was daylight. Bridie was there. Bridie was crying.

'Don't,' she tried to say. 'I'm all right.'

It was not Bridie after all, but Judith, and both were gone before she could explain that she was not going to die. She said so, however, to the long-nosed man when next he was there. He said:

'Of course not. You're doing splendidly. We're very pleased with you.'

'Tell them so. They think I've been dead a long time. Where are they?'

'We've sent them home. But they'll come soon and see you.'

'Some children . . . their mother . . . I don't know who they are . . . I missed the boat, you know, though they paid. They said all the things and did all the things, and answered all the letters. But I had to stay . . . for the children. It was the Visitors . . .'

'You mustn't talk so much if you want to get well.'

'Oh, but I shall get well. I've got a lot to do only I can't remember what it is.'

The emerald glowed again on an older woman who was writing in a book. She came over to ask how Kate felt.

'I don't know yet. I suppose I have pneumonia? Have I been in this bed all the time?'

'No. You were brought up here when they got hold of your family. This is a paying ward.'

The whirligig had stopped but she still swam in and out of consciousness in a haphazard way. When next she came to the surface Douglas was assuring her that the children were quite all right. They had not caught her cold.

'They say you've been asking about them all the time.'

'Have I? I don't remember.'

She could not recall any worry about Timmie and Caroline. Yet it seemed to her that some other children had haunted the nightmare from which she was emerging. As she reached after the memory it vanished for ever.

'I shall never forgive myself,' Douglas was saying in his dreariest voice. 'If I'd realized you were so ill that day . . .'

She shut her eyes, thinking that she could not be bothered with him until she was better. This time she went to sleep and woke to a much clearer scene, comprising the whole ward and the patients in the other beds.

It was early morning. A coloured ward maid brought in a tea trolley. Some women in dressing gowns and hair curlers gathered round it, carrying cups to those who were still in bed. One of them came over to inspect Kate.

'Feeling better, Mrs Benson?'

They knew her name here. To them she was already a person, involved in the present rather than the past; they had recognized that much about her before she herself knew where she was. Nor were they going to bewilder her by insisting that she ought to be somebody quite different.

'You look ever so much better. Dr Ames is very clever, isn't he?'

'Is that the chubby one?'

'Oh no. That's only little Dr Cotteril, the House Physician. Though he's quite clever too. A nice boy. Dr Ames is the Registrar.'

A great spate of activity set in as the night nurses put the ward to rights before going off duty. Beds were made for patients well enough to sit up. Advanced convalescents set off with sponge bags to the bathroom. There was much coming and going with bedpans. A distracted old man rushed in and made for a curtained cubicle but was driven off by a nurse.

'His wife's in there,' commented Kate's companion. 'She's going up to the theatre today. Of course she's under already. Had a shot before the tea came in. He shouldn't come rushing in here just when everybody is perched on the bedpans.'

'He doesn't know what he's doing, poor man,' said Kate.

The unhappy creature had drifted to the tea trolley and was absently finishing up the cold dregs in the cups until Sister came and led him out of the ward.

The tea trolley was wheeled away. A newspaper trolley arrived. The night nurses trooped off duty, smiling good-bye as they went. The day nurses trooped in, smiling good morning as they came. The women in dressing gowns got into bed again and took the curlers out of their hair. Vase after vase of flowers was brought in. Breakfast arrived. A procession with a wheeled stretcher came to remove the operation patient.

Kate knew that she had come back to the world again – a world full of people living their private lives and enduring the common lot.

6

It was a strange world and she liked it better than she would have expected. Hitherto she had always supposed that a ward full of other patients must be an irritating nuisance to an invalid. Yet, when a private room fell vacant, she refused to move into it, preferring to remain where she was.

She and these other women, shut up together like passengers on a ship, knew more about one another than is usual with shipboard acquaintances. Most of them were sustaining, or had recently sustained, some ordeal by pain, terror, or shock. Each had her own way of going about it. Beneath a surface of commonplace chatter, mutual sympathy, high spirits, and valour were plainly discernible. They were a corporate body, on pleasant terms with the nurses but by no means subdued by them nor was there any superstitious respect for the doctors.

'I can't help laughing,' said a massive matron to Kate, 'when little Cotteril tells me things I knew before he was born or thought of.'

From six in the morning, when the first tea trolley came in, till nine-thirty at night, when all lights were extinguished save the emerald over the nurses' table, a slow, quiet, efficient bustle of activity went on. Somebody was always doing something. Something was always being done to somebody.

Patients were washed, given injections, given enemas, given blood transfusions, and trundled off to the theatre. Fresh flowers arrived. Faded flowers were thrown out. Twice a day the newspaper trolley came. Twice a week the library trolley came, also a trolley with writing paper, soap and bath powder. Meals came. Visitors came. Curtains were pulled round beds and pulled back again. Important doctors, with their retinues, trod the ward and stood murmuring round X-ray photographs. New arrivals, flung into a waiting bed, lay for a while in mysterious isolation. They were soon absorbed into the community; their names and case histories were common property before nightfall. Mobile patients wandered from bed to bed, exchanging magazines, knitting patterns, and cooking recipes. Pastors of various denominations flitted tactfully about in search of their sheep. Little bells were rung and Mass was whispered in some curtained corner. Death, pain, and panic were held at bay, not only by doctors and nurses but by humanity, solidly arrayed to defy the foe.

In this sane and tranquil sisterhood lay Kate, so weak that she could scarcely lift her hand, a little stronger every day and every day more aware of the impasse before her. What should she do, where should she go, when she could no longer lie here?

She could not live with Douglas again. He had no genuine wish to live with her. The flat, Ronnie, and Mrs McKintosh suited him perfectly. To leave them would be a sacrifice imposed by convention since any revival of Edwardes Square was now impossible. She could not very clearly remember all that he had said on that dreadful afternoon, but enough survived to settle the matter. Had this break not occurred in their lives they might have continued very well in the path that they had always trodden. He could have escaped from bitterness and self pity by spells of fantasy with some Pamela or other. She could have borne with him by reflecting that she, probably, got more out of their marriage than he did. Although she had, long ago, rejected the Mortimer maxim that all men are silly, she had come to believe that Mortimer women inevitably married silly men, were mysteriously attracted by them, attractive to them. Men of sense, hovering for a while round the bevy of red-haired beauties in the Addison Road, were apt, after closer inspection, to bow themselves out. Douglas had cut a more impressive figure in the world, was far less meek and browbeaten than the average Mortimer husband.

This workable compromise was now at an end. She could not stomach his determination to sentimentalize his own remorse when he supposed her dead. That remorse was very natural; she had felt it herself, often enough, when aware of the astonished compassion with which the living think of the newly dead; she had then perceived the mystery, the pathos, the unfinished pattern of any human life. It was typical of Douglas to falsify this compassion by dismissing, for his own peace of mind, all that she had been and done. It suited him better to substitute an artificial creature, an elfin, poetic girl quenched by poor Michael's death.

She had not been born 'a different person'. She had never betrayed her own nature, the strongest impulse in which was to love and care for children. She would have been the same Kate, no matter whom she had married, more of a mother than a wife, perhaps, but a good wife for a certain type of man. It seemed to her that she would have done very well for some old-fashioned, heroic explorer who, having discovered the North Pole, would come home and beget another child before going off to discover the South

Pole, confident that his wise Penelope would guard his house for him in his absence and would always welcome him back with open arms. Many a man has rejoiced in such a wife, many a woman in such a husband. Sooner than marry Douglas she might have done better to become a Nanny, giving her life to a succession of children and turning to new ones when time stole away the old.

Some way of living apart must be devised which should not shock or distress her family. She had done so already, in a most careless and culpable way, and they were letting her know it.

'You look tired,' she said, when Judith came one day to see her.

'Well, you know, we've all had rather a fright. It's taken a lot out of us. We can't think how you got to the Addison Road.'

'I was delirious. I thought the Challoners' garden was full of black men.'

'It probably was. That house is now a club for coloured students. Thank heaven one of them looked out of the window and saw you! Otherwise . . .'

Otherwise . . . she might have died all over again. They would have been obliged to go through it all twice . . . a funeral . . . feeling sad . . . impossible! One obol is the fare for Charon. Nobody gets two.

'Hazel and Andrew got worried when you didn't come home. At last they rang father up and they all hovered around for ages before doing the sensible thing and going to the police. They upset each other so much that Hazel threatened a miscarriage and her Mummie came flapping up from Leamington Spa and scalded herself with a hot-water bottle.'

'Oh dear.'

'You'd have been traced quicker if you'd had your address in your handbag.'

'I haven't got an address,' muttered Kate.

'What?'

'Hazel is all right, isn't she? There's no danger . . .'

'Oh no. That was just something they dreamed up to make things worse. Then at 3 a.m. they proceeded to ring *us* up.'

'Oh dear, oh dear,' sighed guilty Kate.

The period of canonization was clearly over. She was a real person again and a very tiresome one into the bargain.

'I suppose you thought you still lived in the old house?'

'No. I think I wanted to get to Keritha. I was worrying about Edith and how she's managing without me.'

'Keritha?'

Judith looked thoughtful. Presently she said:

'It must be nice and warm there. Very different from this horrible climate.'

'You get cold north winds in the winter.'

'But the Challoners' house is lovely and warm?'

'Oh yes. Quite.'

'And soon it will be spring. It comes so much earlier there. It must be heavenly. And all those servants!'

'Yes. It's wonderful not having to lift a finger.'

'I don't wonder you were so happy there.'

Kate had not been happy there. She had been desolate and miserable, most of the time, wondering why they did not write. She would have said so if her tea had not arrived just then. Judith poured it out for her, saying:

'Quite nice! And it ought to be, considering what they charge.'

239

'Oh dear!'

They talked about the children for a little, but Judith looked pensive and presently asked what Kate thought of Mrs McKintosh.

'I think she's awful. So do you, don't you?'

'I don't think she's so bad,' said Judith, blushing slightly. 'And she can do no wrong in Father's eyes.'

'Men!' said Kate. 'It's that Scotch accent. I must admit I've been misled by it myself. We Englishry always associate a Scotch accent with honesty, and efficiency and common sense.'

'Well . . .' Judith laughed a little, 'it often is. If that's all you have against her . . .'

'I agree it often is. They're a wonderful nation. But they do have a small percentage of throw-outs and she's one. And I have plenty against her. She's a very indifferent cook. There were cobwebs on the ceiling. And they went to get a whisky bottle from the sideboard which they thought was full. It was half empty. They were quite astonished. Mrs Mac, who was bringing in some underdone chops, gave me a squinneying sort of look. She could trust them not to put two and two together, but she obviously wished me farther.'

'Was this all on the day you were delirious?' asked Judith derisively.

'I wasn't delirious then. And when first I got back you all . . . since when have you decided she's not so bad?'

'All I mean is that Father is provided for. You needn't be in a hurry to find a house or a flat till you're quite strong.'

Judith departed soon afterwards, leaving Kate to be torn between relief and remorse. The demand for a new Edwardes Square had apparently been suspended. Douglas might remain indefinitely in his widower's burrow. The whole family had lived through a night of terror for which her own delirium was not a complete excuse. It seemed to her that some warning had flashed through her mind, when she was sitting in that garden, and that it had been ignored. She had known herself to be ill, and had behaved as though she wished to die. Yet later she had fought her way back to life for some purpose which now eluded her.

Douglas came to see her no more. He was reported to have contracted a chill in which she did not wholly believe. A chill had always been his resource in any difficult situation. He lay apologetically in bed, declaring it all to be too maddening, until the situation cleared up. This chill, said Andrew, who brought her the news of it, was nothing serious. Mrs McKintosh was coping with it. She was giving him friar's balsam.

'How perfectly wonderful of her!' snapped Kate.

'Isn't it?' he said innocently. 'She's really, in her own way, a very capable person. Mother . . . we ought to think a bit where you go, when you leave here. Of course Hazel and I would love to . . .'

'Oh, you mustn't dream of it. Far too much for Hazel.'

'We couldn't be sure of looking after you properly. Besides . . . we've got Hazel's mother still. We all thought you could go with Bridie to some comfortable hotel. But now Bridie's got this offer . . . this chance of getting into the Melchester Rep. . . .'

'Oh no . . . oh no! Bridie . . . her career . . .'

'Personally I'd have thought she'd get other chances quite as good. However . . .'

'A convalescent home for a few weeks.'

'A bit odd . . . when you've got a large and devoted family . . .'

'No, it's not. Sensible. Find one and I'll go to it. I don't mind where I go as long as I'm not a bother.'

'Dr Ames says you've got to be very careful for some time to come. Especially in the spring. So treacherous . . .'

He hesitated and added:

'You wouldn't think of going abroad? Somewhere nice and sunny? As soon as you're fit to travel?'

'Oh no. I've had enough of abroad to last me for a long time. And there's your father . . .'

'He's all right with Mrs McKintosh . . .'

They had all, it seemed, decided to exalt Mrs McKintosh. Kate forbore to remind him of the Haggis Hag, since somebody was needed at the moment to stand by with friar's balsam. In any case he was making off, reminding her that he was in a hurry because the baby would be born in six weeks' time.

'Getting into a flap, are they?' said the woman in the next bed. 'Who's to look after you when you get out? It's always the way. As long as you're on the danger list they'd give their eyes for you. Once you're off it! Whatever did you want to go and get ill for? The very idea!'

'It's very anti-social to get ill unexpectedly,' said Kate.

'I should say so. If you're a Mum, it is. You mustn't get ill without writing round, six months ahead, to let everyone know you mean to be at death's door on 23 January at 4 a.m. exactly.'

Observing her companions and their visitors Kate perceived that her own predicament was not uncommon. The smiles, the tears, the rapturous relief, with which families welcomed the news of a sure recovery, had all vanished by the time that they took their loved one home.

Departures were bleak affairs. The relative who had been

'sent to fetch her away' stood impatiently holding a suitcase, while the ex-patient, shabby, in clothes hastily brought for her, pale, tired, less robust looking than she had been yesterday, scurried from bed to bed. A last word must be said to comrades whom she would probably never meet again, since they were not really her friends although they had recently been united in some mysterious, vital activity. Farewells to the nurses, who had been through nothing out of the ordinary, could be made with an easy, smiling gratitude. These others, with whom something had been shared, got a tacit Hail and Farewell, since some of them had fought their way back from the very wharf of Lethe, back to cups of tea and kindly gossip.

'Good-bye, Mrs Peters. I hope your son gets through his exam . . . Good-bye, Miss Goddard. Here's your magazine. Thank you so much for lending it . . . Good-bye, Mrs Benson! Best of luck to the new grandchild. Six weeks isn't it? . . . Goodbye, Mrs Warburton. I'll try to match that knitting wool for you . . . Good-bye . . . good-bye . . .'

The empty bed was made up. It stood waiting for a few hours. A stretcher trundled in. Another inert warrior was flung into the community to be cured by doctors, tended by nurses, and sustained in the will to live by Mrs Peters, Miss Goddard, Mrs Benson and Mrs Warburton.

Bridie, when next she danced in, was so much taken up with the offer from the Melchester Rep that Kate's future remained for some time in abeyance. Then she suddenly let off a rocket.

'Oh! About you. When you get out of here. It's all settled. Aunt Fanny would love to have you. She rang Andrew up. The scarlet fever is over. Isn't it lucky?'

'Fanny?' shrieked Kate.

'She'll bring you breakfast in bed and everything, and not let you catch a chill. We shall be quite easy in our minds about you.'

'I will not! No, I will not!'

'But, Mother . . .'

'Go to Fanny! How would you like it?'

'I should hate it. But she's your sister. Andrew said you said you don't mind where you go.'

'I won't go to Fanny. I didn't know you were sadists.'

Bridie giggled and said:

'Did anyone ever tell you about the table?'

'What table?'

'Why . . . when you . . . when we were dividing up the things in Edwardes Square she had the cheek to say all the Mortimer things ought to be given to her! The tallboy and those pictures . . . and eventually we fobbed her off by sending her that little table that's been so rickety ever since that man broke it. The awful man, I forget his name, that Judith asked to supper once. And when she found what an invalid it is what do you think she did? Sent it to a very expensive place to be mended and told them to send the bill in to Father.'

'I hope he refused to pay it!'

'Oh, when did Father ever show fight? He just moaned about it and said he couldn't refuse "at a time like this". What was that man's name who broke it? He's quite vanished out of our lives.'

'Fanny shall give it back now,' declared Kate. 'If it's been mended it will do nicely for that space between the windows in Hazel's drawing-room. She will have no excuse for not giving it back.'

'My dear Mother! Who ever got anything out of Aunt Fanny?'

'I shall,' said Kate. 'Andrew shall drive me down there one day. When I'm quite well again and the baby is born. It's light and small, that table. It will go easily into the back of his car. We'll have tea and just as we are going I shall say: "Oh, by the way, as we are here, we may as well take that table back." And Andrew and I will carry it out to the car and drive off. And that's another reason why I shouldn't go near Fanny till I'm fighting fit.'

'But in the meanwhile, you must go somewhere. Personally, I can't think why Judith . . .'

'A convalescent home.'

'That's a possibility. If we find you one, will you go to it?'

'I'll find one for myself.'

'How can you?'

'I'll ask Sister. I'm sure this problem must often arise. She'll know of somewhere. I'll fix it up for myself.'

Bridie looked dubious, as though Kate's power to make her own arrangements must be for ever suspect after her recent escapade.

'As long as you promise not to do anything silly . . .' she stipulated. 'You'd better ask Judith, when she comes tomorrow, and see what she thinks.'

Judith did not come, owing to some nursery crisis, but Brian looked in on her behalf. By that time Kate had held a fruitful consultation with Sister. She was able to give Brian the particulars of an excellent, if expensive, convalescent home on the south coast to which she could be driven straight from the hospital. He gave the scheme a cordial blessing and presented her with a Get Well card from the children and a bunch of small bright tulips.

'Lovely,' she said. 'I do like them small. I hate them the

size of footballs and four feet high. Why can't we leave flowers alone? At Keritha they've planted little tulips all down the slopes below the house. I've never seen them, but I'm sure they must look enchanting.'

'Ah, yes! Keritha,' he said eagerly. 'That does sound a very lovely place.'

He gave her a long, speculative look, while she handed the tulips to a nurse, and examined the children's card, which had a picture of a rabbit ill in bed being nursed by another rabbit.

'Did Timmie choose it himself?' she asked.

'*Ça se voit!* You can't think Judith or I chose it? How is poor Edith Challoner getting on? You were worried about her. Have you heard from her?'

'No. She was never one for writing letters.'

'Really it was rather hard on them, having you snatched away like this.'

'They were very kind to me.'

'They're fond of you. Old friends. Now, this convalescent home: it's an excellent plan for the near future. As long as you need any special care and attention. But what are your plans after that?'

'I haven't made any yet.'

'You've got to be very careful for some time. Very careful indeed. The doctor says so. Especially in the spring. It's so cold, often, in England. March . . . April . . . May even! Frost in May . . . we get it quite often.'

'Oh, I know. I promise to be careful.'

'A warmer climate . . . you won't be up to the exertion of house or flat hunting for some time.'

'No. I'm afraid not.'

The nurse brought the tulips in a vase and put them on

Kate's locker. Brian swallowed once or twice and said:

'We have . . . Judith has had . . . rather a bright idea. But she wasn't quite sure what you'd think of it. We put it up to the others . . . all the family . . . we telephoned. They all approve, so long as you like it. But nobody felt quite sure . . . so I volunteered . . .'

Volunteered *again*? marvelled Kate. After that fiasco in Switzerland? What a man he was for rushing in! It must have something to do with his inner lack of confidence.

'You're worried about Edith,' he suggested. 'You could talk about nothing else when you were delirious.'

'Couldn't I? Who says so?'

'I heard you myself.'

'You weren't here.'

'Oh, yes I was. I came here with Judith and you were raving about an injection for Edith.'

'Oh yes. But I'm not worried now. They've got somebody to give the injections.'

'Still, it's a much better climate than this. And, by all accounts, such a comfortable house. Luxurious! Troops of servants. And the Challoners so anxious to have you. Why shouldn't you . . . for a few months . . . till the summer perhaps . . . till you are more fit to make permanent plans . . .' – Brian's smile was anxious but he managed to maintain it – '. . . why shouldn't you go back to Keritha?'

PART SIX

'AWAY! WE'RE BOUND AWAY!'

The lonely mountains o'er
And the resounding shore,
    A voice of weeping heard, and loud lament:
From haunted spring and dale,
Edg'd with poplar pale,
    The parting Genius is with sighing sent.

MILTON

1

'Yes,' said Kate, rousing herself from her memories. 'Edwardes Square was sold even before I went back, for three months, that first winter. I was ill. I had pneumonia. The family decided that I needed a warmer climate.'

'But you're going back now?' asked Selwyn.

'Oh yes. I'm quite strong again. I dare say I shouldn't have stayed so long if it hadn't been for Edith. Besides, I couldn't live for long anywhere else on my currency allowance.'

'You don't want to go back?'

'Not much. I've grown very fond of Keritha. It's such a friendly place. Not only the people, I mean. They're nice, but I don't really understand them very well. It's the island itself that seems to be full of friends.'

'I know. And when we go away we'll lose them for ever.'

'Oh no! Not necessarily for ever. I'm sure *you* could come back if you liked. Eugenia will be here. Dr Challoner said in the boat this afternoon that he hopes she'll stay on. I'm sure she'd put you up.'

'Ah, but my friends mightn't be here. Somebody might have come and kicked them out.'

'I don't see. How could anybody kick them out?'

Selwyn lighted another of his new cigarettes before answering. Then he said:

'Simply by convincing everybody that they aren't there. That's how they've been kicked out everywhere else. Once it's happened, out they have to go. Think of all the deserted altars in these parts. Mere stones. Once something more. Some progressive fellow turns up and proves, in the interests of ter-ruth, that they're nothing but stones and then . . . "each peculiar power foregoes his wonted seat".'

'Progressive fellows who come here get stung by wild bees,' said Kate. 'Like tax collectors. The people take to the mountain and the intruders get stung to pieces. That's why this island has always been left alone.'

'What co-operative bees!'

'Bees don't like it if little boys tip stones into their nests.'

'Oh. I see. So that's why it's called Keritha. Honeycomb!'

'A polite name. There's never been much honey. Is that Dr Challoner calling?'

'Something's bleating. Sounds more like a . . . No. It's Milorthos Persi. Don't worry. Let him come down here if he wants you. Why should you go up?'

Kate compromised by calling out in reply and remaining where she was.

'Sounds upset,' commented Selwyn. 'Perhaps somebody's told him about Eugenia.'

'Ssh! I think he knows.'

The bleating had ceased and presently Dr Challoner appeared, indignantly waving a letter. The post-bag from Zagros had been flung into their boat just before they started for home. On the jetty at Keritha it was unpacked and the mail for the house set aside. Few letters ever arrived for other destinations. The *dromokopi* were not given to writing home although some sent money regularly to their families.

To receive a letter directly addressed to him on Keritha had surprised him, since Poste Restante Thasos had been the only address which he had left in College. The contents were most disturbing.

'Those records,' he panted as he joined the other two, 'I'd no idea that any of them were valuable.'

'I don't suppose they were,' said Kate. 'Secondhand records never fetch much.'

'Will you read this!'

After a hasty glance at the letter she exclaimed:

'What! Ronnie Sinclair!'

'You know him?'

'He's a friend of my husband's. They share a flat.'

'Does he know what he's talking about?'

'Records. Yes. I expect so. He collects them.'

She read on and handed the letter back, saying:

'Yes. I think there was one of Patti.'

'What has been done with it? You see what he offers? If I'd had the faintest idea . . . I know nothing whatever about music.'

Selwyn suggested that, since it must be a song, it would either be amongst those given to the islanders, or amongst the discards which he and Kate had stacked up the night before. A move was made to the house and the stack was examined. No record of Patti turned up.

'Then Keritha must have got it,' said Kate. 'I wish I could remember . . .'

'I think I do,' said Selwyn. 'It was in French, and they laughed their heads off, but took it because they liked her voice.'

'Probably smashed by now,' growled Challoner.

'I don't think so. There was an argument. They were going to give it to somebody who sings very well herself. On their way . . .'

Selwyn broke off. His jaw fell.

'We must find out who this person is,' said Dr Challoner. 'We must explain that it was a mistake and ask for it back. That woman . . . Eugenia . . . she probably knows who has got it. Let's have her here and ask her.'

Neither Kate nor Selwyn made a move. The same disconcerting notion had occurred to both of them. Despite their murmured protests that the record might now be impossible to trace a summons to Eugenia was presently bellowed through the house. She appeared, looking a little surprised. It was the first time that her new lord had ever addressed her directly and the first time that anybody, in that household, had ever yelled for her with so little ceremony. Standing in the doorway, her hands crossed on her stomach, she awaited his commands.

'Ask her! Ask her!'

'What, exactly?' muttered Selwyn.

'Ask her if she knows who has got that record.'

After a short conversation with Eugenia, Selwyn reported gloomily that the record had been thrown over the bridge.

'Nonsense! Why does she say so? She can't be certain. They wouldn't have selected one on purpose to throw away. You said yourself they wanted to give it to somebody.'

'She's quite certain,' said Selwyn.

'Mrs Benson! Do you believe this?'

'I'm afraid I do. I'm very sorry.'

'I don't. Somebody has got it. Somebody knows it's

valuable and means to hang on to it. I don't trust these people a yard . . .'

He dismissed Eugenia with a gesture and turned on Kate: 'You haven't really told me what she said.'

'Yes, we did,' said Kate, her unlucky temper flaring. 'She said that was the record they offered to the waterfall . . . I mean' – she flushed scarlet – '. . . the one they threw over the bridge.'

'Offered to . . . just now you said they were going to give it to somebody. They don't, surely, think that a waterfall is somebody?'

'I don't know,' sighed Kate unhappily.

'Like spitting,' said Selwyn, coming to her rescue. 'In some parts of Europe, even now, it's supposed to be unlucky not to spit over a bridge if you cross it.'

'Not in the least like spitting. That's a survival. A symbol of sacrifice. To propitiate the spirit of the river. And you said they were taking it to somebody who sings.'

'Well, actually, a waterfall does sing.'

'It sings? What does it sing, may I ask?'

Selwyn took from his pocket the piece of paper upon which he had that afternoon scored the song of Keritha.

'This!'

'I know nothing whatever about music,' said Dr Challoner, waving it away.

'Then how can you know whether it sings or not?'

'You've very nearly got it,' said Kate, glancing over the little score. 'Only it needs half semitones. I've listened to it often enough to know. That plop! at every fifth bar is just right.'

Dr Challoner turned away, convinced that the pair of them were deliberately keeping him in the dark. Until now he had believed Mrs Benson to be a trustworthy sort of person, but he would rely on her no longer. She knew more than she would admit of the mysteries reported by Tipton. On the trip home he had not mentioned them, flinching from so ridiculous a subject, and he was now glad that he had not done so. She would only have told him lies.

A maid announced dinner, which was, as usual, a faultless meal. None of them enjoyed it much. Kate was overwhelmed with horror at her own indiscretion. Selwyn, somewhat to his surprise, felt sorry for her.

'This business on Sunday?' barked Dr Challoner suddenly. 'Why don't they go to church? They're all Christians, aren't they?'

'Oh yes,' said Kate. 'But there's no church here.'

'Why don't they go to Zagros?'

'There aren't enough boats to take everybody. And they like to be all together.'

'What do their priests say to that?'

'I don't know.'

'For hundreds of years,' put in Selwyn, 'they've had to get on without priests and churches. It's only since the Turks cleared out that there were services on Zagros. The church there was used as a mosque before.'

'But this affair here? Is it Pagan or Christian?'

'Christian,' said Kate indignantly.

'Does any priest officiate?'

'No. But it's all just the same as what they do on Zagros. Only there it's at midnight, and we wait till sunrise.'

He decided that he had better see for himself, although he did not relish an expedition before dawn and had previously asserted that nothing would induce him to join it. These two were quite capable of concealing some startling deviation from Christian practice. Their behaviour over the loss of his Patti record was monstrous.

The mere thought of it almost made him choke, nor could he decide which, of three possibilities, was the most repulsive. A valuable piece of his property had been wantonly destroyed by half-wits, for no reason at all. It had been destroyed for an outrageous reason. It had not been destroyed, but filched from him by some sly scoundrel. If such were the case it had never gone over the bridge. He might at least ascertain that. He would explore the rocks in the ravine below the bridge. With luck he might find fragments of a record which undoubtedly had gone over, since he had seen it thrown. These fragments, pieced together, might give Kate and Selwyn the lie.

This resolve put him in a slightly better temper. Remembering that the rocks might be slippery he asked if there were any sand-shoes in the house, which he could borrow.

'Freddie had some canvas shoes with rubber soles, that he used for climbing about in the ravine,' said Kate innocently.

'Those would do.'

'Do you want to climb about in the ravine?' demanded Selwyn. 'You'd better not. Wild bees.'

He kicked Kate under the table and she agreed hastily that there might be some wild bees down there.

'You've had trouble with them?'

'Oh yes. They're a nuisance. Quite a lot of them all over Keritha.'

'Cyanide guns. Two or three puffs from them and nobody need worry about wild bees. Alfred had them here?'

'N-no . . .' faltered Kate.

257

'I wonder he hadn't, if wild bees are really troublesome. Garland Becker found them a menace in Asia Minor, I believe, until he got cyanide guns.'

'They wouldn't be very safe here,' protested Kate. 'There . . . there might be people, children, about, who got a puff as well as the bees.'

'Oh? Of course the local population is always warned before they are used.'

Becker and his team, thought Dr Challoner, would make short work of all this nonsense, if only they could be summoned. Was there no way of explaining, or concealing, Alfred's concubine?

'How much furniture,' he asked, 'will that woman expect to be left for her own use? Not much use her staying here, is there, if I decide to sell all the furniture?'

'Eugenia? Oh, she's got her own furniture. In her rooms across the courtyard. She wouldn't expect anything to be left for her here. But she'll take good care of anything you do leave. If you can't make up your mind about everything this time, you could always come back. She'd look after you and cook for you. You'd always have a housekeeper.'

A housekeeper?

That word suggested an asset rather than an embarrassment: an amenity to be let with the house. He had, indeed, supposed her to be some species of housekeeper himself until he got Alfred's fantastic letter. The whole thing was really quite simple. Becker might come tomorrow, if it were not for that gravestone.

Her bother Alfred must be removed from Keritha and there was nobody to whom such a commission could be entrusted. Nor could anything be done until Potter and Mrs Benson were off the field. He must in future keep all his intentions strictly to himself.

The thought of Tipton in Athens suggested a possible line of action. Tipton, for the next ten days, would be at the Acropolis Hotel. He might know of some firm in Athens which would supply a cross, suitably inscribed, transport it to Keritha, set it up, and throw its predecessor into the sea. A pause in Athens, on the way home, and a consultation with Tipton might be well worth while, so long as he need not tell Tipton exactly what was wrong with the original stone. The fellow would dine out on it for years. No ridicule must be attached to the name of Challoner.

Could this difficulty be settled nothing need prevent an invitation to Becker at which all respectable academics would rejoice, since it meant one in the eye for Spaulding. Somebody else could also get one in the eye. No island could presume to thumb its nose at Becker. The prospect was so attractive that Kate had to ask a question three times before she got an answer. Rousing himself at last he said that he could not imagine what epitaph on a dead city Alfred had quoted.

'Unless,' he added, 'it was a couple of lines of Berytus.'

'Beirut,' murmured Selwyn. 'It had a nasty earthquake in the time of Justinian.'

'But who wrote them?' asked Kate.

'They've been ascribed to Palladas. But that earthquake, it's mentioned by Theophanes, is at least a hundred years too late for him. They had an earlier one, though, I believe. Somewhere round about 350.'

'A.D.,' supplemented Selwyn.

'Earthquakes?' repeated Kate in relieved tones, as though earthquakes were a minor calamity.

'I don't believe Palladas would have objected to an earth-quake,' said Selwyn. 'He was a glum type. A born Has-Been.'

'Then perhaps he meant something else.'

'Oh no. Too glum to be subtle. What really got in his hair was the doctrine of the Resurrection. He thought everybody was getting soft. As for the Athanasian Creed!'

'There is no evidence whatever,' barked Challoner, 'that he took the slightest interest in the Athanasian Creed.'

'I should think not. The Christians were daft. The Neo-Platonists were daft. Anybody who made a fuss about anything was daft.'

Selwyn leant back in his chair and after a while he growled:

'Once I had a vote, dentures, a neurosis and an electric razor. Now I, Potter, lie here having nothing at all! That's what Palladas had to say about people who make a fuss.'

This foolish quip got the reception which it deserved. Neither of his companions was listening.

Kate was wondering whether she had ever, herself, assisted at the funeral of a city, in Freddie's interpretation of the word. Then she remembered the Wardens' Reunions in the late 1940s. For some time after the end of the war these had been held annually in a studio just off Edwardes Square. A miscellaneous rabble of neighbours – women and elderly men for the most part – housewives, chimney-sweeps, schoolteachers, grocers, judges – had met to drink sherry and to spend an hour in synthetic geniality. They had nothing in common save an astonished memory. Once, amidst terror and destruction, they had been so closely united that each had been able to draw upon the strength of all. Now they had fallen apart again into isolated entities. The old jokes were no longer funny, the mutual gratitude had been spent, the tolerant sympathy had flickered out. They wished one another well, but that which they had once been was no more. Had they, over the sherry glasses, silently mourned for it? She thought that they had. It had been a seemlier funeral than some. Brian's prophecy of giggling children at the waterfall crossed her mind and she did what Eugenia would have done: furtively she threw a pinch of salt over her shoulder.

Dr Challoner was brooding upon his private *delenda est Carthago*. Bees! Becker must be cautioned about that and so must the people who put up the cross. A few puffs of cyanide and little more would be heard of a minute citadel which had, throughout the ages, defied the Turks, the Genoese, the Venetians, the Franks, the Romans, which might, if ever the Minoans came so far, have thumbed its nose at Crete.

2

Upon the next day, and the next, no meals were served to the new Lord of Keritha. He had been warned that this would happen, but he had not wholly believed it. Kate, smuggling trays up to his room, could only assure him that it had always been so. For some thousands of years nobody had ever eaten anything upon these two days.

Keritha was mourning the dead. The wind sighed in the pine trees. Even the waterfall sang with a mournful cadence. All the maids had gone home to weep with their families. Eugenia, in her own quarters across the court, was lamenting for her children and their father, gone down into silence.

'Why suddenly now?' demanded Dr Challoner, when his final jug of cocoa was brought to him on Saturday night. 'Those sons of hers! They've been dead for years. Is it in actual fact some kind of holiday?'

'No,' said Kate patiently, 'it's the time to mourn. The people here get over things, in a way, very quickly. They have to. You bury your dead and you go out to milk the goats. But then, in a way, the dead are remembered longer. Everybody cries for them once a year, and nobody cries alone.'

'Where's Potter? Is he crying?'

'No. He's helping me with the eggs. Several hundred of

them. All to be boiled hard and dyed red. I must go back. There's a lot to be done before tomorrow.'

She went downstairs, thinking that it might be better for Selwyn if he did cry. The kitchen was empty. He had finished the eggs and left them ready piled in large baskets. Now she could hear him out on the terrace, banging about and whistling. He was putting up the trestle tables for her, and adjusting the roasting spits further down the slope.

Although grateful for his help she wished that he would not persist in this role of a man to whom nothing in particular can happen. It was glaringly out of place on Keritha, at this season when everybody else was openly acknowledging a common burden of grief. That Dr Challoner should dissociate himself from this general impulse was unseemly but not surprising; by Keritha standards he was a gross barbarian. Selwyn was not. He must know very well what was going on yet dared not take part in it. For two days now he had been proclaiming himself as something less than a man – a creature immune from change, chance, and loss.

She wished too that the lambs, bleating in the kitchen court, did not sound so pathetic. That was one of the local customs which she found revolting. These poor little bleating creatures, who would tomorrow be killed and eaten, always wrung her heart.

This was the last time that she must hear them. Next week she would be gone, for she had no further excuse for staying. They had all said as much in their last batch of letters. She must come back to them. She was needed. Poor Douglas was getting nothing to eat save tinned baked beans, since a successor for Mrs McKintosh had been difficult to find. That fabled treasure had nearly burnt her gentlemen in their beds, setting fire to the flat when the worse for drink. She had now joined Pamela Shelmerdine in the limbo set up for women who might never be mentioned because they had let Douglas down.

To find a housekeeper willing to endure Ronnie's manners was clearly a task for Kate, since Judith, Hazel and Bridie had all of them tried in vain. If Kate came home and saw to it nobody, not even Brian, would again dismiss her to exile. Brian must have been even more tactless than usual. He had misinterpreted their anxiety for her health. Two or three months, in a warm climate, had been all that they had in mind.

They were perfectly reasonable, and the worst embarrassments of that earlier return would not, at least, recur. She was no longer an angel. She might go back, although she could not imagine what she was to do with herself for the rest of her life.

Had the fatal break never occurred she might have continued to do as she had always done, dwindling imperceptibly through her seventh decade. She would have seen to it that Douglas lived in comfort, have visited a few old friends, served on a few committees, treated herself to an occasional play or concert, and lent a hand with her grandchildren. Each year she would have done a little less, have become a less essential person in the community, until she had respectably earned the right to figure as 'Old Mrs Benson'.

Several years must now be filled before she could reach that haven. She was not old yet, and her health was robust, since the pneumonia had left no lasting weakness. How the gap was to be filled she knew not. Those commonplace activities, natural enough had they never been discontinued, could not be resumed quite spontaneously. She must make some kind of life for herself, inch her way into a seat by the hearth, form a few ties which needed no nourishment from the past, collect a little junk as evidence that she was a person. The prospect daunted her. She would rather have stayed on Keritha, although it was now a banquet hall deserted. A banquet in full swing, from which her own place had been removed, promised little.

When Edith died she had meant to stay with Freddie, whatever they said at home. They had stood together at the grave and when they turned away to walk home he had taken her arm affectionately. She pictured his old age, the slow loss of vigour and power, never dreaming that he would follow Edith so quickly. As if divining her thought he said suddenly:

'Maybe not. We don't know, Kate, my dear. Nobody knows what the Visitors have written on his face. I may go tomorrow. And you may tumble unexpectedly into something quite new and strenuous.'

'You mean it's wrong of me to stay?' she asked. 'I ought to go home and chase a job?'

'Oh no. Stay! If They chalked up a job for you, it will come here chasing you.'

Now he was gone and the only job provided by Them, so far as she could see, was to engage a cook-housekeeper.

All the plates had to be piled in readiness on the kitchen table. She had done this last year and then gone to Eugenia's room to ask if seventy would be enough. Freddie and Edith were sitting there, both in tears. This year poor Eugenia would be weeping all alone. Kate left the plates and hurried across the kitchen court, past the bleating lambs, to where a light burned in a window and Eugenia sat, small and withered, amidst lace curtains and solid Victorian furniture. The ikon of the Saviour lay on a bier, surrounded by candles and covered with a muslin cloth on which were strewn fresh rose leaves. With tears pouring down her face Eugenia handed a faded photograph to Kate. The little dead daughter could not have been a pretty child. She had Freddie's thin sharp features. Clad in many frills, posed in a photographer's landscape, she stood as though already lost amongst the shades.

'Bebbies,' moaned Eugenia.

There was no self pity in her grief. She wept for a motherless child, rather than for a childless mother.

When Stephanie died, remembered Kate, Judith cried and said: Poor Aunt Stephanie! And I said: No! Poor us, to be living without her. And she said: But it's much worse to be dead than to be alive. She was only ten, but she was right. Ah, but why can't Selwyn mourn as they do here? If he could think of that poor girl, torn away from her children, crying for them, then . . . oh, then he would be so sorry for her, he would exert himself. He'd never leave them in that . . . he'd make a home for them again, in Stockholm where his friends are . . .

'Bebbies,' repeated Eugenia, taking another picture, a snapshot of two boys playing with a puppy. 'Ai! Ai!'

Ai! Ai! Oh dear! The parsley is all withered in the garden. Suddenly Kate recalled Freddie's voice saying that, as though he had just walked into the room. It returned to her with a clarity only possible, perhaps, in this haven where the dead were never sentimentalized. She saw Freddie again, pale, quiet, and saw the strange, sharp firmness of his smile. She began to cry too, with her head on Eugenia's shoulder.

'Ah, Freddie! Freddie!'

'He was a man,' wailed Eugenia. 'A great rich man. He lived in this fine house and he ate what he pleased and he did what he pleased. He took great pleasure in his life. In the morning he would come downstairs in his beautiful dressing gown, and call for this and for that, as the fancy took him, and I would bring it to him very quickly. And now . . . now . . . he lies there and never knows if it's night or morning.'

'Heaven?' sobbed Kate.

'The soul goes to Heaven. But who wants to be nothing but a soul? No pleasure in it. A thin life, that, for a man. Ai! Ai! Have they brought down the cheese for tomorrow?'

'I don't think they have.'

'The lazy scamps. They've forgotten it again.'

'I'll go and see.'

Kate went up to her room for a coat and a torch. Midnight was gone, but they would be awake up at the home farm. Nobody on the island slept that night.

She felt her way up the track, listening to the sigh of the wind in the trees. It was clear and warm. The moon, which would be full tomorrow, had already vanished behind the mountain, but the sky was full of its light and there was a sheen of moonshine on the sea.

At the farm there were lights and voices and the same universal ceaseless wailing. As she drew nearer a chant arose; it was one of those laments which Freddie had collected and translated for her. She waited on the threshold listening. A woman sang a verse or two so sadly that it seemed indecent to break in with demands for cheese. But then the voice broke off to inquire negligently about a button which was to be sewn onto somebody's coat.

I shall never really understand them, thought Kate, tapping at the door.

A girl came and promised that the cheese should be left at the house early in the morning. Beyond her Kate could see the room, the candles, the ikon on its bier, and the silent people assembled there. One face turned towards her for a moment. It was Selwyn, sitting between two old men. He had found companions at last. She did not think that he recognized her. He was fathoms deep, entirely surrendered to sorrow.

As she stole away the song rose again, carried on the light breeze away over the sea towards the morning. The moonlit shimmer was gone, and in the east the darkness had changed its hue.

An hour before sunrise she knocked at Dr Challoner's door since he had signified his intention of attending the morning's ceremony. He came downstairs lamenting the fact that he had no thick overcoat. The morning air was chilly and he would certainly catch cold. Eugenia, as if she understood what he was saying, came forward with an odd-looking hooded cloak.

'Freddie's,' explained Kate. 'He always used to wear it. It's quite true, you'll need it.'

It was better than nothing, though he did not much like the look of it. He muffled himself up in it and they set out.

The whole island was astir. People were coming along the track from the waterfall and down the path from the home farm. There were groups ahead of them trudging eastward. Sleepy children tugged at their mothers' hands. None had been left behind; even the youngest babies came. A very old man travelled pickaback, on the shoulders of the young, who took it in turns to carry him. Weary with their night of weeping, unusually silent, they flowed on as thought drawn to their goal rather than making for it.

'They've all got guns!' marvelled Dr Challoner. 'Why?'

His voice, in that hushed throng, sounded harsh and alien. Kate made no answer, nor were there any bows or greetings as they joined the assembly. Freddie's cloak got a few glances of recognition. He writhed to think of the absurd figure which he must cut in it and added another mark to his score against Keritha. He now hated the place with the venom usually reserved for those who had worsted him in an argument on his own subject. Presently he broke the silence again:

'There's Potter! Carrying that old man.'

Kate clenched her teeth against the temptation to say: Shut up!

In a perfectly clear sky, day imperceptibly conquered night. No rosy clouds in the zenith heralded the hidden sun; light from some unrevealed source was distilled, drop by drop, into the air. Colour deepened in a world which had, as yet, no shadows. The smell of spring, the flowers of Keritha, grew stronger. Down below the rim of the world the bright horses, new harnessed, were rearing and plunging, eager for their day's journey. He was coming. He was mounting his chariot, haled on by Old Time, who would never allow him to be a single minute late. He was coming.

On a little headland, the eastern spur of the island, the people of Keritha stood waiting in front of a narrow crack in some rocks. There was some stir inside. Dr Challoner, by now a little subdued, asked in a breathy whisper who was hiding in there.

'The old man,' whispered Kate. 'The oldest man on the island.'

Nobody else looked that way. All stood motionless, gazing out to sea. A baby cried, mewing faintly, and was hushed. Keritha waited. The flat sea floor waited. The whole world waited.

It happened very suddenly.

A spark, a long beam, and the sun leapt out of the sea as an old, thin, far-away voice shouted the message down the years:

'*Christos anesti!*'

BANG! BANG! BANG! BANG! went a score of guns as a thunderclap of joy broke over Keritha. *Alithos anesti!* He is truly risen! The news was shouted again, and again, until everybody had told it to everybody else, and the echoes of it hummed between the mountain and the sea.

BANG! BANG! . . . ang . . . ang . . . 'He is truly risen,' cried Eugenia, falling on Kate's neck.

'*Ke tou chronou!* And next year too . . .'

'Risen!' squealed the children.

'And next year too,' bellowed a huge rustic, seizing Dr Challoner and kissing him on both cheeks.

BANG! BANG! BANG! BANG! Behold we live and take joy in living. He is so good that He is stronger than death, BANG! BANG! . . . ang . . . ang . . . e-esti. . . chronou . . . ang . . .

It was incredible that so few people could make so much noise for so long. The sun was clear of the horizon and sailing upwards, a dazzling disc, before the last shot was fired and the tumult died away in laughter and embraces. A general movement began back towards the house. Some of the men had already gone on to kill the lambs.

'Let's wait here a little,' suggested Kate. 'Let them all go on ahead. Eugenia has gone. She'll see to everything. I don't want to get back till that messy business is over.'

Dr Challoner sat down on a boulder and straightened his tie, which had been pulled round to the back of his neck. He was quite dazed by all the kissing and man-handling to which he had been subjected. Kate sat beside him. The very old man was carried off on the back of a great-grandson.

'They say he's over a hundred,' she reported. 'They remind me of some old people I've seen on a vase somewhere. An old man carried by a young man. Who would they be?'

'Anchises and Aeneas probably.'

'Oh yes. Aeneas carried his father out of burning Troy. They do manage, somehow, to look like people on a vase, don't they?'

'I can't say that I see it. The people on vases suggest a much higher level of civilization.'

A little girl ran up to them, flung her arms round Kate, and said breathlessly:

'*Alithos anesti!*'

'*Efharisto, poullaki mou. Ke tou chronou!*'

Kate hugged the little creature close for a moment. Her affection for children seldom took the form of caresses or demonstrations of tenderness. To see them happy and thriving was enough for her; if they wished to be hugged, she obliged them, for their satisfaction rather than her own. Now the weight and warmth of the child in her arms soothed a hunger which had come upon her during that uprush of life which all had shared a few minutes earlier.

'What did you say?' said Challoner.

'I said: Thank you, darling! And next year too.'

The child, when released, flung herself upon him, disarranging his tie again, and assuring him that Christ was truly risen.

'Go on,' exhorted Kate. 'Thank her!'

'*Efharisto!*' growled the spokesman of civilization. 'Is that how you spell it?'

'No. It's the way it's pronounced.'

His outlandish cloak was evidently familiar to the child. She put a small fat finger on it and looked doubtfully at the strange face inside the hood.

'Milorthos Frethi gave us eggs,' she suggested.

'There will be eggs,' promised Kate.

Reassured that nothing was going to be changed, the little creature bowed to them and trotted off.

A Stay-at-Home, thought Kate. When she grows up she won't leave the island.

The crowd was thinning rapidly. In a few minutes the two foreigners were left sitting solitary by the sunlit sea. Fumes of gunpowder now drowned the scent of hyacinths.

'How far,' asked Dr Challoner, 'does this go on in other parts of Greece?'

'I've never been anywhere else at Easter. On Zagros they fire off guns. But they have it at midnight, not at sunrise. And I believe they kill the lambs on Saturday, and cook them in some special way, instead of this barbecue. Nicer, I should think. Here the meat is almost raw.'

'I was thinking of cooking. I mean as a religious observance.'

'Oh, where there's a church the priest comes out, and calls, like the old man did.'

'Then, if they had a church, all this business would be quite commonplace?'

She assented, a little doubtfully. By her the last half hour could never have been described as commonplace. The moment of sunrise had moved her deeply on all the Easters which she had spent on Keritha.

'Not worth attention, really,' he decided. 'I can't see anything on this island which calls for the slightest attention.'

Smiling a little, she conceded the point. She did not really want him to think Keritha worth attention. He had much better go away and tell other people, people like himself, how dull it was, and then nobody would ever deem it worth exploitation. Eugenia, ending her days in the gracious empty house, would guard the memory of those two who had loved the island. The seasons would pass. The harvests would be gathered – food enough for the *klisouriasmeni*, and the mallows would wither in the garden. The north winds would blow. The spring flowers would blossom again, and the fruit trees, almond first, and then the plum and the peach. The people would weep, as all men must, rejoice as all men will, and nothing would ever be changed.

She rose and suggested that they might now return since the lambs would be roasting on their spits.

'How long does this beano go on?' he asked.

'All day and all night.'

'You mean we've got them on our hands for twenty-four hours?'

'I'm afraid so. And they eat without stopping. They eat enough for a year.'

'Then I must go on as best I can with trays in my room, I suppose.'

'Oh no! You must eat with them. They'll be shocked if you don't.'

'I can't stand much more of it. The row when the sun rose . . .! My head is still going round. These people are nothing to me. I'm nothing to them. And . . . they smell.'

'But, you see, they think of you as taking Freddie's place. And you are their host.'

'*What*? I'm paying for all this?'

'Freddie always did. They're very poor. They can just

manage to live off the island. It's so fertile they can get their own food and sell enough on the barer islands to buy the very few things they need to buy. But they couldn't afford a feast like this out of their own pockets. Of course the ones who go away send home money.'

'If they had a spark of ambition they'd all go. Why do they stay here to starve? I think you might have warned me.'

'I'm sorry. It never entered my head.'

'I shouldn't have stayed over the weekend if I'd realized.'

'Oh, you'd have had to stay. Think of all there is still to settle. You haven't really decided yet about most of the furniture.'

'I've decided to leave it here. Too much trouble to shift. Can that woman read?'

'Eugenia? I think she can. Greek, of course.'

'If I make any further decisions I'll get someone to write a letter for me telling her what I want.'

It struck him that he had better perhaps accept his role of the new Lord of Keritha, and endeavour to look genial. These festivities might be a tedious, exhausting imposition, but some civility on his part might dispose Eugenia, later, to accept his orders should he decide to let the house. She need know nothing about Becker save as a friend and guest of the house. Investigations might thus be carried out with little trouble from wild bees. In which case the monstrous banquet now being held upon the terrace would be the last joke played by Keritha upon strangers.

The noise of it was audible a long way off, as the mixed smell of hyacinths and gunpowder gave way to that of roasting meat. Somebody was playing upon queer little bagpipes. Fifty people were talking at the very tops of their voices. The island soil had turned bright red; it was littered ankle deep in dyed egg-shells. The maids, hurrying from the spits to the tables, crunched over them and the children continually threw down more.

Boisterous shouts greeted the host. He was conducted to a place at the head of the longest table. Eggs were thrust at him by a dozen hands. One maid ran up with a plate of smoking meat and another with a fresh supply of wine from Freddie's vineyard. The little bagpipes played, over and over again, a single phrase on four notes.

'I think I know this tune, if you can call it a tune,' he said to Kate.

'I expect you do. It's the first half of God Save the Queen, and it's played in your honour. As for the other half, those are all the notes that pipe has.'

She dived under the table, snatched away a child who was eating Milorthos Persi's shoelaces, and carried him back to Maroulla, his mother. He had been new born when she first came to Keritha. She had gone with Edith to visit Maroulla, and had got her first taste of Coca-Cola.

'What a big boy he is,' she said. 'And now . . .'

She pointed to a swaddled parcel in Maroulla's arms and would have said that his nose was out of joint had that not been too difficult in Greek.

'Now, he is no longer the bebbie.'

'And you are going away!' said Maroulla. 'We shall be sorry. Next Easter you won't be there. But we'll remember you.'

'Yes. And I'll remember you. I shall think of you all in Stockholm, next Easter.'

'Stockholm? Is that a place in England then?'

'No. I meant London. I shall be in London.'

'That must be a fine sight, London, at Easter.'

'How many people in London?' put in another woman.

'About eight million, I think.'

'Ah-h-h-h!'

They sighed to think of the gorgeous noise made by eight million people upon learning that Christ had risen.

'What do they eat?' asked Maroulla.

'Eggs,' said Kate. 'Often they are gold and silver! Chocolate, you know, covered with gold and silver paper.'

'Ah-h-h! And they throw it down and dance on gold and silver? Look out, Anna! Your Kiki is going to be sick.'

'Little stupid! You gobbled too fast. Now you've wasted all that lovely meat.'

'Ah, there's plenty more today. They can throw up as much as they like, the children, and there'll be another plateful. Oh, listen. Kostas is going to sing *The Tell Tale*.'

Comparative silence fell as an old song was sung at the expense of couples supposed to be courting. It had but one verse, but in each repetition a new couple was named.

'Lakis kissed Eleni,' carolled Kostas, while everybody turned to laugh at the blushing pair.

> 'Only the night saw them, and a star.
> So how does everybody know about it this morning?
> The star set into the sea and told the waves,
>> And the waves told an oar blade
>> And the oar blade told the sailor,
> And the sailor came home and told everybody.'

'That Lakis,' commented Maroulla. 'What I'd like to know is if there's anybody he hasn't kissed.'

'Yannis kissed Despina . . .'

'Mrs Benson!'

Kate became aware of an appeal from the host.

'What's that they're singing?'

'Just a folk song. The *Koutsombolis*.'

'The rhythm! It's got a rhythm . . . it reminds me . . . Meleager . . . *Nux hiere kai luchne . . .*'

At Kate's shake of the head he offered a translation about holy night and a lamp, the only witnesses of two lovers' vows.

'Oh, it's the same song, probably,' said Kate, who was not paying much attention.

She tried to stand between him and Maroulla so that he should not be shocked by what was happening. That the swaddled newcomer should be suckled was natural, but the two-year-old, who had already feasted upon Dr Challoner's shoelaces, was now getting the breast.

'Vasilis kissed Anna . . .'

This simple joke lasted for a long time, while the assembly munched on, filling itself to the brim and shouting with its mouth full. Plates went back and forth to the spits, pitchers of wine were brought from the house, also many bottles of Coca-Cola, which most of the children preferred. The crates which came over with the goat had been specially ordered for this feast.

When everybody, according to *The Tell Tale*, has kissed everybody else, a new tune was struck up by the pipes, a fiddle and a drum. A long line of girls danced across the terrace, their hands clasped and crossed, their hair flying, and their light feet crushing the egg-shells.

'Gold and silver in London,' sighed Maroulla. 'In all the streets where they dance! How beautiful!'

Kate remembered a poem which Freddie had quoted, last Easter, or perhaps the Easter before. It was not in Greek, but he had insisted that it was not by an Englishman. It was about bagpipes, and a gold-and-silver wood, and queens dancing. He said that there is a 'happy townland', which we all believe to be somewhere, although we never find it. The people here, on Easter day, came perhaps as near to finding it as anyone ever does.

'I wish I could see it,' murmured Maroulla.

'Next year I'll send you some gold and silver eggs from Stock . . . I mean London.'

Again she had nearly said Stockholm. She had never been there and had no wish to go. She was tired, and she had been thinking too much about Selwyn's children. He ought to take them back there, where he had friends, and he ought to make his beautiful bowls again.

These junketings were too much for her at her age. She was beginning to feel quite dizzy, and poor Dr Challoner looked as though he might fall to pieces at any moment. He was, she noticed with surprised approval, making some effort at civility. When people spoke to him he said thank you instead of begging their pardons. He now knew two words of Greek.

Taking pity on him, she whispered that soon, perhaps, they might both slip away.

'Thank heaven for that. Will this really go on till dawn tomorrow?'

'Yes, and then they'll all troop off to work, just as usual. Now, aren't those girls pretty, dancing? You must agree they're like girls on a vase?'

'They might be, if it wasn't for the row and the mess and the egg-shells.'

'Well, nobody would put all that on a vase. But I suppose it was always there, when girls danced, don't you?'

'What? Row and mess and egg-shells?'

'Why, yes. What kind of girls were they, dancing on vases?'

He frowned. He had never supposed that girls dancing on vases were real girls at any time.

'They were ... er ... maidens ... Good heavens! Look! Just look! There's Potter dancing too!'

4

Two days later they bade farewell to Keritha. Dr Challoner had announced his decision to leave the house more or less fully furnished. He had no more time to waste; he had got the jewellery and would dispose of the rest at some later date.

Kate and Selwyn did not exactly receive their marching orders, but he offered to take them with him as far as Thasos in tones which implied that his house thereafter would be closed to them. Since transport to Thasos was not always easy to secure they accepted the offer and made faces at one another behind his back.

On the last morning Selwyn went up early to say goodbye at the home farm. The visit, and the task of looking cheerful, cost him some effort; his heart was heavy at the prospect of leaving Keritha. He went, however, because he felt grateful to his friends there. He stayed for half an hour, laughing and talking, and charmed the children by drawing a picture of their kitten.

Coming home he made another sketch. A goat and her kid, on a high rock, were peering down into the ravine. These two had often posed thus, to the delight of Kate, who had remarked on it and declared that they were typical of the island. When he got back to the house he took the sketch to her room and gave it to her, saying:

'Here's some of our friends on Keritha.'

Kate was charmed, but told him that he ought to send it to Hagstrom.

'I did it for you. As a matter of fact it wouldn't do for glass. It's too solid.'

'You were drawing all yesterday.'

'Yes. I . . . I'm sending something to Hagstrom.'

'You will? I'm glad. I was hoping . . .'

'Yes,' said Selwyn, sitting down on her suitcase.

'Oh, don't!'

She spoke too late. The suitcase collapsed beneath him.

'Now look what I've done!'

'It doesn't matter. We can tie it up. Get some rope.'

He went off in search of rope while she salvaged the contents of her crushed case. The news that he meant to get in touch with Hagstrom so much pleased her that she could easily forgive him, although their intimacy was punctuated by mishaps of this kind, ever since the disaster to her table.

The tie between them was not easy to define. His sorrow and his future were continually in her mind, and had become almost a personal concern to her, yet she was not particularly fond of him. The bond had not sprung from liking or preference, as is the case in most friendships. The effort to scan fully the life and lot of another person is seldom made unless attraction or sympathy lead the way. Once it has been made a claim is established. She had thought him disagreeable until she knew his story. Having learnt it, she ceased to ask herself whether she liked him or not.

He came back with some rope which he had got from Eugenia and put her suitcase into an efficient strait waistcoat.

'But what about the Customs?' she complained. 'It would be just like them to make me undo it all.'

'I'll be at your elbow, all the way to England, and I'll tie it up for you again. In London I'll buy you another. A lovely Potter-Proof Suitcase.'

As he tied the last knot he added:

'As a matter of fact I came to ask you a favour. Now I doubt if it's a good moment.'

'Ask anyway,' said Kate, putting her passport into the bucket bag. 'I'm in a softened mood.'

'It's two favours, really. First: when we get back, would you go and see the boys?'

'Paul and John? At that place near Guildford? I certainly will.'

'Thank you. Second: I think I ought to make a home for them again. But I'll want somebody. Some woman. Could you tell me how to find someone?'

'Some sort of housekeeper-nanny? Yes, indeed. You'll need somebody like that.'

'Just to start us off.'

'I'm sure I can find somebody.'

'It would have to be someone who didn't mind going to Sweden for a bit. If Hagstrom will take me back I'll have to go there for some time, I think.'

'Why not? Sweden is a very nice country, so they say. I'll start looking around as soon as I get back. And you must take me at once to see the boys.'

'I knew you would. You're very kind.'

He stood up and tested his handiwork by swinging the suitcase about.

'I'm so glad, so delighted,' said Kate, 'that you've . . .'

'Come into circulation again?'

'Yes. Oh, don't! Don't sit on my other suitcase. Sit on a chair. Good heavens! There are plenty of chairs in the room.'

He came to anchor in a solid-looking chair.

'Last week,' he said, 'when everybody was crying, I felt able to . . . I mean, I knew how they felt, and they knew how I felt. And then, on Sunday, when the sun rose and he shouted, I suddenly came to life.'

'I know. I've felt that every year. It's only here . . .'

'I saw the sun rise, once, on Delos.'

She went into the bathroom to look round it and make sure that she had left nothing behind. Only here! she repeated to herself, only here! With the wardens, through the Battle of London, in hospital with those other women, through pain and fear, she had known herself at moments to be absorbed into some other, mightier Person. Only here, on the eastern spur of Keritha, had she known it through joy.

'What were you saying about Delos?' she asked when she came back.

Selwyn laughed and shook his head.

'Had a funny feeling on Delos.'

A bellow rose from the terrace below.

'Potter! Mrs Benson!'

'Hark at him!' said Selwyn. 'Where's he going after Thasos?'

'I think he's going to Athens. He says he has some business with that Mr Tipton.'

'What a horrible idea! Challoner and Tipton! I shudder to think of what goes on.'

'POTTER!'

'*Adsum!*' said Selwyn, poking his head out of the window.

'It's time we started.'

'Oh? Where?'

'Thasos! Thasos! We shall miss that boat for the mainland.'

'Oh well, there's another next week.'

He drew in his head and Kate reproved him.

'I've half a mind to feed him to the dolphins. Know what he did? He tipped Eugenia.'

'He didn't!'

'He did. She was puzzled. She asked me what the money was for. I said to make those cakes . . . you know, the cakes they make for the dead. Sort of iced cakes. For Freddie and Edith.'

'*Koliva?* Now that was clever of you.'

'He's a menace, that old brute. What say we tip him into the sea between here and Thasos? I've a funny feeling that we ought to. Nobody would know. Yorgos wouldn't tell.'

'Unethical, I'm afraid. But he has been intolerably rude.'

'More than rude. You know, I think he hates Keritha. He'd like it to be dead.'

'He certainly hasn't a good word to say for it, I can't think why.'

'As long as it's alive he'll have to be afraid that there's something dangerous about poetry. All his life he's been pocketing the stuff on the assumption that it's dead.'

'I dare say, but I'm sure he sees nothing poetic about Keritha. Come along. We really must go. We've got to catch that boat ourselves.'

He picked up her suitcases and carried them downstairs. Their farewells to Eugenia had already been made and she had retired to her own quarters, but all the maids were assembled in the hall. Kate kissed them and so, much to their amusement, did Selwyn.

Dr Challoner was already sitting in the boat, furious at

the delay, when they came down to it. Their luggage was stowed away. They shot off from the sweet-smelling slopes of Keritha. The house vanished, but they could still see the smoke, curling up through the trees, until they turned westward to round Zagros.

Selwyn looked back no more. Sadness seized him again, as it often must upon the long hard road ahead. He endured it, waited for it to pass, knowing that, in time, it would release him.

Kate, too, was silent, meditating upon his problems. A housekeeper-nanny should not be very hard to find. She knew exactly the kind of person for whom she must seek; not a young woman, not a fussy, conventional old one. To be ideal she should have some measure of education and intelligence, so as to give companionship of a sort to Selwyn until he picked up with his friends again. She must be used to living abroad and able to tackle housekeeping in Sweden.

There was a danger that such a person might become a burden and an embarrassment to him later on. He would only need her for a year or two while that forlorn household was finding its feet. So soon as they no longer needed her she must fade out of their lives, nor must there be any likelihood that he should feel obliged to pension her off. Means of her own she must have, and kinsfolk, to whom she could eventually retire.

People who share a bad time, she reflected, have a way of drifting apart when the bad time is over. There is no estrangement, no loss of regard; some instinct bids them take up separate paths. We live on several levels and there is one upon which nobody, save a saint, can live for long. A run-of-the-mill sinner can explore it for a brief period – a fact which had become painfully clear at those wistful

Wardens' Reunions. Selwyn, Paul and John must not be saddled with a saint, but for a time they would need a friend who could do more than cook their dinners and mend their socks.

A clergyman's widow, she thought, and dismissed the idea. A clergyman's widow would do nicely for Douglas and Ronnie; she knew of an agency which dealt in them. Any kind of widow would be a mistake for Selwyn; there was too much bereavement in his household already.

'Where is the oil bought, for this boat?' demanded Dr Challoner.

He was unusually talkative, and disturbed her meditations by asking a number of questions which he had never troubled to ask before. He wrote down the answers in a little book. What was Eugenia's surname? Who owned those donkeys on which he and Selwyn had first ridden up to the house? How many beds were there altogether? Bed linen? Blankets? She answered him absently as they rounded Zagros and sped north again.

Selwyn, she perceived, would need some explaining, even when she had found a suitable person. Paul and John were easy. Any woman with a motherly heart would understand what they needed. Selwyn might strike a stranger as unprepossessing. He looked peculiar and he broke things. Words must be found to explain how nice he really . . . Nice? She checked herself. This person must be able to understand that it mattered little whether he was nice or not. Such a question is superficial when we really consider what anybody else has to bear. Do we ask whether a drowning stranger is nice before we throw him a life-line? Yet it would be difficult to present him as she saw him herself. Nobody perhaps could do so who had not spent this week with him on Keritha.

She must plead his cause through the children. Poor Paul! Poor John! They cry when they see their father, and he said: 'It's very sad.' But soon, soon, that will be over. We'll get you out of that bleak place and there will be a happy home for you in Stockholm . . . Stockholm . . . gold and silver eggs next Easter . . . the sun on the water always makes me sleepy.

Selwyn, his grief easing a little, turned to her and asked: 'Why are you smiling?'

'Am I smiling?'

'You were just now. You've got your Edwardes Square face. You're planning something for your children.'

'Ah no. My time for that is over.'

'It never will be. "Fish gotta swim and birds gotta fly".'

'I was thinking about gold and silver eggs. Easter eggs. I promised to send some to Maroulla next year. Do remind me.'

'If you're there, next year. Or I'm there. I will. We must send them lots and lots so they can throw gold and silver paper down everywhere and make a gorgeous mess.'

'That's the idea, I think. On Keritha. Next year.'

She turned to take a last look at it and saw nothing save dancing waves. The happy townland had slid beneath the rim of the world. Her lips formed the greeting: *Ke tou chronou* and her eyes suddenly filled with tears. She wiped them away indignantly as though refusing to believe that Time could be an enemy and she herself, perhaps, the first of the living to weep for Keritha.

THE HISTORY OF VINTAGE

The famous American publisher Alfred A. Knopf (1892–1984) founded Vintage Books in the United States in 1954 as a paperback home for the authors published by his company. Vintage was launched in the United Kingdom in 1990 and works independently from the American imprint although both are part of the international publishing group, Random House.

Vintage in the United Kingdom was initially created to publish paperback editions of books acquired by the prestigious hardback imprints in the Random House Group such as Jonathan Cape, Chatto & Windus, Hutchinson and later William Heinemann, Secker & Warburg and The Harvill Press. There are many Booker and Nobel Prize-winning authors on the Vintage list and the imprint publishes a huge variety of fiction and non-fiction. Over the years Vintage has expanded and the list now includes both great authors of the past – who are published under the Vintage Classics imprint – as well as many of the most influential authors of the present.

For a full list of the books Vintage publishes, please visit our website
www.vintage-books.co.uk

For book details and other information about the classic authors we publish, please visit the Vintage Classics website
www.vintage-classics.info